Chained

Books by Eileen Brady

The Kate Turner, D.V.M., Mysteries
Muzzled
Unleashed
Chained

Chained

A Kate Turner, D.V.M., Mystery

Eileen Brady

Poisoned Pen Press

Copyright © 2017 by Eileen Brady

First Edition 2017

10 9 8 7 6 5 4 3 2 1

Library of Congress Catalog Card Number: 2017944324

ISBN: 9781464209536   Hardcover
     9781464209550   Trade Paperback

Poisoned Pen Press
4014 N. Goldwater Boulevard, #201
Scottsdale, Arizona 85251
www.poisonedpenpress.com
info@poisonedpenpress.com

Printed in the United States of America

To Logan Grant Biggs—I'd forgotten how joyous life could be until you smiled and captured my heart.

"Nature teaches beasts to know their friends."
—*William Shakespeare*

"Dogs never bite me. Just humans."
—*Marilyn Monroe*

Acknowledgments

I'd like to thank the staff at Poisoned Pen Press, Publisher Robert Rosenwald, and Editor-in-Chief Barbara Peters for their support of writers everywhere. A special thank you to my editor, Annette Rogers. Your thoughtful advice on Dr. Kate Turner's love life was greatly appreciated. I'm thrilled with the beautiful cover by Holli Roach. Kudos to the hardworking employees of the Poisoned Pen Bookstore in Scottsdale, Arizona, for arranging the events and signings that promote my books. Always gracious and helpful, they make this independent bookstore a warm and inviting place for readers and authors—and the refreshments are delicious.

There's nothing like the input from a critique group to keep you on your toes. I'm grateful to each one of the Tuesday night Sheridan Street gang—Art Kerns, Sharon Magee, Charles Pyeatte, Sonja Stone, and our fearless leader, the incomparable Betty Webb.

The unwavering support from my husband, Jonathan Grant, means everything to me, especially when I'm frantically trying to meet a deadline. I'd like to give a shout-out to fellow veterinarian, Dr. John Hynes, who's been an enthusiastic supporter of my work from day one. Many thanks also to my sister and fellow author Rosemary Simpson for the lengthy afternoon phone calls commiserating on the woes of being a writer—they've been a welcome if slightly crazy diversion.

My wonderful readers are always on my mind. In each book I work hard to make you laugh, relate some veterinary medicine, and offer an intriguing mystery to solve. Feel free to contact me at eileenbradymysteries@gmail.com. I love hearing from you.

Throughout my life pets have always comforted me with their unconditional love. My cat and dog family members are convinced they help me write by lounging on my desk chair and showering me with fur. Wouldn't trade it for the world. Finally, I truly believe that the human race is only at its finest when it shows compassion to all living creatures who share our beautiful yet fragile planet.

Prologue

He was luscious. Skin the color of thick, dark honey paired with tousled blond hair and a lazy smile that made you smile back. Flynn moved among his fellow men like a king—a young Alexander the Great—conquering everyone and everything around him.

Funny and confident, yet understanding and compassionate. To be with him was intoxicating, addictive.

The world turned cold when he wasn't around. The scenery went from rich colors to black and white.

Flynn was too good for his own good.

Too irresistible.

Which was why he had to die.

Chapter One

I must be out of my mind.

Why I let my receptionist squeeze in a veterinary house call the morning of the wedding, I had no idea. As maid of honor I needed to be dressed and in place for a last-minute rehearsal at one o'clock. Instead of relaxing, I'm in an old pair of scrubs rushing to see a dog with a lump on his back.

I'd graduated from veterinary school with a degree and a massive amount of student loans—about one hundred and fifty thousand dollars' worth. Because of those debts I didn't have the luxury of turning down work. That's how I ended up in New York's beautiful Hudson Valley running the Oak Falls Animal Hospital for absentee owner, Doc Anderson. While Doc enjoyed his round-the-world cruise, I held down the fort. As a relief vet, my job was to make money, not waves. After a bumpy start, things had settled down and I found I enjoyed meeting his pet-loving, and sometimes eccentric, clients. On the downside, as the only veterinarian, I survived on a steady diet of stress, lack of sleep, and frequent helpings of pie.

"Let's go, Mari." My veterinary assistant had run back into the hospital for some last-minute supplies plus her emergency bag of potato chips. I gunned the animal hospital truck engine and draped my stethoscope on the rearview mirror. Eight o'clock Saturday morning in Oak Falls and I was already behind schedule.

"Got it, Doc." Mari slammed the passenger door, pulled on her seat belt, and gave me a thumbs-up. She'd already programmed our destination into the GPS, so with any luck we'd be at our appointment in about forty minutes. In case of delay, however, my maid of honor dress, swathed in plastic, swung back and forth from a hook directly behind me. We zipped along on a two-lane secondary road that paralleled the highway. Flashes of russet and gold foliage punctuated the stands of trees lining the road. Few people ventured out this early on Saturday morning. Even though Halloween was around the corner, today's weather prediction called for sunshine and a high of sixty degrees—a glorious Indian summer day to be enjoyed to the fullest before winter hit.

"Right turn in five hundred feet." I slowed down the battered F-150. Our GPS spoke in a clipped British accent. Whenever I heard it I felt like offering him a cup of tea.

Our appointment was in a very rural area outside of town. Here the homes were separated by several acres, interspersed with farmland. I noticed all the properties along this stretch of road bordered New York State Park land. Dense stands of evergreens reached for the sky, creating puddles of green at the base of the gray-blue Catskill Mountains.

"Destination on the left."

A long gravel driveway dotted with pine trees brought us to a modern log cabin home, complete with soaring roof and oversized glass windows, nestled in a slight valley.

Mari's big brown eyes opened wide. "Very nice."

I had to agree with my technician. This place was stunning.

The builder had cleared a strategic part of the wooded property, exposing the killer mountain view. Off in the distance a narrow dirt road ran parallel to a crumbling stacked stone wall that separated the adjacent fields before it disappeared into the parkland—probably a service access trail of some sort.

I slid the stethoscope out from behind the mirror, retrieved my doctor's bag from the crowded backseat, and followed Mari to the front door.

• • ● • •

Before I could ring the doorbell we heard a menacing growl from inside. A human eyeball stared at us through a round peephole cut into the massive entry door.

Knowing some people out in the country were a little skittish about strangers appearing on their doorstep, I waved a greeting. "Hi. I'm Dr. Kate Turner from the Oak Falls Animal Hospital."

Before I got most of the words out the heavy alder door opened and a slim young woman in jeans and a sweater greeted us over the barking of a large gray and white Malamute.

"Samantha Miller. Come in, please. Stand down, Jack." Obviously well trained, the dog immediately quieted down, although a suspicious rise of hair along his hackles remained.

We pushed past the big dog who was intent on sniffing us and vigorously poking at various private parts through our coats.

"Cut that out, Jack." Samantha held her dog's muzzle for a moment, then let go. An apologetic look rose in his dark doggie eyes. "You have to forgive him. We don't get a lot of visitors." The cozy smell of freshly brewed coffee perked me up. Jack stayed close to his mistress, the top of his head coming up to her waist.

As we moved into the kitchen area I was struck by how beautiful the inside of the cabin was. The ceiling rose to a crazy height, with gigantic peeled logs spanning the entire length of the house from one end to another. A two-sided stacked fieldstone fireplace soared up to the roof. The open kitchen gleamed with stainless steel appliances and polished gray granite. White walls and dark wood floors unified the spaces. A vision of the chipped laminate countertops and old yellowed appliances in my rental apartment flashed into my mind—along with my student loan payment schedule. Oh well, someday.

Mari stood thunderstruck. "Do you live here alone?"

"Only on weekdays. My husband works in the city but he's here late Friday through Monday morning." Samantha didn't seem to resent my assistant's rather personal question. "I work for a software company, so all I need is the Internet and my computer."

I glanced again at the Malamute and observed a clump of fur sticking up along his back. "So, is Jack my patient? He looks pretty healthy." At the sound of his name the handsome dog turned toward me, the black mask of his face expectant.

"Yes, I feel horrible." His owner reached out and immediately Jack nuzzled her hand. "I didn't notice anything until last night when I touched his back right there." She made a gesture toward the spot I'd noted.

"Well, let me take a look." Mari stepped in and held the approximately eighty-five-pound dog while I began my exam. After quickly determining his general health, I started walking my gloved fingers through his thick coat. As soon as I separated the sticky hairs I knew we had a problem.

"He's got a jagged laceration here that's infected."

"Oh, no." His owner sounded guilty.

"Are there any barbed-wire fences around that he could have slipped under?" Malamutes and huskies are breeds notorious for taking off and exploring, often without their owners.

"There's a whole length of it up by the forestry trail leading into the state land. He got away from me a few days ago and disappeared for almost a half an hour. He wouldn't come when I called and I got frantic. Finally, I gave up and decided to call my husband, but that's when I saw him running down the hill toward me."

"I'm going to clean it and start him on an antibiotic. Can you give him pills?"

"No problem, as long as it's in a wad of cream cheese." Her warm smile suggested she'd been down that route with him before.

"Cream cheese? Lucky boy, Jack." His plume-like tail wagged on hearing his name.

With my clipper blade I carefully trimmed around the wound to expose the cut, scrubbed it with betadine solution, and followed with a saline lavage. After I disposed of my gloves I put Jack under house arrest—leash walks only and close observation for any change of mood or odd symptoms. Although tetanus is rare in dogs, it was still on my radar.

"Does it need stitches?"

"It's infected now so we can't suture it. That would trap the bacteria inside and make it worse. It should heal fine in about two weeks and when the fur grows in you won't even be able to find it. I'm going to give him a long-acting shot of an antibiotic to get a jump start on the infection."

"Jack doesn't have any problem growing hair, that's for sure." To prove her point Samantha pulled a tuft of grey fur off her black sweater.

The sturdy guy had been a great patient. He'd barely moved as long as someone scratched his ears.

Our work done, we began to say our good-byes. Mari e-mailed Samantha the wound instructions and scheduled a recheck in one week. Thanks to Jack's cooperation and Mari's efficiency, we were now right on schedule. As I pulled on my coat I asked, "How long have you had him?"

"Since he was a puppy. We named him Jack for Jack London, the writer of *Call of the Wild*. He's always been adventurous, digging up stuff, and bringing all kinds of things home." She tucked a random strand of dark hair behind her ear. "I think he got hurt while fetching me a present."

"What kind of present?" Mari momentarily put down our laptop to button her coat.

"Let me show you." She walked over to the fireplace and picked something out of a wicker basket by the woodpile. "This is his latest. I guess it's from a deer."

She placed a bone in my hand.

I felt a jolt in my stomach. The bone I held didn't come from a deer. It was human.

My simple house call had suddenly morphed into something way more complicated.

● ● ● ● ●

After I confessed my suspicions about Jack's present, Samantha freaked and immediately began phoning everyone from 9-1-1 to the local forest rangers. Mari tried to reassure her that the bone probably was from an old Indian burial site. As a local she'd heard of several grisly discoveries made by unsuspecting homeowners. I wasn't so sure.

In my freshman year in college I'd taken several anthropology courses, and even gone on a dig with other students in my class. One of our assignments was to catalogue a cache of bones from a large Native American burial mound.

The arm bone Jack the dog found felt heavy and much thicker than any of the bones I'd handled. My instinct told me this was no ancient artifact.

Who had died and been buried in those deep dark woods?

Chapter Two

The bride and groom were a couple of pigs.

"Here Comes the Bride" spilled out from the portable speakers as the bride trotted down the aisle. Lace anklets circled her four hooves while a fluffy white veil attached to a flower-encrusted headband cascaded over large pointed ears. I'd barely made it in time. As Dr. Kate Turner, the official maid of honor, I carried a bouquet of carrots, Swiss chard, and edible nasturtiums. The groom lifted his snout and sniffed appreciatively in my direction.

Yes, I was a member of the wedding party for two potbellied pigs, the real ones who go "oink." I served a dual function—personal veterinarian to the couple and emergency medical support. I'd been told to wear something flowing and romantic. Since that description didn't match anything currently in my closet, I borrowed a vintage flowered chiffon dress from my office manager, Cindy, and stuck sprigs of baby's breath in my hair to make a floral crown. The diverse guests sitting under the white party tent included a parrot, plenty of dogs, two annoyed cats, several snakes draped around their owners' various body parts, and a whole bunch of potbellied piggies. Most of my fellow staff members from Oak Falls Veterinary Hospital were here to lend their support and eat free food. Even our shy kennel boy, Eugene, had shown up and sweetly volunteered to help keep the party area "tidy."

Why were the pigs getting married, you might ask?

The truth—it was a shotgun wedding, their owner joked.
Six little piglets were expected very soon.

• • ● • •

Accompanying me to the celebration as my friend—and not as
a date, as I emphatically reminded him several times—was Oak
Falls police officer and pre-law student Luke Gianetti. In his
black suit and blue shirt he was undoubtedly the best-looking
guy in the place, rivaled only by Angel, the groom, resplendent
in his top hat and curled tail.

Nancy Wagner, the owner of the pigs, was the brains behind
the party. All proceeds from the publicity surrounding the event
would go to local animal charities. One of Nancy's wealthy
friends provided her gigantic home overlooking the Hudson
River for the affair and a chef acquaintance had offered to cater
the event at cost. Everything was lovely, even if Penelope, the
bride, ended up eating part of her veil.

Unaccustomed to such high heels I concentrated on not falling
over as I walked down the aisle, with the pregnant bride trotting
directly behind me, obviously not happy with my slow pace.
Straining on her leash, she used her snout to goose me along.

When the ceremony was over and the guests were milling
around, I snuck away for a quiet stroll. The Hudson River
sparkled in the distance. The freshly mowed grass of the expansive lawn grew lush and green, even this late in the fall. A mild
breeze kicked up that green smell of cut grass. I slipped off my
party shoes and climbed a small knoll for a better view. At the
crest a pitted stone bench rewarded me with a place to sit and
a spectacular view of the winding river dotted with sailboats.
Mother Nature always puts on a show, if only we take the time
to stop and look. Puffy clouds like mounds of whipped cream
floated across the blue sky.

"A majestic sight, isn't it?"

Luke had come up behind me while I was feeding part of
my bouquet to one of the four-footed guests wandering the
fenced-in grounds.

"Absolutely." Another potbellied pig tore the last of the carrots out of my grasp. "Okay, guys. There's no more food." When I waved my empty hands they got the picture. "So, Luke, did you enjoy the ceremony?"

"I was moved."

"Really?" My eyebrows raised in disbelief.

"Literally." Luke pointed to a pig rooting around further down the hill. "That big brown one over there, the one with the polka-dot bow tie, shoved me with his head until I moved over." He proceeded to give me a reenactment, complete with snorting and grunting that made me crack up.

"Well, I worked this morning, so it's time for me to kick back." Music drifted in the air from the party below. I tilted my face up to the sun. "We should enjoy this weather while we can."

"How about getting some lunch and having our own picnic up here?" Luke held out his hand to me.

"That sounds wonderful." When our fingers touched, our eyes locked for a moment. Although our official status was "friends only" there had always been something....

Carefully, I slid my shoes back on, his arm steadying me. Unfortunately my right heel immediately sank into the soft earth.

"Those things aren't meant for this kind of walking," Luke commented as we picked our way down the grassy slope.

"I've got sneakers with me if I need them, along with my emergency bag, in the back of the truck." We reached the bluestone pathway that led back to the main building but I didn't let go of his arm.

"Always prepared." He smiled at me, eyes crinkling in the corner, making him even more attractive than usual. Our off-and-on flirtation flamed into the on position.

"Where are you parked?" We strolled along arm in arm as if we had all the time in the world.

"Almost at the end of the driveway. You?"

"Right near the house. One of the perks of being in the wedding party."

Luke waited while I scraped the caked dirt off my high heels. A wall of climbing roses, their petals fading, lined the pathway to the catering tent.

It felt nice walking alongside him, our arms linked together. Feelings that I didn't like to admit were still hanging around, took me by surprise. Luke and I hadn't seen each other for over a month and those circumstances had been less than pleasant. Today it almost felt as though our platonic friendship might morph into something more. Maybe I finally was ready to trust someone again. Six months had passed since my last romance had crashed and burned and I'd sworn off dating for a while. But a picnic near the river sounded like the perfect way to catch up on things—all kinds of things—and maybe start something new.

Two lookalike young women approached us carrying plates piled with food.

"Hey, Luke," the taller one said, "Want to join us at that table?" She indicated with her chin a picnic table underneath a nearby tree.

"Thanks, Paula, but Dr. Kate has dibs on me." He introduced me to both of them, first Paula, then her sister, Patty.

"Suit yourself," Paula said in a snotty voice. "Why didn't Dina come with you today?" She stared directly at me when she said it.

What? To hide my confusion I gave her a stiff but polite smile.

"She had to work. I texted a picture," he answered.

He was back with his old girlfriend? It took all my willpower not to glare at him. When did he send her this text—while I was walking down the aisle holding my carrot bouquet?

Whatever warm and fuzzy emotions I'd been feeling about Luke disappeared. As soon as the sisters were out of sight I let go of his arm.

"Back with Dina?" I kept my voice deceptively casual.

"Yeah, about a week ago. We decided to give it another try." Luke looked everywhere except at me. "You still seeing that anthropologist guy?"

I'd been Skyping with a former boyfriend now working at a dig in Africa. Our relationship was purely platonic, but I wasn't going to admit that to Luke. "You mean Jeremy?" Not to be outdone, I pulled my phone out and made a big deal out of checking my messages before I replied. "Yes."

"Hey, you told me this wasn't a date. In fact, you were pretty darn clear about it." Luke sounded annoyed.

"That is correct," I replied, my words very precise if a little too loud. "So no damage done."

"Right. No damage done." By this time we were facing each other, the tension between us practically shooting off sparks.

Before the situation escalated I heard Nancy, the owner of the cloven-footed bride and groom call out to me. "Kate, we need you for some pictures."

Without a good-bye I turned away from him and started down the pathway, annoyed at myself for feeling so steamed up. Reluctantly I let Nancy guide me toward the wedding arch where the rest of the bridal party and several photographers waited.

"But my hair," I started to protest. "Can't I take a minute to—?"

"Don't worry, it looks great." She rearranged one of the pieces of baby's breath still stuck in my hair. "Besides, everyone will be looking at the bride."

I thought she was being sarcastic but then I realized she was absolutely serious.

Today was all about the "oink."

• ● ● ● •

Fifteen minutes later we were finished and Luke was nowhere in sight. I headed to the table set aside for the veterinary staff from Oak Falls Animal Hospital and found most of them getting ready to leave.

"This was a lot of fun. You look lovely, Kate." Cindy, my receptionist, busied herself putting leftovers into the ziplock bags she'd brought. My jacket and purse lay on the bench next to her.

"Thanks for keeping my things." During the photo session my mind had gone over and over this situation with Luke. Watching Cindy I decided the perfect place for him and our non-relationship was in a virtual ziplock bag.

"Did you like the dress?"

"Yes, thanks for letting me borrow it." I twirled in front of her, letting the flowered chiffon float around me. I'll take it to the dry cleaner's tomorrow." Although I'd been especially careful, I was worried about a few areas touched by various wet pig noses.

"How did the pictures come out?" I'd asked the staff to take photos, figuring no one would believe this wedding unless it was documented.

"Great. I've already posted some to my Facebook page. Check your phone. I sent a bunch to you."

"Thanks. I'm sure my Gramps will get a kick out of them." Sure enough, when I scrolled through my messages there I was—walking down the aisle, one carrot sort of flopping out of the bouquet and right behind me the pig bride on a leash in all her pregnant splendor. We both were smiling.

Waving good-bye to everyone I surreptitiously glanced around again for Luke. Not seeing him, I took the coward's way out and texted him thanks for joining me today.

I'd already sent it and climbed into my truck when my phone rang.

"Dr. Kate? This is Samantha Miller. You saw my dog, Jack, this morning."

"Of course, Samantha. Is everything okay?"

"Yes." She sounded a bit embarrassed. "The police came out to my place and I showed them the bone…and I wanted you to know they found…they found the rest of a body in the hills behind the house."

Her voice choked when she told me.

"Are you alright?" That peaceful setting around her house probably didn't feel peaceful anymore.

"I guess so. My husband is on his way home. But I wanted to tell you…"

Her voice broke off.

"Samantha? Are you there?" I could hear Jack barking in the background. "Hello?"

After a moment she got back on the phone. "Sorry. There are a bunch of officers milling around outside. Anyway, they don't think these are very old."

"Oh." That was what I thought when I saw it but I hadn't wanted to needlessly worry her.

"We have a portable electric heater so I plugged it in on the deck for them to use, and that's when I overheard them say it."

A chill ran down my back. "What did they say?"

"They said they think whoever it is was murdered."

Chapter Three

On the drive back home I pushed Luke once again out of my mind and instead thought about my client, Samantha. Here she was living in this beautiful cabin in the woods, far away from the chaos of New York City, and what happens? The police uncover a murder scene practically in her backyard. From personal experience I knew the stress and anxiety a brush with violence could spawn. Hopefully, together, the young couple could put this terrible news behind them.

When I got back to my place around four-thirty, Buddy, my ecstatic dog, demanded attention. I took off the borrowed dress, hung it up, made a mental note to take it to the dry cleaner's, then took him for a walk behind the hospital. Every squirrel required a bark. Being a King Charles spaniel, nothing escaped his doggy attention. With darkness coming on fast we didn't linger. Buddy got a treat and I grabbed a handful of corn chips. Between the close contact with the pigs and Samantha's news, I desperately needed a shower, so that became a priority.

Wrapped in my terrycloth robe I stepped out of the bathroom and towel-dried my hair. The sun had set, the apartment windows no longer reflecting its rosy glow—which reminded me to check the time. I had only five minutes before my Skype "date" with Jeremy Engles, a former college boyfriend I'd reconnected up with through Facebook. I pulled on my favorite soft sweats and fuzzy purple slippers. A quick brush through my hair and a dash of lipstick and I was camera-ready. Given my current track record with men I thanked my lucky stars that Jeremy was zillions of miles away in Africa. A strictly electronic relationship suited me fine for now. While waiting for the Skype connection, nervous energy prodded me to straighten up the bookshelf and clear the top of the desk before I sat down in front of the computer monitor.

Mr. Katt, our hospital kitty, lingered in the office doorway, his tail straight up and twitching, watching me. A feline decision definitely was in the works.

"Come on. Come here, Mr. Katt." I patted the corner of the desk.

He looked away in distain, but it was all an act. The next moment a plump load of furry feline landed full-force on my lap. As soon as I stroked him, his purr motor began to rumble. Mr. Katt was a "hit and run" artist, famous for his sneak attacks on the staff. Periodically he also demands attention, then, after a few moments, scoots off. Those were his terms and I had long ago surrendered to them.

Petting the cat relaxed me a little. I still wasn't sure how I felt about these so-called Skype dates. Jeremy and I had met while undergraduates at the University of Pennsylvania, and had gone out for three months before calling it quits and going back to "friend only" status. After graduation I headed to Cornell University for veterinary school while he went to New Mexico to work on his master's degree. Now a full professor of anthropology with a doctorate, he currently was on sabbatical working a dig in North Africa through his university.

He'd disappeared from my life for five years and now had roared back in.

The glare from the harsh overhead florescent light bounced off the screen so I turned it off and lit a nearby corner lamp. Its flattering glow softened up the room.

Right on time, Jeremy's face appeared on the screen, a little out of focus. In fact, between his shaggy long hair and giant beard, all I could really see were his eyes.

"Hi Kate. You look especially nice tonight."

"You look pretty good yourself. What I can see, that is." He appeared to be sitting in a tent. His bushy beard was a running joke. Most of the men on his dig had simply stopped shaving because of the lack of available hot water.

"Are your clients still saying you resemble…you know, Meryl Streep? Because in this light, I agree with them." His face moved closer to the camera distorting his features.

Surprised he remembered, I absentmindedly pushed a stubborn strand of damp hair behind my ear. "Yes, I get that periodically, although I don't see it."

"Take it as a compliment. The only famous person I resemble at the moment is Bigfoot."

We shared a laugh before I asked, "How is work going? No more duststorms I hope."

"Not since I last spoke to you. But I've got some great news. Our dig is going on a government-ordered shutdown in two weeks, so I'm coming back to the States."

My face froze for a moment. "How wonderful. Your parents will be happy to see you."

"Well, it's poor timing for them since they leave on a month-long tour of China two days after I return."

"That's too bad."

"Every dust cloud has a silver lining," Jeremy said excitedly. "Now you'll have me all to yourself." His sly grin flashed under all the beard hair, but I noticed the corners of his eyes didn't crinkle up.

"My flight gets into JFK late Friday night," he continued. "I'm going to spend that Saturday and Sunday with my folks and then drive up to see you on Monday morning. I'll e-mail you all the details."

Jeremy was coming to Oak Falls?

"Did you hear me, Kate?"

"You mean two weeks from this Monday?" I hoped he hadn't heard the panic in my voice.

"That's right. I can hardly believe it."

"Neither can I." My mind scrambled around for something else to say. I'd kicked around visiting him on his dig sometime, but suddenly "sometime" was only two weeks away. "Uh, when's the last time I saw you in person?"

"At least four or five years ago. Can you believe it?" He put his hand on the screen, inviting me to place my fingers on his.

"That's a definite no." Excited and anxious I blurted out a random thought. "I can't take much time off work, though. I'm the only doctor on staff."

The picture started jumping in and out, probably from a storm thousands of miles away.

"Sorry, you're fading. See you soon." Jeremy waved and blew me a kiss as the connection continued to fail. Outside, the windows were icy black.

"See you soon," I repeated to the empty screen. Our Skype session was over.

Annoyed at not being the center of attention, Mr. Katt hurtled off my lap, navigating several obstacles to arrive at the top of a bank of cages before staring down at me like the Sphinx.

My perfect long-distance flirtation was about to unravel like a cheap sweater in a hot dryer. It was easy to have a relationship with an image on a screen. Real guys and real life promised to be way more messy.

Chapter Four

Monday morning rolled in with threatening black clouds and multiple brief thunderstorms. I didn't mind. After a crazy weekend of pigs with bow ties, human remains, and obsessing about Jeremy's visit, it felt good to get back to work. Mari and I had a full schedule of house calls, so I stocked my doctor's bag and checked our supplies while she updated the computer and went over the appointments with Cindy, our receptionist.

It wasn't until we were in the truck and on our way that I remembered to ask my veterinary assistant if she'd heard anything about the mysterious remains found in the woods. I figured she had a direct information link through Cindy, whose sister was married to Oak Falls Chief of Police Bobby Garcia.

"Any news on the victim?" I stared at the road ahead, my windshield wipers squeaking with each swipe as the rain stopped and started.

"Not yet. Cindy said it looks like animals disturbed the grave and scattered some of the bones. But someone else told a friend of mine the State Troopers think they've recovered almost the entire skeleton." She steadied our laptop as we bounced along the back road.

A strong gust of wind shook the truck and whipped a broken branch across the blacktop. Now rain pelted down full-force on the windshield, the drops landing sideways.

"Well, I hope they can find out who it is soon, for their families' sake."

"So do I." Mari glanced out the truck window as the trees waved back and forth along the road.

For a while we listened to the downshifting of the truck and the howl of the storm.

"Did you hear about the guy and the bear?"

"No." A changing traffic light had me slowly come to a stop.

"I guess Fish and Wildlife got some anonymous complaint about someone keeping a bear on his property."

A double spray of water shot out from the tires as we went through a deep puddle. Concentrating on the road I didn't keep up my end of the conversation, but Mari kept on without me.

"I'm not surprised at anything people do anymore," she commented.

"Is it a cub?"

"Don't know, but I'll keep you posted."

The GPS politely reminded me to make the next right-hand turn. "By the way, what's our first call about?" With the weather so bad I wanted to make sure we brought everything we might need inside with us. That would avoid getting soaked running back and forth to the truck.

Mari refreshed her computer screen before clicking to a different page. "This note from Cindy says a pocket pet got into some tar. You've seen them before. Client's name is Mary Ellis."

Despite the weather I almost slammed on my brakes. That name rang a very loud bell.

"Mari," I warned my technician, "if my memory is correct, we're in for an interesting experience."

Mary Ellis and her family were one of the very first appointments I saw after Doc Anderson hired me to run his practice. After I met them I guessed that interacting with his human clients was one of the many reasons Doc decided to go on a round-the-world cruise.

Recalling that appointment made me realize how much had happened in my professional life in the last six months. Let's see, I'd stumbled on two bodies, helped solve a different murder of a client and friend, and almost gotten killed. Twice.

The highlight of my social life, on the other hand, was being maid of honor at Saturday's pig wedding and having a Skype date with a guy I hadn't seen since college. Winning a prize for the lowest point was finding out that Luke had gone back to his high school sweetheart.

Which proves I don't get out that much.

• • ● • •

Ten minutes later we parked in front of a familiar house. Careful not to land in a puddle, I slid down off the driver's seat, stethoscope wrapped around my neck. Once on the ground I opened the extended cab side door to get my doctor's bag. Mari closed the laptop, placed it in a hard case so it wouldn't get wet, then followed me up to the front door.

In no time at all it was déjà vu all over again.

A teenage boy with a buzz cut answered the door. He nodded solemnly and turned back into the house, the hint of a smile on his lips. We followed him through the entryway and into the living room.

"Where's the patient?" I asked with trepidation.

He pointed to a large glass bottle in the living room with coins lining the bottom. For a crazy second I wondered if he wanted me to count them. On closer look I saw one of the coins move. My guess was that my little patient didn't get into some tar. He was trapped in a jar.

"Your hamster is…?"

"In there." The teen sheepishly reached behind him, then with a flourish held up a large hammer. "Do you need this?"

"Put that hammer away, Tommy." Mary Ellis, his mother, appeared at the kitchen door holding a wiggly toddler in her arms.

It was all coming back to me.

"Hi, Dr. Turner. I'm so sorry to have to call you again." She leaned over and put the squirming boy down. "Damien, say hello to our veterinarian."

Damien eyed me suspiciously. Resplendent in Superman pullups and what looked like his mother's red bedroom slippers, he clutched part of a jelly donut in one grubby hand. "Peanut's in the bottle," he yelled, before dragging his feet along the carpet.

"Now, Damien," his mother admonished him, "use your quiet voice."

The toddler grinned at her. Two seconds later he screamed out his new favorite phrase. "Peanut's in the bottle. Peanut's in the bottle."

Mari nudged me and muttered, "I'm never having kids."

Another piercing scream from Damien announced the arrival of a young girl about six or seven years old wearing a poufy ballerina costume covered in spangles. She grimaced at her brothers before pirouetting smartly across the room, narrowly missing the bottle containing my patient.

"Okay. What happened?" I directed my question at Mary Ellis but noticed Tommy the teenager had suddenly become extremely interested in his shoes.

"Well," Mary sighed, "I told the kids it was time to empty the change jar so they could buy a treat at the grocery store."

"Candy! Candy! Candy!" Damien screeched, reaching a new decibel. In a flash he stuffed the last of the donut in his mouth, stuck out his fingers and started shuffling toward his sister like a zombie. She shrieked and hid behind her mother.

"Damien, stop trying to give Angela a shock."

His sister, keeping her distance, stuck out her tongue at him.

The toddler must have learned that by rubbing the slippers on the rug he could generate static electricity. Pretty smart of him, I thought—annoying, but smart. "So, Mrs. Ellis, you were saying…" I tried to get more of a patient history but suspected I was fighting a losing battle.

"Peanut was in his plastic roller ball." She pointed to an orange see-through ball on the carpet, its two halves resting near the leg of the coffee table. "I don't think it was closed tight enough because Tommy said Peanut got out."

I took a side-glance at Tommy, who had enough common sense to look back down at his sneakers.

"Anyway, the bottle was laying on the rug and the next thing we knew the little guy ran inside and he won't come out."

I couldn't blame him.

"Peanut's in the bottle," Damien commented, the remaining jelly from the donut smeared around his mouth. From the color of the leftovers on his face I suspected raspberry.

"Are you sure you don't need this?" Tommy lifted the hammer up again in anticipation.

"Eeewwwww," Angela whimpered. "I can't watch."

Mary stroked her daughter's back before continuing the bizarre story. "We tried bribing Peanut with hamster food but Damien squished his peanut butter sandwich into the bottle and it got stuck in the narrow part of the neck. I mashed most of it out with a wooden spoon, but it made a disgusting mess. When we turn the bottle upside down now, all the junk blocks Peanut from getting out." Mary comforted her daughter and glared at her oldest who still held the hammer at the ready.

"No hammers," I said as forcefully as I could.

Tommy reluctantly abandoned the weapon on the dining room table.

Dodging Damien, who tried to poke me with his electric finger, I got down on the living room rug and took a good look at the situation. Two bright eyes stared at me from behind assorted change, lumps of bread, and a slimy wad of peanut butter. Despite all the excitement, Peanut looked perfectly fine.

"Maybe we could suck him out with the vacuum cleaner?" Tommy sounded hopeful.

"Eeewwww! Don't be so gross." His sister squealed and covered her eyes.

"Gross! Gross! Gross!" Damien repeated at top volume, keeping up his end of the conversation.

As much fun as this was, it was time to get down to business.

"Can someone bring Peanut's habitat in here?"

Mary gestured to Tommy who made a face before disappearing into the back of the house. When he returned, I was happy to see they had followed the suggestions I'd made during my last visit. Their hamster now had a plastic tunnel, a nice thick nest of bedding material, two water bottles attached to his wire cage and Peanut's favorite thing—a large exercise wheel.

"This is a very nice home for a pocket pet," I told the family.

"He's cool," Tommy volunteered. "Peanut sits in my hand and takes food from me."

"We love him," Angela whispered from behind her mother.

Damien, for once, had no comment.

"Mari, can you go get the duct tape from the truck?" With a nod of gratitude my assistant took off at warp speed.

Tommy's eyes opened wide. "What are you going to do?" I figured all kinds of bizarre scenarios involving duct tape were taking place in his mind.

"I bet you didn't know that duct tape is used in medicine for a bunch of things. Good things, like closing a wound in an emergency, acting as a temporary sling, even removing warts."

"Cool."

"Eeeewwwww!"

When Mari came back I asked everyone to go into the kitchen so I could work.

"Duck, duck, goose," Damien flapped his arms and began to quack. Despite myself I had to laugh. This toddler was growing on me…like a fungus.

"Do we have to?" Tommy begged his mother.

She glanced at me and raised her eyebrows in an unspoken question.

I didn't cave. "Everyone out."

"Let's go, kids." She made an about-face and put her hand on Tommy's shoulder. "Come on, guys. Let's make some popcorn for our guests."

The entire family traipsed out of the room, but not before Damien got his final two cents in at the top of his impressive vocal register by screaming, "Popcorn! Popcorn! Popcorn!"

Mari raised her eyes to the heavens. "Thank goodness."

"It's only temporary, so don't get used to it." I took the roll of duct tape from her hand.

"What are you going to do? Break the bottle?" For a moment Mari sounded a lot like Tommy.

"No. I'm going to perform a veterinary magic trick. The vanishing hamster." For emphasis I waved the duct tape in the air like a magic wand. Mari didn't seem impressed.

First I opened the door to Peanut's habitat, took a few morsels of his dry food and crushed them in my hand, releasing the delicious odor of hamster kibble goodness. Next, I carefully reached back inside and sprinkled the pieces where he could see them. A quick search of his bedding uncovered a few hidden blueberries and a sliver of carrot. Those went on top of the dry food. When I snuck a surreptitious peek into the bottle I saw two black eyes watching me. I spun his wheel. As soon as it clicked he lifted his head, eyes shiny with interest.

"That got his attention." Mari leaned closer to the bottle.

"Good." I took a few pinches of bedding material and sprinkled it near the cage door. Trusty hemostats made it easy to lift out most of the debris from the neck of the bottle, creating a clear passage. Once that was accomplished I slid the habitat as close as possible to the opening in the bottle.

"Duct tape, please."

Mari pulled several strips off and cut them with her bandage scissors.

Trying not to jostle the bottle too much I duct-taped the cage to the bottle, doubling it over where the two parts met so nothing sticky would touch the hamster's fur. Satisfied I stood up.

"What next?" Mari asked.

"Abracadabra. Drum roll, please." I waved my stethoscope over my invention.

The expression on her face suggested I had lost my mind.

"Just kidding. Let's turn day into night."

We pulled the heavy drapes across the living room window and flicked off the lights. The room was now quiet and dark.

I was counting on the little guy getting bored in the bottle and deciding to go home to his yummy food and beloved wheel. Meanwhile, we needed to give him some privacy.

"Hey," I whispered to my assistant. "Want some popcorn?"

• • ● • •

Twenty minutes later Mari and I were stuffed with popcorn and had listened to Damien chant that all-time favorite, "Peanut's in the bottle," about a million times.

When we stood up I told everyone except Mari to be quiet and stay put until I checked on my patient.

On tiptoe I opened the kitchen door. The squeaking of the exercise wheel signaled success. Without turning on the light I stealthily made my way into the living room, cut the duct tape with the bandage scissors, peeled it away, and quickly closed the cage door. Success. Thankfully, no one was any the worse for wear, except maybe Mari.

Despite my command, everyone suddenly burst out of the kitchen with a tired Mom unsuccessfully trying to herd her rowdy kids back inside.

A cheer went up when I turned on the lights and they saw Peanut in his cage, happily scampering away. Angela managed several pirouettes before Damien gleefully began rubbing his borrowed slippers on the rug.

Time to leave.

Tommy obviously was disappointed that no hammers had been involved in the rescue.

I went over a little basic hamster care with the kids while Mari entered the bill into the computer.

Relieved everything had gone well, Mary Ellis escorted us toward the front door. Mari couldn't stop herself from asking a question.

"You seem so cool amid this chaos," she said. "How do you do it?"

"What chaos?" A rattling noise behind us turned out to be the giant glass bottle, now hamster-less, which one of the kids had rolled down the hall, aimed directly toward us. The leftover coins clinked against the sides with each full revolution. Instinctively, Mary blocked it with her foot.

"I hate to tell you, but this is a good day," their mom confessed.

"I'm never ever having kids," Mari swore under her breath.

"Buzz." Damien's fingertip touched my hand. A crackle of static electricity zapped between us.

The toddler stared at me, waiting for my reaction.

I didn't flinch. Instead I slid my shoes back and forth on the carpet, held up my index finger, and slowly inched toward him. "Buzzing you back."

A cascade of giggles erupted from him and kept up even as we closed the front door.

Mari sprinted to the truck ahead of me. I waited on the porch, checking my pockets to make sure I hadn't left anything behind. The rain began to fall harder before I dashed down the driveway trying to avoid the puddles and rivulets of water streaming along the slight incline. With one move I threw open the truck door and leaped into the driver's seat. The windshield had fogged up and the inside of the cab smelled like damp wool with just a hint of overripe banana. After I stowed all my gear behind my seat, I started the engine and set the controls to defrost.

Next to me Mari kept staring at her phone. From the expression on her face I knew something had happened.

"Anything wrong?" I turned on the windshield wipers to clear the glass.

"Cindy texted me. They think they've identified the remains. There was an inscription on the watch." Her eyes were wells of darkness. "Chief Garcia is helping provide dental records to the investigators working the case."

I let the truck idle. "Someone local?"

"Yes. Everyone thought he went out to California, to Hollywood." She sounded like she was in shock, her words garbled. "He's not supposed to be dead."

The rain hit the windshield with an icy slush that smeared the view. A gray-white fog hovered above the tree line.

"What was his name?" I asked as gently as possible.

"Flynn," she answered.

"His name was Flynn Keegan."

Chapter Five

Our long and now sad day finally ended but the rain kept up a steady drizzle. We made it back to the Oak Falls Animal Hospital looking like two drowned rats. My straight blond hair lay plastered to my head while Mari's darker locks had exploded in a cumulus cloud of curls. Our final house-call client had been an easy vaccination, a sweet but gigantic dog terrified to get into his owner's car. Since Jumbo the Mastiff weighed as much as his owner, the dog always won the argument.

A few seconds after we left their home the skies opened up for the third time that day. They say third time's a charm but we both got soaked in a ferocious cold downpour. Periodic bursts of sleet made the driving conditions slow and hazardous. Both of us were relieved when we finally made it back to the hospital. Only Cindy's car remained in the parking lot. Everyone else had left. We zipped in through the side door used for walking the dogs. After dumping our equipment in the treatment area, I made a beeline for the warmth and comfort of my office and portable space heater. Mari followed right behind.

The office was dim but I didn't have the energy to get up and turn on the overhead lights.

"You look like a young Meryl Streep, only wet," my assistant quipped before sinking into a chair in my office.

"Thanks a lot, Mari," I replied, sarcastically. This was the supposed resemblance to the famous actress that Jeremy had mentioned and that had turned into a running joke with my staff and clients. "Your hair looks like Damien zapped you good."

"Please, don't remind me—I never want to hear *Peanut's in the bottle* again." Mari stomped her dripping sneakers on the floor. "My feet are freezing."

"I feel like I took a cold shower with all my clothes on." Clinging damp pants began to stick to the black leather desk chair. The entire room started to smell pretty funky.

Cindy poked her head in. "Let's go, ladies. I made you hot chocolate." Seeing no activity on our part, she pointed at the door. "Now."

Following orders we marched into the surgery suite where to our surprise she had set up a little picnic on one of the stainless-steel tables. Hot bright beams from above focused down on a pair of stools, each covered with a towel. Blue placemats and two mugs of cocoa with a peak of whipped cream on top beckoned to us. It smelled delicious.

"Thank you, Cindy. You're too good to us," I told her. Mari and I sat down and soon the combined heat of the surgery lights and drinks warmed us up.

"Cozy now? I figured you could use some cheering up." Ever mindful of the utility bills, Cindy waited a beat before switching off the overhead spots.

"That was perfect." I'd begun to feel a little sleepy from the sugar and the chocolate and the heat.

"All right, you two," she announced to us. "I'm going to take off. Kate, I walked Buddy for you."

"Thanks again."

"See you tomorrow—and put your raincoats and boots in the truck. I'm not going to do this every day." Cindy walked down the hall toward the front door, turning off lights as she went.

"Yes, Mommy," Mari called out.

"I can't hear you," she joked. The slam of the front door left us alone in a darkened hospital.

"She's right," I said, not moving.

"She's always right," Mari agreed, "but I still have to give her a hard time once in a while."

We clicked off the remaining office lights and brought our cups to the sink in the break room.

"I'll wash," I volunteered. "The hot water will feel good on my hands."

While I cleaned, Mari checked the countertops, straightened out the treatment area, and made sure we were ready to close up. No lab samples to put out tonight. She stowed our house-call gear away and placed the remaining vaccines with its ice pack back in the refrigerator.

The hospital felt uncharacteristically quiet, until an unexpected roll of thunder made the windows rattle. The next clap of thunder was quickly followed by the familiar sounds of driving rain and wind.

"Want to stay until the worst is over?" I asked.

"Sure. Lucy and Desi will be fine."

Mari wasn't referring to the old nineteen-fifties television show. No, she'd named her beautiful pair of Rottweiler dogs after the famous Hollywood couple. Because of her working hours, she'd installed self-feeders and multiple water bowls in her kitchen, as well as a king-sized doggy door out to the fenced-in backyard. She lavished attention on them, referring to the dogs as her fur children. Her boyfriend insisted she loved them more than she loved him, and he probably was right.

We walked the short distance to my attached apartment in Doc Anderson's converted garage. The sound of the rain echoed even louder under the metal roof. Exhausted, I dropped down on the old chenille sofa while Mari took the recliner. Buddy greeted us with a slow tail-thump. He moved just enough to rest his head on my foot.

"There might be some dog hair on that chair," I warned.

"No kidding."

I wasn't exactly known for my housekeeping skills.

Together we listened to the steady staccato of raindrops. I wrapped a soft plaid blanket around my shoulders and handed another to Mari. Without prompting, she told me about Flynn Keegan, the person found dead in the woods.

"I was always envious of Flynn in high school," she confessed. "He was gorgeous, popular—everything I wasn't. Everyone loved him. You knew he was destined to succeed at anything he set out to do."

"Sounds familiar. Most of us know someone like that."

The softening rain pinged a gentle rhythm. We both listened, lost in our own thoughts.

"Can I ask you something?" My assistant stretched out her legs.

"Sure."

"Seeing that arm bone the other day creeped me out." Mari involuntarily rubbed her hands together. "Now I feel even worse because I knew Flynn and his mom and sister."

Unfortunately, I understood only too well how she felt. After I discovered two of my clients dead during a house call, I'd had nightmares for weeks. The only consolation I could offer were some very personal words of wisdom.

"You know my Gramps often came across bodies during his arson investigations. He told me the way he dealt with it was to believe that the dead chose him to find them, so he could help tell their story."

"But a dog found Flynn's arm." There was a shaky quality to her voice as she pulled the blanket tighter around her body.

I thought about that for a moment. "Did he like animals?"

Her reply came slowly. "I think he did…I'm pretty sure his family had a dog."

"Maybe that's how Flynn wanted us to find him. Maybe he wouldn't have minded at all. Think about it."

A tiny smile curved her lips and her face relaxed. She began to experiment with the recliner lever, and the seat lurched backward.

"You know, somehow that makes me feel better."

"I'm glad."

Once more we drifted into silence, listening to the slowing patter of raindrops on the roof.

Her next question drifted up from the depths of the chair. "Do you think they'll find his murderer after all these years?"

I took a long drink of water before I answered. "When did he leave Oak Falls?"

"Let's see. I was a freshman in high school when he was a senior. My impression is he left town a couple of months after he graduated."

I could hear her softly counting.

"That would be ten years ago."

"Ten years is a long time. I'm not sure who will end up doing the investigation."

"So it won't be our local police?"

"Honestly, I don't know. I'll ask Luke when I see him." I didn't say *if* I see him. "Better yet, Cindy can find out for you."

"True." With a jolt the recliner jerked back up to its original position. Mari slipped off her blanket and folded it on the sofa. "This is so weird, Kate. I think that Flynn's graduating class has their ten-year high school reunion in a few weeks."

We both knew one member who wouldn't be there.

The staccato beat of raindrops on the metal roof faded to a periodic ding. "Sounds like the storm has tapered off."

Mari brushed some dog hair off her pants. "We need to lighten the mood here before I go home. Let's change the subject." Her mouth scrunched up in a half smile. "So when is Jeremy coming—and is he staying here with you?"

Jeremy?

Rats. I'd forgotten all about him.

After Mari left I drifted off to sleep on the sofa, so when the phone rang I was tempted to let it go to voice mail. However, the name on caller ID made me wake up fast.

"Hi, Gramps. Everything okay?" My grandfather usually stuck to a specific pattern, calling me every Sunday evening like clockwork. I prayed nothing was wrong.

"Everything is fine on this end." His voice sounded strong and clear, thanks to a new medication for his smoke-induced chronic obstructive pulmonary disease. After more than two decades in the NYC fire department his lungs had paid the price.

My watch read nine-thirty. In my Gramps' world, nine-thirty was like midnight.

"What are you doing up at this hour?"

"Late night poker game. I couldn't leave without giving the boys a chance to win back some of their losses."

"Did they?" I sat up on the sofa and rubbed my face. The blanket slid onto the floor.

"Of course not." He laughed at the absurdity of my question.

I realized the rain had completely stopped. With a stretch I rolled my shoulders. "So, anything else new since I spoke to you last?"

"I should ask you the same question."

Oops. I didn't like the implication in his voice.

"What's this about a body being found in the woods near Oak Falls? Or did that slip your mind?"

Buddy stirred next to me then pushed his nose under my hand. Phone calls made him jealous. "Hey, I was going to tell you about it after they identified the remains." I tried to sound self-righteous to cover my tracks. It didn't work.

"How come the newspaper mentions you?"

Shoot. I hadn't had any time to check the news. "One of my Saturday morning clients showed me a bone that her dog brought home. I told her to call the authorities."

"Okay. So do they have an ID?"

"Yes. A local boy named Flynn Keegan. No one knew he was missing. Everyone, including his family, thought he'd gone out to L.A."

"The paper said he'd been gone for what, nine or ten years?" An arson investigator for twenty-plus years in New York City, bodies and murder were nothing new to my Gramps.

"Sounds about right. I really don't know that much about it."

"Let's hope it stays that way." This time the disapproval in his voice was obvious. "It was a homicide, I suppose."

"If the town gossip mill is correct. Official cause of death should be released soon." I got up off the sofa and stretched again. "Don't worry. This is one murder I'm not getting involved in."

Buddy jumped down, eager to go for his nightly walk.

"Promise?" Gramps made me feel like I was ten years old.

"Yes, I promise." Unfortunately the inquisitive little girl he had raised lurked deep inside me and crossed her fingers behind her back, just in case.

There was no immediate reaction from my Gramps until he said, "Katie, my love. Now why don't I believe you?"

Chapter Six

When my alarm clock went off the next morning I wanted to throw it across the room and go back to sleep. Although that would have been lovely, there was work to do. When I let Buddy out, cold air woke me up in a hurry.

Thirty minutes later, armed with steaming cups of coffee, Mari and I braced for more bad weather. Loaded down with raincoats, umbrellas, and two extra pairs of boots stashed in the back of the truck, we thought we were prepared for the worst. But good old Mother Nature decided to surprise us and, instead of the predicted rain, served up sleet and frigid winds. The stinging glacial gusts that whipped around the corner of our next house call made me wish I'd worn an arctic-rated ski mask.

"Pretty soon we'll be battling the snow." Mari adjusted a gigantic fluffy muffler to cover her nose and mouth after we reached our client's porch. With a gloved hand studded with ice crystals I pushed the doorbell. "How Much is That Doggie in the Window?" cheerfully chimed back at us.

The two figures that opened the door appeared as snug as bugs, if bugs wore hand-knit sweaters. Handsome in a diamond-patterned argyle sweater, Little Man gave us his customary Chihuahua greeting—a teeth-baring lip-curling snarl. His owner, Daphne Davidsen, wore a matching human-sized outfit and offered us an effusive welcome. Both topped off their outfits with colorful golf hats festooned on the top with a mock black-and-white golf ball.

"Come in, come in please. It's getting very cold out there." Although christened Daphne, everyone called her Daffy, for obvious reasons. She stepped gracefully aside and guided Mari and me into the foyer. We all pretended Little Man wasn't emitting growls from one end and poisonous dog farts from the other.

"Did you know the first golfing club in the United States was founded in 1786?" Daffy volunteered. "In their honor we are wearing replicas of one of those early golf costumes."

"Of course you are." Mari's voice popped up over my shoulder.

As usual, I had the impression of stepping into an alternative universe, a world where everything coordinated. All flat surfaces, such as tables, sideboards, and even the fireplace mantle were littered with trinkets, figurines, and lace doilies. Velvety curtains covered the windows and even the chairs wore skirts.

• • ● • •

Daffy and her Chihuahua dog were among my favorite and most frequent house-call clients. After an exam a few months ago revealed an infection in the anal gland of her beloved pooch, she decided to schedule appointments every two weeks, whether he needed them or not. So, faithfully, twice a month, I checked the problem area and trimmed her Chihuahua's nails. I suspected Daffy liked having the company.

"How is everything going? Any problems with your sweetie pie?" Little Man's giant bat ears twitched and his eyes malevolently swiveled from Mari to me, and back again. We followed his owner into the kitchen and waited in front of the island where we routinely did the exam. Daffy placed her pet on the countertop that was covered in newspaper and draped with a green towel. The dog stood as quiet as a statue, the golf cap riding at a jaunty angle on top of his shiny, bald, head. All he lacked was a putter.

"Front or back?" During each visit my assistant and I had to outmaneuver six pounds of unhappy dog. We had our strategy down pat. Sometimes I wondered if Little Man thought we were here to play some kind of bizarre game with him.

Mari pointed to the dog's head so I circled around the back, getting into position for a sneak attack. Our patient's nose was too small for a regular muzzle. Instead I took a thin strip of gauze from my pocket. Because Chihuahuas are tiny but have big heads and skinny little legs, we always handled them with extra care. My assistant dangled her keys in front of him as a distraction while I slipped the customized gauze noose over his nose and tied it behind his ears. Now protected against sharp teeth, I scooped him up with a flourish and pressed him into my body. Used to the whole thing by now, Little Man barely protested. Instead he emitted a half-hearted growl, then submitted to the inevitable with an air of wounded dignity.

My exam revealed nothing to be concerned about, so after a quick butt-cleanup and nail-trim, our work was over. We handed the now-happy dog back to his owner.

A quick wash and we all were back to normal. Well, a version of normal.

As always, a pile of chocolate chunk and oatmeal raisin cookies waited on the dining room table along with fresh coffee and a pitcher of milk. Every time we visited Daffy I said I wasn't going to have any cookies—and every time my resolve goes right out the window. Today was no exception. The sleet storm had let up and a peek through the lace curtains told us our weather had significantly improved. Thin rays of sunshine tried to break through the gray clouds and momentarily lift our spirits.

After a pleasant chat with our hostess and way too many cookies, Mari and I got up to leave. That's when she said something unexpected.

"My friend, Eloise, noticed Luke Gianetti with his old girlfriend the other day." Out of the corner of my eye I saw Mari give me a sideways glance.

"Yes, I know all about it." Strangely my vocabulary and throat simultaneously dried up.

Intent on spilling her juicy piece of gossip, Daffy continued. "They were in Rhinebeck at that new Thai restaurant—Bangkok

Nights. At least I think that's what she said. Eloise passed them as they were leaving, otherwise I'd know more about it."

Upon seeing the expression on my face, Mari jumped into action. While steering me firmly toward the front door, she countered, "That's interesting, but Dr. Kate and Luke are only friends."

Our client scratched her chin in a judgmental fashion.

"In fact," my assistant continued as we scrambled to put on our coats, "she has a new boyfriend named Jeremy. Someone you went to college with, isn't that right? " Mari checked the room as she spoke to make sure we had all our equipment.

"Very interesting." Daffy's quick mind started processing the new information.

My assistant continued to babble away. "He's coming for a visit next week."

I stopped dead in the hallway. "Just a sec, I think I left my bag…"

Mari handed me the laptop. "Stay here, I'll get it."

An unexpected grumble of thunder rumbled above us—so much for the sunshine.

"Is your new boyfriend going to help you solve the murder?" My client's grossly magnified eyes stared at me through thick reading glasses. "I hope so. Flynn was such a sweet boy, very considerate."

Temporarily trapped until Mari returned I asked, "You knew Flynn?"

"Of course, dear." Surprise was in her answer, as though it were obvious she knew everyone in town. "He always did little jobs here and there to earn extra money. Such a good-looking young man too, and so popular with the ladies. Young ladies and older ladies, if you know what I mean." She gave me a magnified wink.

Mari arrived and proceeded to nudge me forward.

"Wait a minute." Despite the promise to Gramps to stay out of this murder, curiosity got the best of me. I splayed my hand up against the wall in case Mari tried to push me along. "Daffy, do you remember which ladies Flynn was popular with?"

This time our hostess demurely hesitated. "It's been quite a long time."

Almost ten years. I figured a lot of juicy gossip had flowed under the old bridge in that time.

"But you've got such a good memory." I praised her shamelessly.

Mari shot me a look. I could see the corners of her mouth twitch.

Flattery opened the floodgates. "Well, there were several girls in high school, then that drama teacher. Odious woman. All of the ladies at the bridge club wondered about that one." To make sure we got the point she raised her fingertips to her forehead and tapped vigorously a few times. "Of course he also delivered groceries to the late Mrs. Alberts, God rest her soul. It took a very long time for him to help her unpack them, what with her unfortunate drinking problem. Sometimes over an hour." She cocked her head and nodded for emphasis before continuing. "I also heard a rumor he was in some kind of relationship with Alessa Foxley—the ex-model who owns Phoenix Nest—but that was just a rumor, so I won't dignify it by repeating it."

Whatever else she said was muffled by a crash of thunder, followed by the familiar din of raindrops.

"Dr. Kate, maybe you can find out the truth—like you did before."

"Good idea," chimed in my assistant.

"I don't think so." This time I hustled Mari out, after a quick thank you to our hostess.

For the second day in a row we sprinted to the truck, dodging the downpour. I could vaguely make out Daffy and Little Man through the foggy truck windows, standing at the door waving.

• • ● • •

On the way to our next appointment road conditions became so bad all I could do was stare at the white center line and concentrate. Our clothes were practically steaming, thanks to the truck's defrost setting. My tight waistband persistently reminded me of my lack of willpower.

"Hope that stuff about Luke didn't upset you too much." Mari paused in the middle of her data entry notes.

"No, I'm okay."

The wipers made a soft squeaking sound as they went back and forth. *Luke and Dina*, they repeated, *Luke and Dina*. Only last Saturday I'd been flirting with him at the wedding, not knowing he'd started up with his ex again. I could kick myself.

Mari seemed to sense my thoughts. "Luke is water under the bridge, Kate. In less than two weeks Jeremy will be here. Aren't you looking forward to seeing him?"

"Absolutely. Jeremy is a lot of fun."

"Luke is back with his ex so the coast is clear now. Right?"

The coast is clear? Even though it made no sense I still felt angry with Luke. Why did he keep going back to his high school sweetheart when it never worked out? First love like theirs must create some very tight emotional bonds, chains that should have loosened up by now.

Mari continued without any feedback from me. "Jeremy is an anthropologist, isn't he? Maybe he can help you solve Flynn's murder."

I downshifted as we started descending into the valley. "I'm not going to investigate Flynn's death. I've got enough on my plate."

"Are you sure?"

"Sure."

We rode for a while in silence until Mari changed the subject. "Did I tell you about the bear?"

"You mentioned something."

"Oh. Well, I found out more details. Crazy Carl has it."

"Who is Crazy Carl?"

A large puddle loomed on the edge of the shoulder.

"Crazy Carl is one of our homegrown oddballs. Always talking about conspiracies and aliens and some new get-rich-quick scheme. He's got a big place over by Sheckter's Ridge that he inherited from his parents."

A double spray of water shot out from under the tires and sprayed both sides of the road.

"So," Mari continued, "word is he trapped a bear in his horse paddock and is trying to teach it to dance."

"What? That's terrible." I hated hearing stories like that. "Did someone call New York State Fish and Wildlife and report him?"

"Yes. One of his neighbors turned him in. My friend told me the authorities are supposed to go over and check it out but they're shorthanded at the moment. This isn't the first time Carl's done something dumb like this. A couple of years ago he was fined for keeping a family of bobcats."

"Let's hope he learns his lesson."

Her answer came after more potato chip-crunching.

"I wouldn't bet on it."

More puddles of water glistened on the lower parts of the road. A traffic light glowed red in the distance. Easing up on the gas, I carefully slowed down the truck.

"Listen, Mari. Sorry I'm so touchy. Between Luke and now Jeremy…" I left the sentence unfinished. "It's been a while since Jeremy and I have seen each other. I don't want to factor a murder investigation into his visit."

"Yeah, Cindy filled me in."

"I've got no idea what conditions were like on his dig in North Africa. This will be the first time he's been back to the States in quite a while." We idled waiting for the signal light to change. "His dig has been suspended, so there will be plenty of things on his mind."

My assistant turned back to the laptop screen trying unsuccessfully to stifle a snicker. "Oh, I don't know. Bet he'll have one particular thing on his mind."

I didn't dignify her implication with an answer.

By Thursday, any charm associated with the changing of the seasons had vanished. Day after day brought more sleet, icy winds, and gray skies to the Hudson Valley. Weather reports proved unreliable. Slip-on rubber boots became my norm, since things often turned drastically different from hour to hour. To make matters worse, a flu-like virus struck several staff members. Cindy and I ended up being the only two left holding down the fort.

The sound of my steps echoed as I walked through the empty lab into the reception area. Cindy sat manning the phones. One hand held a fragrant cup of mint tea while the other grasped a wad of Kleenex. A discrete pile of used tissues filled her waste-paper basket.

"How are you feeling? Are you sure you're well enough to come to work?" I'd talked to her yesterday and she had sounded awful. Her hoarse voice today actually was an improvement.

"I feel better than I look." Since her face had a greenish tint, I was relieved to hear it.

"Do we have any appointments this afternoon?" The weather forecast called for sleet and possibly hail later in the day.

She glanced at the computer screen, and checked some notes. "Only one recheck. The sick people aren't up to seeing anyone and the people who feel okay don't want to risk being exposed to any sick people."

"That sounds about right." I sat down in the empty waiting room on one of the plastic reception chairs. It smelled like disinfectant.

She blew her nose, took another sip of tea, and looked miserable.

An SUV pulled into the parking lot as close to the hospital entrance as possible. The figure that emerged appeared ready to climb Everest, completely encased in colorful ski clothes and a face mask. However, I immediately recognized her canine companion who looked perfectly at home in the winter chill.

When the door opened, a big Malamute pushed his muzzle into my hand and thumped his tail against the chairs lining the reception area.

"Hi, Samantha," I said. "I'm glad to see Jack is feeling so good. Let's go into the exam room."

They both followed, Jack shaking little pellets of water off his coat and Samantha divesting herself of layers of clothing that now must be unbearably hot.

Once in the exam room I knelt down on the floor and let the dog love wash over me. Jack wagged and wiggled, showing no anxiety in visiting an animal hospital. Working my way front to back I checked his lymph nodes and listened to his heart, and then took a good look at the healing laceration on his back.

"This looks fantastic." I noted the hair regrowth and smoothness of the scar tissue.

"Yes, he's back to his normal self and tricks. I can't believe it, but he took off up the mountain again the other day."

Remembering her beautiful home and the woods at the edge of her property, I could imagine it was quite a temptation for Jack to run free. All those delicious odors and wildlife just waiting to be found must be hard for a dog of his breed to resist.

"Did he go back to the gravesite?" I hoped he hadn't disturbed the crime scene by digging a hole.

I could hear the frustration in her voice when she answered. "You bet he did. I followed him this time. He even tangled with a piece of the old yellow caution tape."

"Hey. What's going on in that dog brain of yours?" I playfully tapped him on the noggin and stared into his bright brown eyes.

"Beats me." His owner called his name. Jack bounded over to her and promptly sat on her boots.

"Well, the wound has healed completely, no signs of infection. We don't need to see him again until next year for his vaccinations and heartworm preventative."

"Great."

"Anything else I can help you with?" I sat down at the desk adjacent to the exam table and began to make a few notes in the office computer.

"Actually, I do have some questions, but not about my dog."

I swung my desk chair around.

"Do you happen to know if there has been any progress finding out what happened to Flynn Keegan?"

Her voice sounded concerned. "I haven't heard anything. The investigation isn't in the hands of the local police. Why do you ask?"

She hesitated for a moment. "Last time I chased after Jack, he led me right back to the…where they found his body. People have been coming up there and leaving things—flowers, pictures, a wooden cross. That's when I noticed it."

"Noticed what?"

"I hope you don't think this is strange, but I'm a gardener."

My face probably betrayed my puzzlement.

"I saw a climbing rose on one of the trees close to the burial site. A Rosa rugosa."

A vine in the woods…maybe I didn't understand the point.

"Someone planted it up there. It's not a native plant. When it's in bloom it's a beautiful variety filled with blossoms. There was one late flower left on the branches."

"So someone planted it there?" I repeated.

"Yes. I'm sure of it. And the color of the petals was white."

I still wasn't sure what she was driving at.

This time her voice became impatient as though I was a child who didn't understand a lesson.

"My guess is the name of that particular climbing rose is Iceberg," she explained. "A white rose is for remembrance."

• • ● • •

After Samantha left I thought about her discovery. I highly doubted that the investigators on Flynn's murder noticed a climbing rose, especially one that wasn't blooming. If Samantha's hunch was correct, whoever killed Flynn might have been remorseful and planted the vine nearby, like you'd place flowers on a grave.

If true, that detail pointed to a local—maybe a local who loved him.

"Cindy, let me know if anyone needs me. I'll be in my office." I disinfected both hands from the bottle on the counter and hurried back to the office computer to finish some paperwork. Behind me, my poor receptionist answered with several sneezes.

The local newspaper lay on top of the desk so I opened it up. Mr. Katt took advantage of that opportunity by catapulting from the top of the bookshelf and onto the page I was trying to read. Our hospital cat specialized in appearing out of nowhere like some feline ninja. Trapped at the desk I slid the front page out from under his substantial kitty rear end. There must not have been much news around because the editor rehashed yet another article about the happy family Flynn came from and how mysterious his disappearance was. It went on to comment how ironic it was that his high school graduating class reunion would take place soon at the popular Lakeside Hotel. Underneath the story a small notice gave details on funeral plans and the memorial luncheon planned for this Saturday.

The obituary revealed something unexpected and a little spooky. His birthday was the same as mine, same day, same year. We'd both been newborn babies in delivery rooms worlds apart.

What did they call it—your Fate? Or Karma?

Fate had brought me to Oak Falls through a veterinary help wanted ad.

That same Fate had kept Flynn Keegan in Oak Falls through the actions of a killer.

Chapter Seven

On the day of Flynn's funeral, Cindy closed the animal hospital so the staff could attend. First a religious service would be held at St. Steven's Catholic Church in town, and directly afterwards a celebration of his life had been scheduled for friends and family. That meant I was off an entire Saturday morning and, knowing Jeremy would soon be visiting, I took the opportunity to deep-clean my apartment. The sofa cushions yielded a treasure trove of coins, dog treats, lint balls, and stray chips. Annoyed at the noisy vacuum cleaner, Buddy retreated to his dog bed and watched me with a baleful eye.

When I opened all the blinds, bright sunlight revealed a horror show of fingerprints, dog paws, and unidentified stains on the windows. Armed with dishwashing liquid, glass cleaner, and a grapefruit scented all-purpose cleaner, I systematically attacked everything that didn't move.

Pretty soon my apartment vibrated with the contrasting rhythms of dishwasher and vacuum cleaner set to the staccato drumming support of the washer and dryer. The loose change banging around with the clothes rang out like clashing cymbals.

The good news about living in a small space is that it doesn't take much time to clean. By noon, I was finished, only waiting for the last load of sheets to dry.

All the elderly appliances were now sparkling clean, however the refrigerator remained suspiciously empty. I decided to reward myself for a herculean cleaning effort by eating a big bowl of wonton soup and some shrimp dumplings, courtesy of our local Chinese restaurant, the Lucky Garden. Once full, I would then tackle the grocery store. Usually I order takeout but today I felt like treating myself by sitting down and relaxing at one of Lucky Garden's streamside tables in the glassed-in porch.

To my surprise the restaurant parking lot was jammed with cars and trucks and even a few emergency vehicles. Lucky Garden had built an attached private meeting room for group gatherings, bridal showers, and the annual Oak Falls Ladies Bridge Tournament. Maybe one of those groups was holding a meeting? I considered going somewhere else but hunger won out.

The inside of the restaurant proved to be fairly quiet with only a few couples and families munching on eggrolls and sipping soup. A heady fragrance of sesame and ginger stimulated my appetite. I weaved my way toward the glassed-in porch, where one other couple huddled together, taking advantage of the relative quiet and seclusion. No crowd in here.

Having memorized the menu by now, I waited for a server, glad that the biggest task of the weekend, cleaning the apartment, had been completed. When I heard footsteps approaching, I swiveled in my seat, ready with my order.

"Kate, I knew that was you." Mari stood in front of me wearing a black-and-white printed dress.

Astonished, I blurted out, "I thought you went to the funeral."

"I did. Now I'm at the memorial service luncheon." She sat down opposite me.

"Here?" The choice of a Chinese restaurant seemed a bit strange.

"Of course. Flynn delivered takeout for Lucky Garden since forever. He worked as a server all through high school." She seemed astonished I didn't know any of this. "Why don't you come and join us?"

I shook my head. "No, that doesn't feel right. I don't know the family and I didn't know him."

"Flynn's grandmother asked me to invite you. Besides, you're not going to get any food for a while if you stay out here."

She had a point. I hadn't seen a waiter this entire time.

"Besides, it's more of a party for Flynn, a time to remember him. You'll see."

"Alright. But I'm not going to stay long."

We made our way toward the restrooms then through a door marked "Private." I could hear the din coming from behind the door, the Beach Boys playing at top volume, with a chorus of people singing along.

Mari was right. The scene definitely felt more like a party than a memorial gathering. A large color photograph of Flynn rested on an easel in the front of the room and smiled out at the crowd. Several rows of tables had been pushed aside to clear a dance space.

To my surprise our receptionist, Cindy, waved to me as she danced the twist with her brother-in-law, Chief of Police Bobby Garcia. Her very pregnant sister watched and clapped to the music.

Several groups of people clustered at the remaining tables. My eye was drawn to the woman dressed in black sitting in a wheelchair, a wistful expression on her face, who waved at Mari. The clear blue eyes and chiseled nose marked her as Flynn's mother, Lizette Keegan, who looked very much like her son. A teenage girl stood directly behind the chair, texting nonstop. Although dressed in shades of black, the many studs, safety pins, and skulls on her jacket and jeans made me think black might be her everyday color of choice. The nasal piercing and silver dumbbell over her eyebrow tended to confirm my guess.

Idly, I wondered why they were playing oldies from the sixties at a young man's service.

"Come on," Mari directed me to the buffet table, skillfully navigating past an enthusiastic dancing couple. It looked like the Lucky Garden supplied most of its menu for the event. I soon spied my favorites and loaded up a plate. By this time I was starving. We grabbed two empty seats next to an elderly lady chatting amicably with a frail-looking man wearing motorcycle boots, a heavy black sweater, and a checkered do-rag around his forehead. Flynn's mom was nowhere in sight. After a quick nod hello, I dug into the food. Mari, by now stuffed with Chinese food, opted for sliced pineapple, a fortune cookie, and a mixed drink with an umbrella in it from the bar.

Someone must be using an old playlist, I thought, because now the crowd was listening to the Grateful Dead.

The three big guys all in leather sitting at the far end of the table got up in unison. One of them glanced at the frail man next to me, before placing a finger onto an old healed wound on the bridge of his nose. His black eyes glittered with menace. That caught my attention.

Before I could note anything else, the men silently walked away. Strange behavior, I thought at a memorial service.

"They don't write them like that anymore," the do-rag dude, unconcerned at the veiled threat, loudly pronounced to the entire table.

I turned my attention back to him. From the little I could see of his face, which was covered with a gray-streaked beard, he looked to be in his late fifties, early sixties. Peeking out from under a heavy sweater were blue prison-style tattoos on the bony knuckles of his right hand that said BORN. The thin left hand, tapping along with the music, revealed another set of tats that spelled out BADD. How long ago were they inked? I also found it curious he stayed bundled up in the overheated room.

When the music stopped, the older woman at the table took the opportunity to introduce herself to us. "Hello. I'm Sophia Keegan, Flynn's grandmother. My son, Antonio, God rest his soul, was Flynn's father."

Mari quickly spoke up. "Hi, Mrs. Keegan. I'm not sure if you remember me. I'm Mari Attwater, Teri's daughter? I used to babysit Fiona."

"So good of you to come, dear. I spoke to your mother a few days ago." After a moment Sophia looked past Mari to me.

"Uh, Kate Turner. I'm here with Mari. I never met Flynn, but I am so sorry for your loss." Even as I spoke the socially accepted phrase, it felt inadequate. "He must have been a wonderful person to have so many friends here."

His grandmother smiled. "Flynn was a golden boy. Only on loan to us for a little while from God and his heavenly kingdom."

"Amen, sweetheart." Leaning in and giving Sophia a quick kiss on the cheek, the older man in motorcycle boots nodded good-bye to us and carefully made his way into the crowd. I noticed how his clothes hung off him like he'd had a recent weight loss or illness.

More guests stood up to dance, clapping to the music.

My eyes drifted over to the huge likeness of Flynn, blond, handsome, his grin infectious. "Golden Boy" suited him, right down to the thin gold chain around his neck.

Mari downed the rest of her umbrella drink and took off for the dance floor. I took the opportunity to grab seconds from the buffet table.

After several songs Mari came back, another cocktail in hand. Now overly full of Chinese food, I started to leave, but before I could make my move, Flynn's grandmother gestured for me to come sit next to her.

"Excuse me, Kate. You're the new veterinarian who's working at Doc Anderson's place, right?" Sophia continued, demanding my attention. "Didn't you discover that poor girl Claire's killer? I seem to recall…"

"Yes. She's the one," Mari spoke up enthusiastically. "Maybe Kate could help you find out what happened to Flynn."

Horrified by Mari's suggestion, I put my head down and silently opened my fortune cookie. Sophia's hand reached out and touched me on the arm. "Now that might be too much to ask. The policeman who contacted my daughter-in-law didn't sound too hopeful."

Her fingers were lumpy and swollen at the joints.

"That's so kind of you," I began, "but I really don't know much—"

Mari happily interrupted. "Don't let her fool you. She has some kind of weird talent for solving crimes."

I gave Mari an icy stare to try and get her to cease and desist. It didn't work.

"You know she's solved two different murders."

I felt like making it three by murdering Mari if she didn't quit talking.

"Maybe Kate could sit down with your family—"

Now it was my turn to interrupt. "Mari, please let it go for now. Okay?"

By that time it was too late.

Sophia invited both of us to her daughter-in-law's home for a chat. I felt guilty turning her down after attending the memorial luncheon and chowing down on all the free food. She glanced at her watch. "Let's make it five o'clock. Kate, you can meet our entire family." Flynn's grandmother then stood up and hugged Mari. "Thanks for bringing her today. It's a sign, I think."

A sign?

Solving a crime that was ten years old? I should have let her read the fortune hidden in my cookie. "Roads that look promising often lead to dead ends."

Two hours later a sobered up and embarrassed Mari stood with me outside Flynn's family home.

"Sorry, Kate," she told me for the umpteenth time.

"It's okay." I didn't want to admit a tiny part of me was curious to hear what the family had to say.

The house was a modest brick in the ranch-style that was very popular in the fifties. Not particularly New England in style, the home looked like it had seen better days. The Keegans' faded red front door was unremarkable except for the black wreath hanging above a worn brass knocker.

A familiar person opened the door, recognized Mari, and gave her an almost imperceptible nod. I, on the other hand, received a suspicious stare. From Mari's description and my observation at the memorial service I recognized her as Flynn's younger sister, Fiona.

Although she'd changed her clothes, the color black still appeared to be most of her wardrobe. Despite the cold, she wore a thin short-sleeved t-shirt over silver-studded black jeans, with a black fake-fur vest. Her uncovered arms sported numerous tattoos, seemingly random in choice and most poorly executed. A shame, since Fiona could have been an appealing girl if she lost the attitude and most of the Goth-like makeup.

"Hey, Fiona." Mari made no attempt to hug or comfort her in any way. She'd warned me ahead of time that the girl she used to babysit didn't like to be touched.

"Hey."

With that nominal greeting Fiona motioned us into the house. A noticeable lack of color was the predominant color scheme. Empty beige walls blended into the beige carpet in the hallway. Positioned in distinct clumps in the tan living room were three generations of Keegan women. The only man present sat in a brown faux leather recliner in the corner, his feet elevated, with an annoyed expression on his face. He reminded me of an old football player whose muscle had turned to fat.

Lizette, Flynn's delicately beautiful mother, welcomed us from her wheelchair. Grandmother Sophia sat on the sofa furthest from her daughter-in-law, while Fiona leaned against the living room wall, arms crossed in front of her.

"Would you like something to drink?" Sophia asked us.

For a crazy moment I thought they were offering us more cocktails.

"I'd like a cup of coffee, black, if you have it." Mari sat down and smiled at them all.

I also sat, feeling terribly awkward, already regretting my decision to come to the house.

"Make that two coffees, thank you." I genteelly folded my hands in my lap.

There was another one of those silences until Mari spoke. "Lovely church service. Very moving."

The entire group nodded except Fiona who began to text, the clicks of her messaging the only sounds in the room.

At that moment Sophia returned with a tray and two steaming china cups and saucers. Mari thanked her and put both on the small table between our chairs. I sensed tension between grandmother, mother, and daughter. Sophia's warm expression vanished as soon as she returned to the sofa. Looks of annoyance were equally directed at Lizette and Fiona. The man in the corner, she ignored.

There was no way I was going to initiate this conversation.

To my surprise the guy in the recliner started the ball rolling.

"Don't think I know you, but I'm Bruce, Flynn's stepfather." From my angle I mostly saw the top of his head with greasy receding hair slicked back behind his ears.

"Correction. If you actually married my daughter-in-law, you'd be his stepfather." Sophia's bitter statement dropped like a bomb in the middle of the room.

"We can't afford to get married what with the benefits and everything. You know that." Lizette sighed in exasperation and helplessly looked around the room for confirmation.

Now Sophia angrily folded her arms in front of her.

As if on cue, Fiona weighed in. "What's your love life got to do with anything? My brother is dead."

Mari picked that moment to speak, which was pretty brave of her. "Your grandmother invited Dr. Kate and me here to see if we could help in any way."

"Like any of you care. You're the reason he left in the first place. He hated all of you." Fiona spewed out her harsh words before storming out of the room and slamming the hallway door. The family declined to comment, ignoring her outburst as if this were a daily occurrence.

Bruce made a half-assed effort to get out of the recliner but Lizette stopped him. "Honey, leave her be. She needs some time to herself." Her fingers fluttered in futility.

Obediently he collapsed back down, scratching his head. For a moment I thought he was going to say something, but instead he cranked the chair back into the full reclining position.

Compared to the rest of the family, Sophia sounded like the voice of reason. "As you have been told, I have asked Dr. Kate to look into Flynn's death for us." She turned and focused all attention on me. "How does this work? Do you want to ask us questions?"

I sensed multiple eyes staring at me. Should I address what Fiona said? Her outburst might have been truthful or merely a dramatic version of the truth. The Keegan family dynamics certainly were odd. Resentment bounced between them like balls of heat lightning.

The five of us sat in the beige living room on beige chairs trapped together. All of them nervously waited for me to answer Sophia. I needed to say something.

"Well, I never met Flynn. Why don't you start by telling me a little about him?" The tension eased up on hearing my simple request, but winnowing out the truth, I suspected, would be a whole different ballgame.

No one volunteered to begin, so I directed my first question to his mother. "Where did he grow up? Here in town?"

Sophia and her daughter-in-law eyed each other before Lizette spoke. "I moved to Oak Falls when Flynn was only a baby. Tony had been killed in a helicopter crash. Sophia suggested we move into one of her rental properties."

"I'm in the house directly next door," Sophia explained. "Flynn lived there with me until he was ten or eleven, right up until Fiona was born."

"Why was that?" I tried to keep my voice nonconfrontational.

Lizette shifted in her wheelchair, smoothing down the tan blanket draped over her knees. "I have MS, multiple sclerosis. The type I have is called waxing and waning—so sometimes I am very bad and other times I feel almost normal. After we moved here I became very sick and could barely stand. My mother-in-law took care of Flynn while I tried to recover. It was a horrible time for all of us."

"Not so horrible when you felt good. Or do you forget the parade of boyfriends in and out of here? Pretending you didn't have a son. Shame on you," Sophia bluntly interjected. There was a stunned silence from Mari and me. No one else batted an eye. They'd obviously heard that story many, many times before.

Lizette sighed again and wearily put her head down.

Sophia directed her next comments to me. "Did you listen to the music today? Those were the songs Flynn and I danced to. We would twirl around and around. I taught him the Twist and the Mashed Potato and all the crazy sixties dances. So much fun, we had so much fun." Her eyes glistened with tears yet unshed. "My sweet grandson."

Her daughter-in-law fiddled with her nails.

"Who took care of you, Lizette?" I asked. How, I wondered, did Bruce figure into the family picture?

"My husband's survivor benefits and pension paid for my health costs and home nursing care," Lizette explained. "I also received Social Security benefits for Flynn. Although Sophia took care of him most of the time, I'd try to see him every day if I could."

Sophia harrumphed and frowned.

I secretly blessed Mari when she asked the next question.

"Fiona and Flynn have the same last name. Was Antonio Keegan the father of both of your children?" A flicker of something passed between Sophia and Bruce.

"No." The answer came from a different side of the room.

We all looked up.

Fiona had returned without anyone noticing.

"No. Flynn's father was killed in Afghanistan. He got a purple heart and a commendation for bravery. My father is sitting on his ass in the recliner over there. I'm not sure he even has a heart." Like a dark vengeful shadow she glared at Bruce, daring someone to contradict her. When no one rose to the bait, she mumbled something inaudible and stalked out again, this time without slamming the door.

"Fiona is upset. She doesn't mean it. Please forgive her," Lizette pleaded. She gripped the sides of her wheelchair and glanced over at Bruce, whose face was slowly turning bright red. "I'm joining Sophia in asking you to find out what you can."

Obviously, this was not the "normal happy family" of everyone's dreams, the family extolled in the newspaper articles I'd read.

What had life really been like for Flynn, the town's "Golden Boy?"

• • ● • •

After the second uncomfortable family blowup, Mari and I made a lame excuse to leave. I promised to do what I could. Truthfully, I hoped the police would step in and I would be able to step out of the picture. More toxic family situations, I didn't need. After my own mom and brother had died in a hit-and-run accident, I'd been lost in a funk of anger for years, hating my father for his perceived indifference until my grandfather rescued me. It had been twelve years since I'd spoken to my own father. I didn't need to vicariously revisit all that pain.

Once back home I decided to concentrate on Jeremy's surprise visit. Bolstered by a glass of cold white wine and a piece of chocolate, I wandered around the apartment, viewing it with a critical eye. Buddy followed me, not sure what the heck I was doing. First I needed to set Jeremy straight on my odd living arrangements. Old Doc Anderson had converted the hospital garage into one big room with no privacy whatsoever. Used primarily as a "crash pad" to stay in when he saw a late-night emergency, function definitely trumped form. After his wife died, Doc added a kitchenette, sold their home, and moved in. Nobody thought it would be permanent. That was fifteen years ago.

Feeling somewhat guilty I sent Jeremy a lengthy e-mail explaining my living situation and tried unsuccessfully to set up another Skype session before he got on a plane back to the States. There was nothing to do now but wait. And clean. Again.

No way did I want him to stay here with me in this cramped space. Too much togetherness so quickly would make me uncomfortable.

With the weather still rotten, I didn't relish driving to the grocery store, so I searched the kitchen for something to eat.

Forgotten cooked pasta in a gooey clump and a crusty open bottle of marinara sauce didn't look that appetizing, or healthy. In the freezer I discovered a package of peas and another of white corn, but I had the vague suspicion I'd used one or both of them as emergency ice packs.

Not much lurked in the pantry cabinet other than sugar, salt, and granola bars. However, sticking my hand behind some flour, I uncovered a half-full jar of peanuts and a can of chicken wedding soup with those little meatballs. Wine and peanuts as an appetizer followed by a main course of soup...I've had worse dinners.

Buddy woofed for one of his dog bones.

We both settled down on the sofa and crunched away. That scene in Flynn's home kept haunting me. What must it be like to live in a constant cauldron of anger and despair? Maybe the murderer was closer to home than anyone thought.

Still thinking about the Keegan family, the chime of my phone caught me by surprise.

Hungry?

Of course, I texted back

Open the door.

Buddy began barking before I could read the response. It was just like Luke to pop up unexpectedly, especially when I was wearing sweats with my hair a mess.

"I didn't think I'd see you so soon." I opened the door and he rushed by me, raindrops sliding off his coat, his hair dripping. Two paper bags oozed the very familiar odor of Chinese takeout. Obviously, he hadn't agonized over our argument at the potbellied pig wedding like I had. But why would a guy just back with his girlfriend keep stopping by my place?

Since Luke had been here many times, usually with some sort of takeout, he knew exactly what to do. I joined him in the kitchen area, while he put the bags on the counter and took off his wet coat.

"Where should I put this?"

"Go ahead and hang it on the extra chair." He looked like he'd taken a shower in his clothes. I threw him the towel that I'd used earlier to dry my hair. "Be my guest."

"Thanks." Blotting and rubbing vigorously, he dried off his face and head, which left some hair sort of standing on end a bit. Darned if he didn't look even better that way.

"You know tonight isn't Thursday." I decided not to mention I'd been to the Lucky Garden for lunch today and spoken to the Keegan family. It would spare me another argument about staying out of police business.

He glanced up from his plate. "I took a makeup class. Thought you might be hungry."

Luke and I had gotten into the habit of sharing Chinese food together on Thursday night, after his pre-law class at the community college. That was also my late night at the hospital and by the end of the day I often felt too tired to move. Our habit started months ago when we were trying to solve a murder case and had continued, as we'd became friends. What I thought might grow into a serious relationship had now crashed and burned.

Buddy followed Luke to the kitchen table, confident that a morsel of chicken would somehow end up in his mouth.

"Did you get my text about having to leave after the wedding?" I couldn't believe that was already a week ago.

"Yes. No problem. I had to run, too." He plunged his eggroll into the sweet and sour sauce.

Not to be outdone, I put a large spoonful of hot mustard on my eggroll and took a bite. After about a second my eyes started to water and my throat lit on fire.

"So, I hear you're expecting some company soon." Luke scooped fried rice onto his plate and lifted a piece of chicken with his chopsticks.

With my throat still burning from the mustard and my face turning red, all I could do was nod.

"Is Jeremy going to be staying here? In Oak Falls, I mean?" He eyed me with a curious expression on his face.

Still unable to talk I chugged a glass of water since I didn't have any milk in the house. When that didn't work I tried to put out the fire in my mouth with some steamed rice. Tears dripped from my eyes.

"Are you okay? I'm sorry. Maybe you don't want me asking you any personal questions.

I wiped my sweating forehead with a napkin. "No, no it's fine. He'll be visiting me for a few days."

"You're probably looking forward to that. It's been a while, hasn't it?" This time he didn't even pretend to be subtle.

Recovered from the mustard attack, I speared a forkful of Chinese vegetables. "Yes." After my one word answer, I innocently smiled at him and continued to eat. If he wanted more information from me he was going to have to work for it.

"Well, I hope everything goes well for you. You deserve it."

"Thanks." Strange to be having this conversation with him, considering there were so many times I'd wished…

"Sorry." Luke snuck a quick peek at his watch. "I've got to go." He jumped up and carried his paper plate over to the garbage.

This was our pattern. Sometimes our Thursday evening get-togethers would be social and stretch out for a few hours and sometimes they ended up a terse eat-and-run.

"Wait a minute. Can you tell me anything about the Flynn investigation?"

He paused. "What do you want to know?"

"Well, I know they are calling it a murder." I started closing the takeout boxes and putting them in the refrigerator.

"First of all, it's not our case, not our jurisdiction. I can tell you Chief Garcia is releasing a statement to the press tomorrow that the preliminary findings show death by blunt force trauma to the skull. My hands are tied on this one." Luke put on his damp coat and stood in front of the door. "It's been almost ten years since he disappeared. I highly doubt anyone will ever solve this."

"That dovetails with what the family was told." Since he'd been nice enough to bring me dinner, I confessed that I'd been to Flynn's memorial party earlier today. "His mother and grand-mother asked me to find out what I could—informally."

Our eyes met. "I don't envy you."

"Tell me about it."

Luke hesitated for a moment. "Don't get me wrong. I hate that it was Flynn. We went all through high school together. I still remember how good he was in the senior play, *Romeo and Juliet*. He was Romeo, of course."

"Of course." I gestured toward the newspaper on the coffee table. "They've got more pictures of him in today's paper. What a really great-looking guy."

"Yeah, more so in person, although I didn't hang out with his crowd much. My thing was sports, until I tore my rotator cuff a few months before graduation."

"That must have been rough on you."

He shrugged and dug into his coat pocket for his gloves. "I think it hurt my dad as much as it hurt me. All those visions of me as a pitcher for the Yankees evaporated overnight. Anyway, getting back to Flynn. He always had a bunch of guys with him, what we'd call a posse today. Maybe you can start by talking to them."

"Good idea."

He moved to open the door, saying, "I'm sorry for his family, but now they have some kind of closure." Luke bent down to say goodnight to Buddy who responded by rolling over on his back. Just as quickly as he had arrived, Luke was gone.

• • ● • •

After Luke left I cleaned up the kitchen before sinking back down on the sofa. Time to veg out for a while. Near the television remote, Flynn Keegan, Oak Fall's "Golden Boy" stared at me from the local paper, the dream of a bright future stretching endlessly in front of him on that day so long ago.

Closure. Sometimes there is no closure. If I were his mother I would have preferred the fantasy of her son living it up in Los Angeles to the cruel reality.

If I were the killer, I think I'd be on my guard.

Chapter Eight

Monday morning found me on a very different kind of house call, featuring a lot of bull.

Literally.

My patient today was a tranquilized sixteen-hundred-pound breeding Scottish Highland bull and, from underneath the view wasn't that great, if you get what I mean. Smelling that musky, funky unneutered male bovine odor had lost its appeal after the first thirty seconds. A sneaky little breeze rustled some dead leaves and blew dust into my eye as I lay on my side in the dirt visualizing the damage. I was cleaning a puncture wound just above his hairy left rear fetlock since their usual large-animal vet wasn't available.

"Need anything else, Kate?" Mari's face materialized next to me, a wad of gauze in her hand.

"I'm good, I think. Just a little more trimming and I'm done." His owner had noticed her prized male limping, but the cause had been hidden in the double coat of long wavy hair cascading down his legs. Haggis, my Highland bull patient, was a particularly handsome example of this ancient breed, with long curved horns and shaggy blond bangs to die for.

Those long horns, which grow on both the males and females, were most likely responsible for this injury, probably some long-forgotten bovine dispute.

Satisfied with my work, I folded up the sterile surgical kit and slid out into the weak sunlight. Our patient had been confined in a metal stay-pen for his and my protection, and I could tell the mild tranquilizer I'd given him had begun wearing off. This king of the pasture wanted out. Now.

"Can we release him?" asked owner, Alessa Foxley. She and her property manager, Gene Russell, were standing ready to take over. Her fifty-acre place called Phoenix Nest was what used to be called a "gentleman's farm." The animals decorated the scenery, lived long lives, and all had names. Haggis was a perfect and lucky example.

Gene opened the metal pen gate staying well back from the bull's three-foot-long horns. By his side their border collie waited for a command. With a quick hand signal, the dog moved into the corral and gently encouraged the bull toward the opposite gate. Hesitant at first until he saw his lady cows waiting in an adjacent pasture, Haggis slowly lumbered toward them. Once safely in the next enclosure, Alessa opened the final gate and let the reunion party commence. Maneuver completed, the two humans did a high-five. Although in his late sixties, the wiry Gene acted as spry as someone several decades younger.

"That's pretty slick." Mari began gathering up our gear. "Good teamwork."

"Thanks for coming out, guys." Gene called out his good-byes and began walking toward the barn, the border collie following close behind. I began the semi-futile attempt of brushing mud and dirt off my coveralls.

Alessa strode over to us, picture-perfect in her Ralph Lauren country wear, accompanied by four well-behaved German shepherds. An ex-model-turned-New York City-corporate-lawyer, she had jumped into her weekend country life here in the Hudson Valley with both designer leather boots. Perfect classic features made-up to their best advantage, with salon-streaked blond hair pulled back in a high ponytail, she radiated rich, cool, and confident woman.

"So, what do we do for Haggis now, Doc?" A deep bellow and snuffling noise made us turn around. We all stood and watched the small fold move away from the gate. The bull wasn't wasting any time. Post-op for only a few minutes, he was already bossing around his little harem.

Unlike some of my clients from the city, I knew Alessa didn't mind getting her hands dirty, so her printed instructions were pretty detailed.

"I'll leave you with an ointment to use only if you see any redness or oozing. If you can lavage the wound twice a day, using a steady stream of saline, that would be fantastic. There was no evidence of tendon damage that I could see, so I would expect the lameness to resolve in a few days. Our X-ray shows no hoof wall involvement either." The patient, now oblivious to us, started searching for the last few sprigs of green in the pasture, none the worse for wear. Both wide pastures surrounded by dry-stacked bluestone walls and dotted with stately trees were tranquil in the weak afternoon sun.

We walked over to the truck where Mari waited, busily entering everything into the computer. "Thanks for your help, by the way," I told Haggis' owner.

Alessa laughed. "I grew up on a dairy farm near Watertown. All of us kids helped out. I'm a lot tougher than I look."

"That's a big leap, from dairy farm to living in New York City. How did that happen, if you don't mind me asking?"

"My parents encouraged all five of us to go to school. I started at the community college, modeled for a while in the city, then transferred to NYU. Later, I went to law school." She pulled off her work gloves. I noticed her nails were cut short. "My oldest brother still runs the family farm. Weekdays, I work in the city and come up here on the weekends. Gene and his wife, June, live here full-time and help me run the place."

"Maybe it reminds you a little bit of home?"

"Oh, you have no idea." The tone of her voice made me look up. It didn't sound happy at all.

Haggis interrupted the moment with another loud bellow.

"He sounds back to his old self." Alessa grinned at me. The shepherds sniffed and explored around the corral, never venturing too far from their mistress.

"A model patient." I began to put my equipment away. "I'll e-mail my records to your large-animal vet so everyone will be up-to-speed on your guy."

"And I'm almost finished with the paperwork. Sorry, but the connection was slow," Mari explained, her eyes on the computer screen.

I leaned against the hood of the F-150, peeled off my coveralls, and put them in the back of the truck.

"I'm curious," I asked Alessa. "I've seen the Highlands, the dogs, and a few horses. Are those the only animals you have here?"

Her eyes narrowed for a moment. "Not by a long shot. The rest are in the back behind the barn. We've got sheep, some milk goats, and, of course, the hens for eggs. A few beehives, two peacocks, a bunch of ducks out by the stream, and Gene stocked the lake with various fish..."

"No dairy cows?"

"No, the Highlands are my bovine fix. They're pets, really, and actually very friendly. I've even got a waiting list for my calves."

"I'm done." Mari ran Alessa's credit card and handed our client a printed receipt.

"That's fantastic you can do everything from the laptop."

I checked the detailed instructions before handing them to her. "Modern technology. Plus, you don't have to try and decipher my handwriting." We both laughed. Sadly, my handwriting over the years had become illegible to everyone, including me.

Alessa tucked her paperwork into her designer jeans pocket and asked, "Hey, weren't you guys in the news a while ago? Do you mind me asking about the grave you found?" The question came out of nowhere, but everyone around Oak Falls liked to gossip. A recent resident to town, I didn't think she'd be interested in a local murder. My assistant also seemed a bit surprised.

Something jogged my memory as I attempted to recall my conversation with Daffy. She'd mentioned something about Phoenix's Nest and Alessa, the former model who'd hired Flynn to do odd jobs.

Since I didn't reply right away, Mari answered her question. "That was a difficult day. Our house-call client's dog was the one who actually started it. He brought a bone home to his owner and when Dr. Kate saw it, she recognized it as human. After that, the police took over."

"Are the police still hanging around over there?" Alessa's steady gaze revealed nothing but a casual interest.

I thought that was another odd question, but this time I responded. "I'm not sure."

"They are sure about the remains?" Her voice was emphatic.

"Definitely. I know you can't believe everything you read in the newspaper but this time you can. The victim was Flynn Keegan, a local boy. I think you knew him?"

"I did know him." There was a strained quality in her voice. "Flynn helped us out a few times on the farm. He seemed like a good kid."

"A very puzzling case."

"Yes." She kicked a stone with her boot. "Did they find a wallet with money in it, or any papers buried with him?"

"None that I'm aware of. But can I ask you why—?"

Before I could finish, she interrupted. "Great talking to you. Thanks for everything, Doc. You, too, Mari." Halfway to the house Alessa turned back toward us and waved, her well-trained German shepherds fanning out behind her in a protective wake.

That was strange.

Why did Alessa ask about Flynn's wallet?

Our client disappeared into her home. Off in the distance I could see the Scottish Highland fold grazing. As I took one last look at the house, I noticed a woman's face appear in a window on the second floor for a moment, watching us leave. When I caught her eye, she disappeared.

The farm appeared peaceful and quiet with no one in sight. I'd have to find another time to question my client about her relationship with Flynn.

We loaded up all our equipment and backed up. Our trip down the driveway stopped abruptly. The big iron gates at the end of the property loomed ahead, tightly closed.

"I'll text them to let us out," Mari said.

While she looked up our client's number, my eyes idly followed the high block wall where the gates attached. When we arrived for the appointment, Gene had been waiting for us in his pickup. I didn't notice the thick roll of barbed wire running on top of the wall as far as I could see. Wires, skillfully camouflaged by paint, and run in a conduit line, probably electrified everything.

"Nice place," Mari commented as the heavy gates started to swing open. She programmed our next stop into the GPS while I waited to go through. Across from us a white panel van pulled onto the side of the road, probably overshooting its destination. As we watched, the driver suddenly turned his wheels hard and made a U-turn, leaving deep tracks in the soft dirt of the shoulder.

With the coast clear, I eased out onto the main road.

"Nice place," I repeated without thinking. My mind was too busy noting that this nice little place called Phoenix's Nest, was protected by guard dogs, barbed wire, and electrified fencing.

Were they trying to keep people out or keep someone in?

Chapter Nine

Some autumns in upstate New York are glorious, the trees covered for weeks in leaves of scarlet, gold, and rust. This wasn't one of them. Day after day we suffered through rain, sleet, icy winds, and gray skies. I almost looked forward to the snow. Multiple layers were the norm since the weather could turn drastically miserable in an hour or less.

On Wednesday the hospital waiting room was warm but empty. With no clients to see I'd been staring out at the parking lot, watching tree limbs swaying and bending with the wind.

Cindy glanced up from her computer. "So, did Mari say anything to you about Flynn? She's been bugging me to talk to you about him."

"You mean using my magic powers to solve a ten-year-old cold case? I told her not to get her hopes up, especially now that winter is almost here."

"Have you spoken to anyone yet?

Her question made me think for a moment. I leaned against the reception counter.

"I talked for a while with the immediate family after the memorial service. Then a few days ago his mother called and she helped set up a meeting tonight at the high school with his old drama teacher."

"What made you choose her?"

"You've got to start somewhere." My elbow slid and almost knocked into the business card holder.

The ringing of the phone interrupted us, but before Cindy could answer it, they'd hung up.

"Must have been a wrong number. That's been happening a lot." My receptionist tapped her pen on a note pad.

Mr. Katt strolled past and jumped onto the reception counter.

Cindy petted him then continued our conversation. "I'm sure whatever you can do to help will be appreciated. Flynn was…" she paused for a moment, searching for the words. "He was like a shooting star. Everyone in town knew he was going to go on to better things and we were proud of him. But I have a feeling some of his friends thought they could ride along on his coattails—feed off his leftovers. After you speak to the drama teacher, maybe you should talk to the three guys he always hung out with."

"In my spare time." I pointed to the empty waiting room. "Just kidding."

Cindy started to answer but the phone rang again. She checked the caller ID then added, "I guess that's all you've got plenty of with a cold-case murder investigation. Time. Plenty of time."

• • ● ● •

Five o'clock and Oak Falls High School appeared deserted. A furious blast of wind turned my new umbrella inside out. While trying to fix it, I stepped in a deep puddle. Cold water cascaded over the tops of my boots and down my socks. My toes now were soaking wet and squishy. Tonight's interview wasn't off to a good start. Wishing I lived in the desert, I flung open the school's front door, already regretting our meeting. The appointment was with Flynn's former English teacher, who also headed up the drama department. According to Lizette Keegan, her son had had a close relationship with Mrs. Vandersmitt, especially after starring in the senior play.

My footsteps made clicking sounds that ricocheted down the high school corridor. Raindrops slid off my slicker, leaving a slippery trail. Those same fluorescent lights found in every school cast flat, yellowish light in the center of the hallway but left deep shadows in the corners. Rows and rows of metal lockers stood guard, probably the same ones Flynn used. Very similar to the ones I'd used. If I closed my eyes, I could visualize this school and these hallways populated with the busy shadows of long-ago classmates.

Lizette's instructions were to meet Mrs. Vandersmitt in the auditorium, where she and her students would be rehearsing for the school's annual holiday show.

A large double door suddenly swung open right in front of me and two vivacious teenaged girls burst out, singing a portion of "The Little Drummer Boy" in harmony. They whooshed right past and disappeared into the ladies' room.

I pushed open the auditorium doors to find a scene of controlled chaos.

On the left side, in front of curved rows of seats, stood a tightly organized choral group singing a cappella under the energetic leadership of a small balding man in a wrinkled gray suit. On stage, paying no attention to the music, was a boy wearing an oversized sombrero hat dramatically reading a Robert Frost poem. More students hung out in clumps or sat scattered in the audience. The majority looked like they were either playing games on their phones or texting, or both, oblivious to everything happening around them.

A blond woman of Amazonian proportions wore multiple layers of clothing wrapped around her like an onion. She strode across the stage, raised a hand to shield her eyes from the stage lights and called to someone in the audience. One of the clumps moved. Eventually, a girl with pink-tipped hair rose and casually made her way to the stage. The boy handed her the sombrero, which was gigantically too big for her small frame. With an audible exclamation of displeasure, she slid the hat to the back of her head where it hung almost to her waist, supported by the strap around her neck.

The two girls who had gone to the restroom now squeezed past me, still singing, and bounded down toward the stage.

When the drama teacher noticed me standing in the aisle, she called a fifteen-minute break in the rehearsal. Once her back was turned, the kids began chucking the sombrero around like a Frisbee.

In a few long strides, she joined me, ignoring the chatter behind her.

"Evelyn Vandersmitt?" I held out my hand. "I'm Dr. Kate Turner. We spoke on the phone."

The hand that shook mine jingled with multiple small bracelets, some metal, others wood, all of them interesting. "Come with me. Let's make this quick." The cloud of floral perfume enveloping her spread like fog to engulf me.

Evelyn marched ahead, students scattering in her wake.

I followed close behind. "I have to ask. What's with the sombrero?"

She kept moving while she explained. Her bracelets clicked like miniature castanets. "Props can't find our storyteller's cap, so they gave us a sombrero to practice with."

Remembering my own high school, it made perfect sense.

We walked together along the hallway until she ducked into a small room marked PRIVATE that smelled like stale coffee.

"Teachers' lounge," she explained. "We shouldn't be interrupted by anyone in here." Taking advantage of the break, she stopped in front of the automatic coffeemaker and stared for a moment at the half-full carafe before pouring a small mug. I watched her sip it—grimace, but drink it down anyway. "Burnt," was her comment.

Unsure how to begin, I was struggling for an opening line when she made my job easy.

"Lizette called and told me all about you." Close up, the forty-something teacher's Nordic features, broad cheekbones, and deep blue eyes were striking. She wore no makeup, except crimson red lipstick, a slash of unexpected color against her pale skin. "Did you know your veterinary assistant was one of my favorite students? She designed and built most of our sets. Never wanted to be on stage. Quite a breath of fresh air from the rest of the monsters." Although she punctuated that last remark with a brilliant white smile, I suspected it wasn't a joke.

"Mrs. Vandersmitt, did Flynn's mother Lizette explain…?"

"Call me Evelyn, please." Undaunted by the bitter taste of the first cup, she poured a second mug of coffee. "Yes, we had a lengthy conversation."

That sounded like a somewhat chilly statement but her face remained composed.

"I know it's been a few years, but can you tell me a little about Flynn? What kind of student was he? What were his interests?" I took my notebook out to jot down anything important.

At first Evelyn said nothing. I thought she was gathering her thoughts, before I noticed her lips move. Was she praying?

"Please give me a moment." She turned away, fingertips massaging a spot in the middle of her forehead.

To break the awkward stillness I got up and poured myself some coffee in a disposable cup. It smelled flat, like it had been sitting around all day. I returned to my seat just as Evelyn turned back toward me.

"Forgive me. I was talking to Flynn." Her voice was matter-of-fact, as though talking to the dead happened all the time.

"Excuse me?" Maybe I hadn't understood what she meant.

"I asked his spirit for permission to speak about him." She plucked at one of her bracelets.

Okay. I'd had weirder conversations. "So what did he say?"

"He said yes. Also, he told me he doesn't care if his murderer is found. It happened a long time ago and all is forgiven."

Doesn't care if the murderer is caught? Not sure how to respond to that, I nodded my head.

Evelyn's eyes glittered. She leaned toward me. "I'm not crazy. I'm channeling the Flynn I knew. It's an old acting trick."

Still not sure what was going on, I nodded again.

With no warning, her arms shot high above her head and wiggled around. Catching my eye, she explained. "It's a body awareness exercise, to help me relax."

Okay. This was definitely weird. I made an effort to keep a nonjudgmental expression on my face.

"Now, how may I help you?" She lifted her mug to those red lips before realizing it was empty. I was curious if she would drink another cup.

"Can I get your more coffee, Evelyn?"

"No. I'm wired enough as it is."

Now, that statement I could agree with.

"Please don't take this the wrong way but are the police positive it's him?" Evelyn asked. "I find this news so hard to believe."

Now we were back on track. "Yes, he was identified through dental records and personal effects that were found at the scene."

"What personal effects? A bracelet?"

This was the second peculiar question from a woman who knew him—a woman who wore a number of wrist bangles. Had she given a special bracelet to her favorite student?

"I'm afraid I don't know."

Her face deflated, eagerness lost for a moment. "Forgive me. I still can't believe he's passed. What a waste for the world."

I seized my opening. "Did you know that he planned to leave town?"

"I knew he wanted to leave. I'd hoped he would wait until he graduated from college but his mind was made up. Since I couldn't stop him, I supplied a list of names and numbers of friends I have in L.A. Our small-town life held no interest for him." She adjusted her vaguely gypsy-looking skirt.

When she spoke, I noticed her bright red lower lip quivered slightly. Something about it mesmerized me.

"I'd also recommended an acting school and told him to call me when he got settled. Of course, he never did."

Footsteps sounded in the hallway outside, followed by laughter as some of the students from the auditorium began to straggle back inside from their break.

Grabbing her attention, I pressed on, "Did you worry when you didn't hear from him?"

She slid several bracelets back and forth on her wrist. "No. We'd had an argument. Flynn wanted to cut all his family ties, reinvent himself. His home life was difficult—I'll let it go at that."

Evelyn's advice had been more personal than professional. "Why did you advise him to wait?" I watched that lip quiver again.

She jumped up, suddenly restless in the small, stuffy room. "He was too immature, too idealistic. They would have eaten him alive out there. Eaten him alive." A sweep of her arm reminded me she taught drama. Was I witnessing a performance?

"Do you remember where you were the day he left?"

She stared at me, a quizzical look on her face. "I've been trying to recall that. I'm really not sure. Traveling perhaps?"

So, she had no alibi. Not even an attempt at one.

"And the nature of your relationship? Would you describe it as…intimate in any way?" My face began to flush as I asked this extremely personal question.

It didn't upset Evelyn a bit. "Of course not. I was his teacher, well, perhaps more of a mentor or muse really. Nothing else— despite what those old biddies in town think." A thick lock of hair escaped over one shoulder. She pointedly glanced at her watch.

Obviously, I wasn't going to learn much more. I decided to pull a question out of left field before she went back to work. "Why do you think he was murdered?"

Her red shiny lips parted, then closed.

What was I missing here?

She tapped her watch dial and stood up. "I'm afraid I have to go."

Disappointed, I poured my untouched coffee into the sink. "Well, thank you for your time. I'll call if I have any other questions." No alibi to check and no recollection of the day Flynn disappeared. Our interview hadn't revealed any motive for murder; instead, only held hints of a complicated relationship.

I stood up to open the door. Evelyn stopped my arm. Her fingers pressed down hard on my wrist.

"You don't understand," she said, her voice hoarse with emotion. "You can't understand because you never met him. I tried to protect him—the world can be a terrible place."

"Of course you did." Strong fingers dug into me. This intense reaction seemed completely out of place for their "student" and "teacher" relationship.

"I used to picture him accepting the Academy Award and thanking me, his high school drama teacher, for inspiring him to become an actor." Tears glistened in her eyes.

"Evelyn." I quietly asked. "Who do you think murdered Flynn?"

Red lips quivered once again in her pale compelling face.

"The person who hated him the most."

"Who is it you're talking about?" I felt trapped, pushed firmly against the door.

"Bruce."

I blanked for a moment.

She moved closer and spat out the words. "That pig, Bruce, Flynn's stepfather. If I could get away with slitting his throat, I would."

"Why?" Fiona had said Flynn hated his family.

"When Bruce got drunk, he'd hit Lizette, even when she was confined to her wheelchair. Flynn couldn't stop it when he was younger but once he reached fifteen and was taller than his stepdad, he told the SOB to stop hitting his mother or he'd kill him. To prove it, he knocked him out cold."

I was horrified. There had been nasty comments but no hint of physical violence when I'd been at their house, but abused women often keep secrets. Had Bruce taken his revenge by offering Flynn a ride out of town and then, in a fit of rage, killed him?

"Did Lizette report the abuse to the police?"

"No. And she begged Flynn not to tell them either."

Finally I'd found a solid motive for murder. An interview with the wicked stepfather was in order. I also needed to verify where Bruce was the day Flynn had disappeared.

Back inside my truck I blasted the defroster and waited for the windshield to clear. I'd learned two things. Flynn's home life had been worse than I thought, and obviously Evelyn Vandersmitt felt strongly about her handsome student. First, I concentrated on the eccentric drama teacher. Was the quarrel about Flynn's plans to leave more serious than she let on? Maybe in her wildest dreams she fantasized about joining him in Hollywood, continuing to be his muse. Stranger things had happened.

As far as Bruce, the stepfather, was concerned, I needed to verify Evelyn's accusations and make sure they weren't a smoke-screen cooked up to divert attention away from her. I also made a note to find out if there was a Mr. Vandersmitt.

Jealousy cut both ways.

And jealousy was a perfect motive for murder.

Chapter Ten

By the following morning the weather had cleared and our appointment calendar started filling up again. After our third client of the morning, Mari and I took a break at the Circle K near the hospital, chomping on potato chips while gassing up the truck.

"How did your interview with Mrs. Vandersmitt go?" Mari's question came out a little garbled due to chip overload.

I snuck a few mouthfuls of my own chips while figuring out how to diplomatically phrase my answer. Dingy, sleet-streaked windows overlooked the gas pumps where our truck stood. The pewter-colored sky above hid its intentions from us.

"I'm not sure. She's a little odd."

"All the teachers are. My class used to say the real Oak Falls High School staff had been replaced by space aliens who were sent to study us and report back to their planet."

"That would explain it," I joked. "You kids probably acted like you were from outer space too."

"Pretty much. But I did enjoy all my drama classes and working on the sets."

"That's what Evelyn said. She remembered you very clearly."

"Nice." Mari began to peel a banana. "Want some?"

"No, thanks. By the way, I think one of your pieces of fruit is hiding out somewhere in the truck. I smelled a whiff of something funky when I got in this morning." That said, I fished around in the small yellow bag for the last chip, thereby fulfilling my daily requirement of fat and salt. "At least I have enough willpower to buy the little size. One of these days I've got to kick this potato chip habit."

"Me, too."

Reluctantly, I rose, cleaned my fingers with a napkin, and tossed everything in the recycle bin. "Ready?"

"Nope." Her hand dove back inside her extra-large bag. "Maybe I should cut this junk food and lose a few pounds in case I run into some of the kids coming back for the reunion."

"You look fine. It's going to be the same people you see in town all the time, so what's the big deal?" Despite her diet, Mari's athletic body never seemed to gain an ounce.

"Not true. I'd say fifty or sixty percent of my class moved away from here."

"That many?"

Before she could reply, the door behind me opened, shepherding in a blast of chilly air.

I heard someone say my name.

A massive bundled-up mound of black leather stood directly behind me. The only human parts showing were two eyes behind round goggles and slices of wind-chapped cheeks. Luckily, I recognized my client's voice. "Henry James? Are you in there?"

Oak Fall's famous baking biker pulled off his knitted skullcap to reveal a shiny bald head. "Haven't seen you guys in a while. Hey, Mari."

Mari waved to him, a half a banana in her mouth.

"You must be freezing, Henry. Isn't it about time to retire the bike for the winter?" I couldn't imagine how cold it must feel to tool around on a motorcycle in this weather.

He put down his helmet then smacked his hands together trying to warm them up before pouring a big takeout cup of coffee. "Yeah, it's been a bad fall for riding."

"Hey, did you have Mrs. Vandersmitt for English when you were in school back in the Stone Age?" Mari asked him.

Henry laughed. "I think all us boys wanted to have some Vandersmitt—if you know what I mean."

"Oh, come on. Stop exaggerating." One thing I'd learned about Henry was he embellished his stories a bit, like the one about a spaceship landing on the roof of the CVS drugstore one night looking for toilet paper.

"Okay. There were rumors floating around. Guys used to say 'red lips—take a sip.'" He turned to Mari and made kissing noises.

"You are such a pig." She pretended to throw her snack at him but reconsidered. Instead, she crumpled up her garbage and tossed it in the pail. "Two points."

"Anybody know if there is a Mr. Vandersmitt?"

Mari shook her head but Henry cleared his throat and answered me. "There was a Mr. Vandersmitt. Legend says he had a heart attack and died after a night of energetic passion."

That did it. Both Mari and Henry collapsed into a fit of giggles.

"Can we be serious for a second?" I faced the two of them and held up my hands. "Is there any chance that Evelyn Vandersmitt was romantically involved with Flynn?"

That quieted them down.

"Why do you want to know? Are you doing the murder investigation thing again?" Henry's eyes narrowed in disapproval.

"Not really. Just curious." I gave Mari a warning sign to stay quiet.

Henry shook a few drops of water off his skullcap before he slipped it back on his head.

"Listen. When Flynn was in high school I was involved with the Hells Angels. Anything I heard you've got to take with a grain of salt cause my memories are kinda warped. But rumor was that kid didn't have any problems getting…some action, if you ladies know what I mean."

"What?"

"Faculty, students, moms, even a biker's chick. But, hey, maybe that was only a rumor." He picked up his helmet and slipped it on. After lobbing this ambiguous statement at us, he hurried over to the cashier, paid for six dollars' worth of gas and a candy bar and vanished into a cold rain.

His memories sounded like a movie of the week fantasy. Separating fact from fiction where Henry was concerned was no simple matter. I put what he said on the back burner and got ready to go back to work.

• • ● • •

Our last client that day turned out to be a real hoot.

We'd been asked for advice about an injured barn owl found by one of our good clients. Since Mari and I were close by, I told her we would swing over and take the owl to the local wildlife rehabilitator.

Many people don't know that they aren't supposed to keep injured wildlife that they find. First, it can be dangerous, and second, it isn't in the best interests of the animal. A licensed wildlife rehabilitator is trained to treat and hopefully release most injured animals back into their habitats.

Which reminded me about something Mari had mentioned a while ago. "Hey, did you hear any more about that captured bear?"

"Nothing yet."

"Well, if you do, let me or Cindy know. If there's a rogue bear loose in a residential area, I want our clients to be warned."

"Sure thing." She put her head down and concentrated on updating our schedule. I drove, thinking about Flynn—his kooky drama teacher, his toxic stepfather, and all the other people who floated in and out of his short life.

• • ● • •

Luke Gianetti's cousin, who was also my favorite waitress at the Oak Falls diner, stood waiting for us in her driveway along with her standard poodles, Jazz and Jewel. The sky had cleared up and pale sunshine shown through the trees.

"Hi, Rosie," I said after rolling down my window.

In her hands she held a large cardboard box. "Thanks so much for coming over so quickly. The dogs found the poor thing when I took them for a walk."

I wasn't surprised, since poodles were bred to be bird dogs, although this beautifully groomed pair of black and white poodles looked like they'd be more at home lounging on a velvet sofa than half-submerged in a rush-filled lake.

"I'll take it." Mari opened the truck's passenger door and Rosie passed the box to her.

"Sorry to run but I'm late for my shift at the diner. Thanks again, guys." With a quick wave she disappeared into the house, the dogs following behind.

The tall box pierced with air holes perched awkwardly on my assistant's lap. "Hey, this thing is heavy. What the heck did she put in here?"

"Maybe a water dish or some food?" I put the truck in gear and turned around in the driveway. "How does the owl look?"

Mari tried to lift up one corner. "Can't tell. I think she padded it with something. Maybe it ran into a window."

Usually barn owls are nocturnal, flying and hunting at night. I wondered how long it had been on the ground before Rosie and her dogs found it.

"Okay. Well, don't bother checking inside. Let's keep it dark and quiet. We should be at the Bird's Nest Sanctuary in fifteen minutes.

I was thinking about Flynn's stepfather, Bruce, abusing Lizette, when I heard a loud scraping noise. It came from the box.

My hands on the wheel, I asked Mari, "What's going on over there?"

"Maybe it woke up."

That noise didn't sound like a little barn owl. A quick look down the road confirmed there wasn't any place to pull over, plus we had several vehicles trailing behind us. Decision made, I put on the flashers and braked to slow down. Thank goodness, it wasn't sleeting or raining now.

"Ouch." Mari pulled her left hand off the box. When I turned I saw a streak of blood on her palm. My guess—it wasn't bird blood. I'd once been trapped in this truck with a hawk. I had a horrible premonition fate was repeating itself.

Miraculously, a small driveway appeared on the right only a few feet ahead. Using the mailbox as a guide, I turned in and came to a stop, just in time to see a large feathered head pop out of the box. Huge yellow owl eyes stared into mine.

The tufts on the ears gave it away. This was a great horned owl—a fearsome predator with dagger-sharp talons. And he wanted out.

"Mari," I kept my voice calm. "Open your door and get as far away as you can. Now."

Immediately she bolted, leaving the passenger door open. Once she was safe, I slid my jacket sleeve down over my hand and waited. The box shook as folded wings pushed up and then out from the cardboard. Most of the magnificent bird's upper body was visible. Somehow, I needed to get it out of the truck before it spread its four- to five-foot long wings and we were both in trouble.

Using my elbow I gently slid the box along the seat toward the open door. A cold breeze drifted through the cabin of the truck. The feathered head swiveled almost one hundred-eighty degrees. Two feet with curved black talons emerged and lifted the bird out of the box onto the seat. Alert eyes searched for the sky.

With my left arm raised to protect my eyes, I gently nudged the now-empty box again with my right arm. Sure enough, the owl got the message. One hop toward the door then both powerful wings unfolded and he flew out of the cab to disappear over the trees.

"Mari, are you okay?"

Her head poked up from behind a rhododendron. "Barn owl, my ass." She scrambled back into the passenger seat, a few leaves stuck in her hair.

I took a look at her hand. Not too bad, but it needed medical attention. "Guess where you're going."

"To the prom?" she joked.

"No." I put the truck in gear and backed up. "But you just gave me a great idea."

Chapter Eleven

Prom night photos, school newspaper articles, the Class of 2007 yearbook—all would help me understand the dynamics of Flynn's high school class, his circle of friends, and perhaps his enemies. He disappeared in August, only a few months after graduation. Someone somewhere had clues as to what happened to him, except maybe they didn't know it.

I planned to call the family and use a request for Flynn's memorabilia as a cover to weasel details of Bruce and Lizette's relationship out of Fiona or Sophia.

Cindy and Mari volunteered to bring me their yearbooks and scrapbooks, while I made a mental note to contact the high school newspaper. The journalism department was sure to have photos in its files and, knowing how most schools operated, they probably never threw anything away. Hopefully, their computer archives would be easy to search, but I didn't count on it. As a last resort I could enlist the help of Evelyn Vandersmitt. Of course, she might have to okay it with Flynn's ghost.

But sleuthing would have to rest on the back burner for a bit since I was booked to the max. The last of my staff had finally recovered from the virus that had laid them low, so things at the animal hospital were getting back to normal.

Mr. Katt perked up now that his personal human staff was back in full force and proceeded to dive bomb Cindy each time she passed by. After one near-miss, our normally bubbly receptionist let out a string of expletives that would have curled Mr. Katt's whiskers, if they weren't naturally curled.

Now that appointments had picked up, Cindy, for some strange reason, decided this was the perfect time to work on all the little repairs and touch-ups the office needed. Our employees were to focus on one part of the hospital at a time. Neon-colored Post-it notes warning of wet paint began popping up everywhere as the staff did random touch-ups to scuff marks in the hospital exam rooms and hallways.

Thankfully, Mari and I had plenty of house calls to make, so we could leave, but not before I backed into a wet wall and got green paint in my hair.

• • ● • •

Our first scheduled appointment was a surprise since we'd just run into him at the Circle K. It turned out to be Henry the baking biker.

Mari remarked on the exterior of Henry James' old farmhouse house as we pulled up. It looked pretty shabby. Built by his grandparents, it was a typical old farmhouse, with bluestone front steps and a wraparound porch in sore need of restoration to bring it back to its former beautiful self. However, restorations cost money and Henry had put that on hold for now. His priority was the big shiny Harley motorcycle stashed in the newly repaired garage.

"How's your hand feeling?" I asked. Mari had insisted that I drop her off at her house yesterday so she could drive herself to the local 24-hour medical clinic.

"It wasn't as bad as it looked. The tetanus booster I got hurt worse than the scratch."

"Lucky you're right-handed. But if it bothers you while we're working, let me know."

Henry's older cat, Dante, was a former unaltered tom whose face and body carried scars from many feline fights. Now a pampered pet, he lived his remaining lives indoors. A look-alike son served as his companion, inheriting Dad's mellow personality and sky-blue eyes.

I rang the doorbell but didn't hear anything so used the iron knocker instead. The sky hung low with gray clouds and the air smelled like snow.

"Hey, Doc. Hi, Mari. Come on in." Henry wore an apron over a wife-beater t-shirt. His bulging muscles and hairy chest made quite a contrast to the tailored cook's apron. Of course, not many bakers sported a bright green snake tattoo that looped around their necks. Despite the incongruities, I'd found Henry to be a pussycat at heart.

We followed him through the plastic-covered living room, which looked frozen in time, into the kitchen where the smell of something baking engulfed us. The warm, yeasty odor spiked with cinnamon instantly made me hungry.

"What are you making?" Mari asked.

"Three different types of breads—banana, zucchini, and date nut." A dusting of flour decorated his ham-like hands.

"Yumm." Mari sat down at the round kitchen table.

"Work first, food later." I wandered over to the sunroom directly off the kitchen, a likely place for a cat to be lounging. Indeed, both felines were curled up on a blanket draped over the sofa. They barely moved when I walked in.

Henry followed, although I knew from experience he'd pass out if he saw his cats get any shots or blood drawn.

"Anything wrong with these handsome boys?" I sat on the sofa next to Dante who reacted by stretching out and rolling on his stomach.

"Could you look at Dante's bad ear? Oh, and Junior needs his rabies shot. Your office sent me a reminder." Henry tried to hide the panic in his face.

Mari and I exchanged glances.

"We'll be fine here, Henry. Go ahead and check your oven." Mari told him. "Make sure to save me a sample."

"Sure." He gratefully took off without glancing back.

"Good job, Mari. I didn't feel like picking him up off the floor." With our squeamish owner safely out of the room, I started examining the older cat whose now-lush coat reflected a nutritious diet supplied by a loving owner.

Meanwhile, Mari removed a rabies vaccine from the refrigerated carry pack, along with a syringe. "Checked both cats' records on the way. Dante is up-to-date. Only Junior needs his vaccine."

While I waited for Mari to draw up the shot, I observed the older cat scratching his head. Remembering his outdoor past, I checked his ears, one crumpled and bent close to his head from an old hematoma wound. Sure enough, my otoscope revealed a mild waxy buildup but no obvious ear mites. I took a swab to make sure and then examined and vaccinated Junior with a tiny cat-sized needle. Getting his injection didn't interfere with his purring. After we finished both cats, father and son followed us into the kitchen, slowly lumbering along like a couple of tiny tigers.

"Done? Everything okay?" Henry turned toward us, a hot tray in his hand.

"Everything's fine. Just keep an eye on that crumpled ear of Dante's and clean it out periodically. Junior is in perfect health."

I stripped off my gloves and put them in Mari's rigid plastic refuse case that held the used syringes. We always brought all our medical waste back to the hospital for proper disposal.

Henry presented us with two plates of freshly sliced pieces of lemon pound cake and what looked like chocolate chip date nut bread, along with a dollop of cream cheese. "Come try this and tell me what you think."

That was one of the perks of doing house calls. Most of our clients felt the need to feed us. The downside to that? Mari and I rarely refused anything.

"Okay, right after we wash our hands."

When I first met Henry I didn't know that his intimidating appearance hid a soft nougat heart. Raised by his two college professor parents who taught at the local community college, he'd been sidetracked during his early twenties, joining a motorcycle gang, to the horror of his middle-class family. Now twenty years later, his mom and dad gone, anxiety had pushed him into therapy. When his therapist encouraged him to take up a relaxing hobby, he chose baking, and to everyone's surprise, had turned it into a mini-cottage industry. Several local stores now carried his "Baking Biker" line of brownies and other baked goods.

Mari beat me to the table. "So good," she cooed after the first bite.

Behind me, the younger cat, Junior, streaked past, put his paw brakes on and settled into the pounce position. "Do they play a lot?" I asked Henry, mid forkful of my homemade treat.

"Until his dad, Dante, has had enough. Sometimes we old guys sit on the sofa and watch Junior tear around the room." Henry's normally chill expression softened watching his youngest cat leap on imaginary prey hiding under the rug.

Junior continued to provide the amusement as we finished our sweet snack.

"Sorry to eat and run," I told Henry when I carried my empty plate over to the sink. "We're slammed with appointments today."

"No problem. I'm glad you got over so soon. They're some bats that hang out under the back eaves and I worried one of them might get into the house." He quickly plunged my plate into a sink filled with soapy water.

"That happens more than you might think. Sometimes bats can become trapped in the house or basement and bite pets or people. Where rabies is concerned you can never be too careful."

Mari rose and thumped her longtime friend Henry on the back. "Really good."

The practiced stoic look he'd cultivated cracked a little.

"Hey, I forgot to ask. Are you really investigating Flynn's murder or were you pulling my leg the other day? Because I might have something for you." Serious now, he turned around.

"Well, I'm more gathering facts at this point, but anything you can tell us would be appreciated by the family." I took a quick look to make sure I'd stowed away all my equipment.

Henry sort of shuffled his pans around, head down. "You guys know I have a bit of a rough past." His voice sounded apologetic.

"Yep. Pretty rough." My assistant didn't hesitate to agree.

"Uh. A couple of months before Flynn left town one of the guys I hung out with got pissed at the kid. Seems he thought his girlfriend had cheated on him, and he suspected Flynn."

Another real clue, finally. "Do you have a name?"

"Legal name? I'm not sure. We called him 'D' because of the real mean streak in him. One time he was high on meth and coke and he messed up a pal of mine—kicked him in the kidneys and crazy-laughed while doing it."

I took a scrap of paper out of my pocket and jotted down some notes. "Is this 'D' guy still in town?"

"Don't think so. As I recall he disappeared right around the time Flynn did. But don't forget, that was a while ago—my memory could be wrong."

"What does 'D' stand for?" Mari asked. She signed off the hospital laptop and waited for it to shut down.

The question hung in the air unanswered the entire time it took for Henry to lead us to the front door. I wondered how reluctant he felt talking about a fellow biker with us. Before I reached for the doorknob he made up his mind.

"Wait." He stuck both hands in his apron pockets. "That nickname sort of described him. 'D' was short for Diabolo, and believe me, that's what he was. When you looked into his eyes you knew who you saw."

He'd confused me. "Who did you see?"

His answer hung in the air, as ominous as a noose in a tree.

"You saw the Devil."

Chapter Twelve

That night I couldn't sleep. Even though ten years had passed since the events Henry described, my imagination brought the evil Diabolo lurking back. Was it a coincidence that bikers showed up at Flynn's memorial service? Maybe they knew something no one else knew.

Something terrible they regretted.

A make-believe video played in my head. In it Flynn lay on the forest floor being kicked over and over by a shadowy figure in leather.

I sat up in bed. What if one of those guys at the memorial lunch had been "D" all along? The massive man with the boxer's damaged face loomed in my memory, his black eyes devoid of feeling staring at me. In my mind he raised a thick finger to the bridge of his flattened nose in an unspoken threat.

That did it. Now completely awake I padded around the bedroom trying to figure out the best way to track down Diabolo. Perhaps Henry or someone he knows could provide a last name. If I had to, I supposed I could get Luke or the Oak Falls Police Department involved.

"What do you think, Buddy?"

As usual my dog gave me sage advice by jumping onto the sofa and curling up. I sat down next to him and pulled my blanket tight.

Like it or not, I faced a major task in trying to reconstruct the past, especially one I had no firsthand knowledge of. A difficult task, I acknowledged, and reached for a leftover glass of water on the coffee table. Flynn's handsome and now familiar face stared up at me from the newspaper. Bikers, a lovestruck teacher, high school infighting—and that was only for starters.

Flynn. Who the heck were you?

Morning light filtered in through the blinds. According to the clock, I'd gotten some sleep despite all the stress. Stretching out under the covers I allowed myself some downtime before getting up and out the door and over to work. Hopefully, I'd be able to juggle my hectic schedule, and investigate this cold case on the side without short-circuiting.

I was pouring my first cup of coffee of the day when Cindy cornered me. "Aren't you getting super excited? Jeremy will be coming to visit pretty soon. I can't wait to meet him." She practically jumped up and down.

Definitely not a morning person like Cindy, I didn't get super excited about anything until after my second cup of coffee. I'd noticed that the arrival of my Skype buddy and former boyfriend had taken on the scope of a national holiday in the eyes of my staff. They wanted all the juicy details.

"Did you decide if he's staying with you?" Cindy had the decency to turn away and pretend to clean the countertop after asking the jackpot question.

Lifting the coffee to my lips I turned back toward my apartment to find the staff obviously expecting an answer. Complete disclosure appeared to be the only way out.

"Okay, everyone. My friend, Jeremy, will be here this Monday, late afternoon or early evening, depending on traffic. He is not staying in there with me," I pointed vaguely in the direction of the apartment, "because it is too small." The next tidbit I lobbed at Cindy. "I have reserved a place for him at the Stanton Inn." As much as I emphasized the word friend, I knew it was futile. The staff had cooked up a tearjerker romantic story starring myself, and a limited cast of characters. With Daffy and Cindy part of the Jeremy/Luke/Kate information loop, I was pretty sure most of the town of Oak Falls got regular updates too.

"The Stanton Inn is lovely." Mari must have been helping Cindy because she suddenly appeared behind her. "That reminds me. You should talk to Betsy Stanton, Dorothy's daughter. I think she went to high school around the same time as Flynn."

Talking to the inn's owners and getting Jeremy entwined in our local murder was not in my game plan. I tried to be diplomatic. "Maybe we can wait until after my guest leaves."

Cindy piped up. "You never know what might happen."

Her words would prove more prophetic than I would ever have guessed.

• • ● • •

Before I knew it another day had ended. Looking out the window I saw only the black night of a moonless sky still with no snow. My workday had been a blur of patients and problems. I'd eaten my lunch standing up. If it weren't for walking Buddy, I probably wouldn't have gotten outside at all.

Frustrated with life in general, I called the one person who always gives me great advice—whether I took it or not. He answered the phone after the second ring.

"Hello, Gramps?"

"Hey, sweetheart, how are you?

Just the sound of his raspy voice made me happy. I sunk into the sofa, wondering why I'd felt so blue earlier.

"I'm fine. Overworked, as usual."

We'd had this conversation before so his wise words were familiar. "You've got to pace yourself. I learned that the hard way."

"I'm trying. One of these days I'll get it right."

For a few minutes we chatted about inconsequential things— the latest gossip at the independent senior facility he lived in, silly stories from the Internet, and everyday stuff. But I couldn't fool him. He knew I had something on my mind.

"Gramps, I've got this situation going on that I'd like to talk to you about."

Through the phone I heard each inhale and exhale. Scars in his lungs from twenty-five years of being a firefighter then an arson investigator made breathing difficult for him. Sometimes the medications worked wonders and sometimes they didn't.

"Trouble with Luke?" His guess was a surprise.

I abruptly sat up on the sofa almost knocking Buddy off his doggy pillow.

"Not even close. Luke is back with his high school sweetheart and for all I know he might be engaged again."

"I'm sorry, Katie." He waited for a moment, probably not sure of what to say. My social life had always been a mystery to him.

"Don't be." That immediate response came out a bit more brusque than I had meant it to be. "Anyway, you were right about one thing. I've gotten myself twisted up in that cold case I told you about."

"Why am I not surprised?" He probably was shaking his head in frustration with me. "How long has this young fellow been missing?"

"Ten years. He graduated high school in June and decided to leave that August. The day he disappeared he left a note on the kitchen table for his mother saying he was on his way to Los Angeles to start the adventure of his life."

A thumping sound came from the phone.

"Is someone else in your apartment?" Hopefully, we weren't on speakerphone.

"It's only Pete. I promised to play poker tonight with a couple of the guys. Anyway, don't worry so much. Whoever did this is probably long gone."

"You've got a point there, but what am I supposed to do? The family asked me to look into it."

Gramps didn't answer right away but when he did it was direct and to the point. "Honey, you could always say no."

After we hung up I thought about what he said. Why didn't I just tell Flynn's family that I couldn't help them? Who am I kidding? I'm not a professional investigator and I'm certainly not going to get paid for my efforts. This crime, as I was learning, wasn't just a simple cold case. It was a frozen solid iceberg-sized cold case.

I didn't have any personal ties to Flynn or his family.

So why did I feel compelled to follow it through?

Chapter Thirteen

The next day, frustrated by my lack of progress and still spooked by the phantom Diabolo, I contacted Flynn Keegan's family. I wanted to get the names of students he hung out with and try to learn more about his final day in town. Bruce and Lizette's relationship was also on my radar. Only Flynn's sister, Fiona, was available and willing to talk to me on such short notice. Last time we met she'd barely said a word to me. This time I needed her to spill the family secrets.

Could Fiona really be as Goth as she appeared? I got my answer when she opened the door. Dressed in black pants riddled with zippers and studs, today her lower lip sported a small safety pin. A cropped T-shirt glowed with gaping skulls while her mouth echoed the effect by becoming a dark hole outlined with thick black lipstick.

My tan cargo pants and brown jacket read "boring," at the polar end of the fashion spectrum. To make up for it, I tried to put some enthusiasm into my greeting. "Hey, Fiona, thanks for meeting with me."

A grunt is all I got in return.

Her crooked finger invited me in and brought me into the foyer. She used her boot to slam the door shut, then marched straight down the main hallway of the house. I followed, wondering about her destination. We stopped in front of a room with one of those joke privacy signs warning visitors to stay out.

After pausing for a moment she took a deep breath and turned the doorknob.

It was a bedroom, stuffy from dust and disuse. From the movie and sports posters on the walls and shelves of trophies, I assumed this had been Flynn's room. Color bathed the walls and stars glimmered on the ceiling. No beige here.

"Flynn's room?"

Fiona confirmed that with a grunt and flung herself on the bed.

I noticed some photographs scotch-taped on the wall above a worn wooden dresser. One captured a dark-haired girl and Flynn in formal wear at what looked like a prom, a fake Eiffel Tower glowing in the background. Another looked like a picture of a very young fair-haired Fiona holding a puppy. There were two funny strips of photos, from one of those machines you find at the mall, featuring Flynn and a pretty blond girl making faces and sticking out their tongues. The last image showed Flynn and a group of guys in swim trunks standing in front of a "Danger. No Swimming" sign. The grins on their faces and their wet hair suggested they'd ignored it.

"Can you tell me about these pictures?"

Fiona reluctantly pulled herself up on her elbows.

"That's senior prom night. This is me with Brandy, our dog, when she was a puppy. She died two years ago. Next one is my brother and Angelica goofing off. Then you've got Flynn's gang, the guys he hung out with all the time. They were quarry-diving and almost got caught by the cops." A hint of admiration penetrated her general gloom.

She stared at me as if daring me to ask another question. Her original passionate plea for me to help find her brother's killer seemed to have dried up. But behind her anger I saw something else—frustration, sorrow, and bitterness. I decided to take a chance and dig deeper.

"It's not easy to lose a brother."

Accusing eyes caught mine. "How would you know?"

Since she had sprawled across most of the bed, I claimed a

spot on the far corner. "My brother and mom were killed in a car crash when I was fifteen. Like you, I didn't get to say good-bye."

I heard her breathing harshly, in short deep bursts.

"Sorry. I didn't know."

"No problem. Don't forget I'm here trying to help solve your brother's murder. Everything you tell me matters."

That got her moving. She sat up, gave me what passed for a smile, and walked over to the photos on the wall I had asked about.

"Okay. So this is a picture of him and Shiloh Alberts. He went to the senior prom with her but they broke up pretty soon after that. I remember she and her mom were out of town when my brother left, because my mom went crazy and called all of Flynn's friends trying to find out where he was." She skipped the puppy picture and went on to the next. "Here's Flynn with Angelica, his on and off girlfriend through most of high school. She was super jealous and possessive, he told me one time."

I wondered how upset Angelica became about not going to senior prom with Flynn.

Fiona paused at the last picture. "These are the guys he basically hung out with twenty-four/seven. Left to right they're Rusty Lieberman, Nate Porter, and Denny Alantonio."

"Were they all in the same year in high school?"

"Yep. Rusty, he's the guy with the red hair, is the smart one; Nate's more quiet; and Denny…I'm not sure if you could label Denny. Maybe the jokester?"

After taking a few mental notes I went and stood next to her. I needed to put the names to the faces. They were all teenagers, mostly the same height and weight, except for Nate, who came up to Flynn's shoulder. "Did the guys have many fights with each other?"

Blank eyes met mine.

"Can you remember any incidents, or something unusual that happened around the time of Flynn's disappearance?"

She scrunched up her face, causing the ring in her eyebrow to play peekaboo.

"Not really. It was a long time ago. They were guys, you know, always punching each other and goofing around. I'm not sure what I can tell you."

"Did any of them come to the house on a regular basis? After school?" In my heart I felt like I was grasping at straws.

Her answer took a while. She stared at the pictures before closing her eyes, at least trying to remember. "I think Rusty came by to study just before tests a couple of times, and Nate used to pop in to borrow Flynn's bike. That, I remember 'cause Flynn got mad one day when Nate didn't return it. The other guy, I didn't see much. Denny had a job after school, I think, at some car dealership."

"That's very helpful." I tried to compliment Fiona as much as possible. The less stress she felt, the more she might recall. "Any idea where most of them are now?"

She shrugged her shoulders. "Rusty is a doctor. My mom told me she saw him the other day and that he'd joined his father's practice. I think Denny started selling real estate because I've seen his picture in ads all over town. His face is even on the grocery cart at ShopRite. Nate lives here in town, still working at the Country Store. I don't think he ever left Oak Falls. Whenever I go in to buy a cone, he's always nice and scoops me an extra big portion of ice cream."

"Does he ever ask you about Flynn?"

A funny look wrinkled her brow. "No.

I glanced around the room one last time. "Alright, I've got plenty to go on for now. Do you mind if I take these two pictures?" I pointed to the prom and quarry photos. "I'll make copies and bring you back the originals."

"Don't bother. Mom's got a bunch more." With a swift gesture, as though she couldn't wait to get rid of them, she ripped the tape off the wall and handed me the pictures. "Can't stand to look at them now. Used to be I'd imagine him having fun in L.A., happy he got out of this crappy little town. That's been replaced by the image of my brother lying dead in the woods."

I knew exactly how she felt.

"Fiona, after my mom and brother, Jimmy, died from a hit-and-run accident, I pretended they were out shopping or running errands and would be home soon. I knew it wasn't true but it was comforting in a weird way. I think everyone has to find their own way of coping with trauma. Have you seen a counselor?"

"Yeah. A bunch."

"Did they help?"

"Some. All I know is as soon as I save enough money, I'm out of here. Flynn tried to escape but didn't make it—but I will." The belligerent tone in her voice didn't invite any dispute. "You know I messed up before he took off. I told him if he left without me I'd never talk to him again."

One more piece of guilt this young woman carried around with her. "Fiona. If Flynn had lived, I'm sure he would have called you."

"You think?" Hope was in her voice.

"I'm positive."

She allowed herself to smile at me. For a moment I saw the resemblance to her brother she'd been hiding under all the makeup.

On our way out I caught her off guard. "One more thing, and I apologize if this is too personal a question. Why do you hate your father so much?"

Her face turned into a furious mask. "Let's see. He hit my mother, my brother, and me all the time for no good reason while we were growing up. I know he's got money but do you think he shares it with his family? No. Instead, he sits on it like a fat frog. Mom had to practically beg for school expenses and clothes and stuff for me."

"Did he ever...?"

Fiona must have read my mind. "When I was nine his good-night hugs changed. They made me uncomfortable. Flynn put a special lock on the inside of my bedroom door so I'd feel safe. Told my dad he'd kill him if he ever touched me again."

Good for Flynn, I thought.

"He hates my Goth look." Her face showed a smug satisfaction. "Good old Bruce gets his pleasure from verbal abuse these days."

The eyes that looked back at me were Flynn's, only buried in mascara and misery. Fiona was coping as best she could. Those black Goth layers camouflaged her pain.

I'd used a rotten attitude and constant sarcasm to deflect the pain of dealing with my lousy father.

With the pictures safely tucked into my purse I left Flynn's childhood home and got into the truck. Before I started the engine I took one last look at the quarry photo. All the guys had defied the rules and dived in together.

Curious that the only one Fiona had seen over the years had been Nate. I also found it odd he never asked her about her brother. Maybe he didn't need to ask because he knew Flynn was dead.

"One step closer," I whispered to the glossy image. "Flynn, just help me get one step closer to finding out what happened to you."

Four figures smiled back at me, frozen in their innocence.

On the way home I detoured into town, hoping Nate Porter, the quiet one of Flynn's gang, would still be around. Ten years was a long time ago, but he might still remember where he was the day Flynn disappeared. The Country Store, where Nate worked, was located in an old farmhouse with a huge wrap-around porch. It sold everything from tourist stuff to exotic specialty foods to local jams and jellies. As a nod to the modern world, a long freezer compartment carried a wide variety of flavors of locally made gelato. Another favorite, the cotton candy machine, stood near a big jar of pickles.

I was in luck. Not only was Nate alone in the store, but he seemed eager to talk to me.

"Yeah, I sure felt bummed out when they identified those remains as Flynn." Nate busied himself by unpacking a box of coffee mugs made in China, emblazoned with the town's name.

"Did you keep in contact with his family?"

His mumbled answer was barely audible. "No. Too painful, I guess."

I never would have recognized Nate from that old quarry picture. The slim, dark-haired boy in the photo had become a man with receding hair and a big beer belly. His puffy red face and mottled nose hinted of too many late nights drinking at the local taverns.

"So, what do you think happened to him?" I asked that familiar question, after he finished stacking the mugs.

He regarded me thoughtfully. "I've been wondering about that myself. The only thing I can come up with is he hitched a ride with the wrong person."

"Was that something you did pretty often?" I tagged behind him as he went into the storeroom and continued to bring out stuff to stock the shelves. "Hitched rides, I mean." According to the posted hours the store would be closing in about twenty minutes. At this rate it might take a few hours to get the answers to my questions.

A short curse word spilled out after he hoisted a particularly heavy box and placed it on the countertop near the cash register. Nate continued to work after catching his breath. "Hitch rides? Sure as hell, we did. In high school the only one who had a car was Rusty. Since his mom always had a meeting somewhere and his dad worked in Kingston, they bought him a sweet ride his senior year. A Jeep, an old one, but hey, it worked. We called it the rocking chair because of the way it rode. You know, back and forth." He demonstrated with his hands and for a moment the shy young boy emerged.

He stopped for a second to search for something on the top shelf.

"How did you wind up working here, Nate?"

A look of surprise, as if it was obvious, was directed my way. "My dad and uncle own this place. I've been working here at one thing or another since I was thirteen. Sort of pre-destined, as it were. I was here in the shop the day Flynn left town."

"Working." Okay, now I had his alibi, but how would I prove it?

"Yeah, until closing."

"Remember any of your customers?"

"Are you nuts?"

To calm him down, I changed gears. "Flynn wanted to go to Hollywood, I hear."

"We all were going to go." His voice shifted and became a bit wistful. "Of course I had big dreams, too, back then but, like most things in life, they didn't pan out."

"What were your big dreams?" I pulled out a stool and sat down while he straightened out the countertop.

Regret flickered in his eyes. "I wanted to be a writer. In high school I wrote all kinds of things, mostly poetry and short stories. My dream was be a famous novelist. Have my picture on the cover of *Time* magazine. Corny, isn't it?"

"No, I don't think it's corny at all."

"Neither did Flynn. He used to tell me that I should go with him to L.A. We'd surf and get suntanned and he'd become a movie star and I'd be a famous writer."

"But life intervened…"

"Yeah, reality has a way of doing that. Now I only drink like a writer." He laughed at his own joke.

"Funny." It really wasn't funny, but I didn't want to hurt his feelings.

"You know, Flynn never lost the dream to make it big. He would have succeeded, too, if only…" Nate's voice cracked and he turned away.

The door chimes jingled as two couples rushed inside to get away from the cold. Laughing together at something amusing, the women immediately focused on the gourmet food while the guys milled around taking in the joke T-shirts and hunting knives behind the glass display counter.

I got up to go. "You're busy. If you can think of anything that might be helpful, anything bothering Flynn those last few weeks, let me know. You can always leave me a message at the animal hospital."

He nodded his head absentmindedly before making an effort and saying in a cheerful voice, "Can I help you folks?"

Before I left I wrapped my scarf around my neck and braced for the cold. Getting into the truck I thought about Nate working at the store from high school to the present. That took up most of his adult life. I didn't see a wedding ring on his finger nor had anyone mentioned a girlfriend. Was marrying some gorgeous California girl another part of his fantasy?

While I drove out of town, I went back over what I'd learned about this member of Flynn's gang. Basically, he came off as a nice guy. Resigned now to what fate handed him, I suspected he used liquor to smooth the waters. That led me to a question about the other two fellows in Flynn's group.

If this was a big-budget Hollywood movie, who would be cast as the villain? Or would some imaginative screenwriter have all of the three amigos strike angry blows at Flynn for pursuing his dream without them?

Chapter Fourteen

When I got home I busied myself with walking the dog and starting a load of laundry. Of all the personalities I'd met who were related to Flynn, his sister, Fiona, resonated with me the most. Hostile and discouraged at the age of eighteen, I supposed her anger struck a chord with me, a very familiar chord. Her life had theoretically changed the most because of Flynn's death. If he had made it out to Los Angeles and had any success, he'd have rescued his sister. Instead of dealing with a hated stepfather and passive mother, her brother would have nourished and supported her with his love.

After the car accident that killed my mom and brother, I was furious at the entire universe and lashed out at everyone around me. Unable or unwilling to deal with me, my doctor dad basically gave up and left me alone to fend for myself at age fifteen. Only four months after my mom died, he moved on with his life by marrying his surgical nurse who immediately became pregnant.

I wanted nothing to do with him. He felt the same about me.

That left Gramps, my mother's father, who offered to take me into his home. He treated me like an injured wild animal and gave me plenty of attention—or space, if I needed it—even when I became particularly obnoxious. Although Gramps worked hard, he made a point to always sit down to dinner with me each night and never missed any event, even minor, in my life. With perceptive counseling and unconditional love, I slowly bounced back.

Bounced back, but not forgiven my father.

● ● ● ● ●

"Hey, Buddy, up on the sofa." I decided to get comfortable and call Gramps. Even at the worst of times it helped to talk to him. My dog snuggled up and rolled over, presenting his belly to scratch. Scrunching up the pillow I settled in and pressed the auto-dial on my cell phone.

"Hello." His voice sounded gravely as usual.

"Hey, Gramps, how are you doing?" We made a point of always talking once a week, even if we didn't have much to say.

"Doing tip-top. I won the poker championship last night—over fifty dollars—but don't tell the staff here because we're supposed to be playing for pennies." He enjoyed breaking the rules sometimes.

"Congratulations. What are you going to do with the winnings?"

"I'm taking all the boys over to Rafferty's Bar next door. We'll jam the place with walkers and wheelchairs and have a great time."

The sight of my Gramps with his shock of white hair guiding all those old guys into Rafferty's Irish Bar would have been funny as all get-out. "Wish I could see it."

"I'll text you a picture." He was very proud of all the things he could do now with his iPhone. Next, he'd be signing with smiley face emogi.

Buddy grunted and pushed his nose into my hand, jealous for attention. "Gramps, do you remember that cold case I told you about?"

Immediately I could feel the atmosphere shift. "Sure. The victim's remains were found in the woods near Oak Falls."

"The sister of the victim is having a lot of problems. She's sad, angry, doesn't know who or what to blame, and wants answers. I feel sorry for her. If you were investigating this, how would you go about it?"

Silence on the other end of the phone meant Gramps was carefully constructing his answer. In a perfect world he wouldn't want me looking into any murder, cold or not. But the world is far from perfect.

"Talk to everyone who knew him and really listen to what they have to say. You'll get a host of different points of view, but pretty soon your victim will come into focus. Next, concentrate on his last few weeks, before moving on to that last day. If the killer was local, you might get lucky."

"And if he wasn't?"

His sigh said it all. "Despite everything you do, no matter how hard you try, the road might lead to a dead end. Correct me if I'm wrong. The police have no DNA evidence. No motive. No nothing. All anyone knows for sure is where he was buried. Right?"

"Right."

"That burial site is an important clue. Why was that particular place chosen? Was it a makeshift grave or dug in advance? Near a hiking trail or completely isolated?"

"Okay."

"And another thing. Lots of times a makeshift memorial springs up at these gravesites. People who knew him, strangers, all kinds of people visit and leave things—candles, pictures, teddy bears, you name it. Take pictures of everything left on that original gravesite. Killers have been known to return to the scenes of their crimes. Look for something unexpected."

"That's a good idea." My comfortable pillow no longer felt comfortable. "I'd like to find out what happened to Flynn, if only to help his sister and the rest of the family."

Gramps didn't reply immediately. A coughing spell caught him by surprise. When it passed he said, "Don't forget the victim, Katie. He deserves justice too."

After we hung up I stared at the old quarry photo one more time. Four boys posing on a sunny day, not a single care in their world. Grinning the easy grin of kids enjoying a lazy summer and getting away with something.

Three of them were alive and one of them was dead. What was it about Flynn that had made him a target for murder?

Most of the detective shows on television I watched featured a murder board. I decided to set up one of my own in the living room using a discarded corkboard stashed in the hospital supply/junk room and a handful of computer paper. Getting into the project, I color-coded and labeled all of my suspects. Next, I drew a basic map of the town with various landmarks noted, took a red Sharpie and marked the roads in and out of town. Now I could locate everyone and move each person around at will.

With my notes in front of me, I began plotting out August 10, that fatal Friday ten years ago. Flynn had decided to leave on a weekday, not a weekend. Probably less confrontation with his family and friends, I figured. At three o'clock in the afternoon, multiple people saw him standing in front of Judy's Place on Main Street. Fiona was still in school and Flynn's mother, Lizette, had been confined to the house recuperating from a bad MS relapse. Stepfather Bruce reportedly had been at work in Kingston.

I could put Shiloh aside since two people told me she wasn't even in New York State that day. As far as the other jealous girlfriend, Angelica, was concerned, I had no idea.

Now for Flynn's gang. First, I concentrated on Denny Alantonio. His uncle's car dealership was located on the outskirts of town, near the junction of the main road leading into the Kingston bus station. According to Fiona, Denny worked at the dealership during that summer, so he would have access to a variety of cars. I wrote car across his paper chest and fixed him to the board.

With pins in hand, I moved to the next suspect, Rusty. What was it Nate said? That Rusty's dad had gotten him a "sweet ride" that summer? In black ink I wrote "sweet ride" on the chart. With no knowledge of his location that day I wrote "car" with a question mark in pencil. For now he'd have to wait on the sidelines.

Nate was easy. I placed him in the Country Store in the middle of town.

That left a wild card, our motorcycle-riding Diabolo, who carried a grudge against Flynn and had plenty of gang friends to back him up. Judy told Luke she'd seen an unusual number of bikers in town that day. I attached a note for myself to find out why.

Something Gramps said nagged at me. Then I remembered. He'd asked if there was a makeshift memorial on the gravesite. Samantha described exactly that when she brought her Malamute in for a recheck, mentioning that people had left photos and flowers. I slapped my forehead. I'd also completely forgotten about the climbing rose deliberately planted by someone.

With my scissors I cut out a vaguely plant-shaped form, wrote "rose" on it and stuck it next to the spot marked Flynn's grave. Still not sure if the rose meant anything, I drew a big question mark on it. To remind me, I cut out a paper cross and stuck it on the burial site with "memorial" written on it.

When I glanced back at my notes more suspects clamored for my attention. Where would I put Flynn's suspiciously dramatic drama teacher or the beautiful Alessa, hiding behind barbed-wire-topped walls? My head started spinning with the bevy of possible murderers running around. Not to mention, verifying all the alibis. At least seeing everything in front of me made the timeline clearer, easier to interpret.

Okay, Flynn, I thought, let's see how cooperative your buddies and friends are.

Maybe they have secrets as deep and dark as the woods they found you in.

Chapter Fifteen

When I got up the next morning, that murder board stared me in the face. Cold daylight made me realize that snippets of information were all I had. I decided to jump into the snakepit and go to the one place in town where you could ask inappropriate personal questions and get away with it, where gossip and rumors swirled in the air as thick as blackstrap molasses:

The Oak Falls Ladies Bridge Club.

When I called my friend, Candy, she quickly signed me up as an alternate player for the next meeting. "Someone always cancels at the last minute. I'm sure we can fit you in."

"Thanks. It will be great to see you again."

"I suspect another motive here, other than visiting me." Her voice bubbled with interest.

Not wanting to drag her into my scheme, I ignored her fishing. "Any chance Mrs. Lieberman or Denny Alantonio's mother will be there?"

"I knew it. You're investigating the whole Flynn Keegan thing, aren't you?"

From the tone of her voice I figured she wouldn't give up easily. "The family asked me to find out what happened, but so far all the trails are ice cold. I'm just trying to clean up some details, that's all."

"Sure you are."

Candy was sounding like my Gramps.

"Well, you're in luck," she continued. "Mrs. Lieberman is a founding member of the Bridge Club. She's been playing for almost thirty years and is an old fireball. There might be a few of the Gianetti family playing, too, if that's of any interest to you. Of course," her voice turned coy, "now that you have another handsome man in your life…"

I hadn't talked to Candy in weeks but, sure enough, she was up-to-date on my personal life, like everyone else in town.

Being nosy about your neighbors was par for the course in a small town.

This time I was counting on it.

• • ● • •

Snuggled in my bed that night I picked up an old paperback book of bridge rules and bidding strategy I retrieved from my bookshelf. Gramps and his friends originally taught me the game and I played all through high school. During college I'd participated in sporadic amateur tournaments and I'd already spent an evening a few months ago with the Oak Falls Ladies. Although they talked a lot, the women in this local club were sharks with their cards and unforgiving of a bad bid.

Before I fell asleep I reviewed the rules on bidding and boned up by playing a few practice games on my phone.

Maybe that's why I dreamt I was in the woods chained to a bridge table, forced to watch helplessly as rows of playing cards dug a deep moat around me, bloody shovels clenched in their skeleton hands.

• • ● • •

Candy called me the next night after work to say one of the club's regular bridge players had dropped out on short notice due to illness. Could I fill in that evening?

Although water still dripped off me from my shower, I told her I'd be there in thirty minutes. Hopefully my wet hair wouldn't freeze on the drive over to her place. Slicking the damp strands into a ponytail, I threw on the first things I saw in the closet and bolted out the door. On the short sprint to the truck, I swear I felt ice crystals forming on the top of my head.

Parking at Candy's place was limited, so most people were forced to park on the side of the road. My F-150 truck ended up at the tail end of a long line of vehicles. I slung my purse over my shoulder and walked along the dark road until I arrived at her driveway. Through the brightly lit living room window I saw women milling around, enjoying the pre-game socialization time before getting down for the kill.

My doorbell rings went unanswered so I walked in. The noise level inside had effortlessly overpowered the bell. Several women clustered nearby cackled about something at an ear-piercing volume.

As soon as I spied Candy circulating among her guests, I pulled her aside. Her streaked blond hair and stylishly short dress paired with fashionable heels made her stand out from the more conservatively dressed crowd.

"If you could point out Mrs. Lieberman, I'd appreciate it." Maybe by talking to the moms I'd get an idea of what their sons were really like ten years ago.

A sea of gray bouffant hair bobbed up and down around me, wearing floating waves of colorful polyester. Candy tugged at my sleeve. "Don't worry. I'm going to introduce you to her."

Before I could agree, I was shaking hands and saying hello to woman after woman, many who were vaguely familiar, probably from seeing them in the supermarket, or at the gas station, or somewhere in town. Three I recognized as clients and another identified herself as Luke's cousin.

"Excuse me, ladies." Candy slipped past my latest introduction and slowly approached two women standing with their backs to us. The taller one had faded red hair streaked with gray.

As Candy made the introductions, I noted that Rusty's mother had the same serious eyes as her son, and they were staring straight at me. Uncomfortably aloof, Missy Lieberman was polite to a fault, most likely saving her quills and arrows for the perfect moment. Her friend, however, chewed my ear off for several minutes asking why her dog rubbed its butt on the floor. Thankfully our hostess rescued me by announcing the start of the round robin bridge games. I cleverly had been paired with an annoyed-looking Missy.

"Dr. Turner. I expect you to strictly adhere to American Contract Bridge League rules." Her request was as subtle as an automatic nail gun. My ass would be grass if I messed up.

"Of course, I'll do my best." The radiant smile I flashed back didn't dent her armor.

"Oh, Missy, lighten up will you?" the round-faced senior to my left interjected while opening a new deck of cards set in front of her. "We're here to have some fun and get away from our husbands."

"I don't believe I've met you." I turned toward the friendly face, temporarily escaping the frowning Missy. "I'm Kate Turner, just filling in for the night."

"Yes, you're the veterinarian. So happy to meet you, I'm Betsy Alantonio. She shuffled the deck like a Las Vegas pro.

Bells went off. I'd hit the jackpot. "Do you have a son named Denny?"

"Yes." Betsy regarded me warily, probably hoping I wasn't one of her son's unhappy real estate clients.

I immediately vanquished her fears by saying my friends gave Denny a glowing review and hinting that I might be hiring him to look at properties soon. Then I secretly thanked Candy for being so efficient.

The silent third member of our table, introduced only as Elsa, sat bolt upright in her chair. Perhaps ten or fifteen years younger than the average player in the room, she appeared scared out of her mind.

We both lucked out with the first game, an uncomplicated and obvious two-heart bid. Betsy played the hand and her frightened partner was the dummy.

Flushed with power at winning the opening game, Betsy began to chat. "How do you like Oak Falls, Dr. Turner?"

"Please call me Kate." I took a sip of water. "It's a wonderful town, very picturesque."

"Humppph."

The grunted comment came from Missy, who Betsy blithely ignored. If her real estate salesman son, Denny, took after his mom, no wonder he was successful.

"Yes, but it's getting a little too picturesque, in my opinion. Sometimes Main Street is so clogged with weekenders I can't do my errands."

That elicited nods of agreement from everyone around the table.

With fingers crossed, I threw in the bait. "Speaking of the town. My grandfather is worried about me. You know, what with the discovery of the body." I made my voice as dramatic as I could stomach.

If I had expected a big reaction I would have been disappointed. The ladies carried on as if bodies were falling out of the sky every day.

"Well, I hate to speak ill of the dead, but Flynn Keegan was not a good influence on his friends. I wouldn't be surprised if he got in with the wrong crowd and met his maker." A sniff followed this bizarre statement by Missy.

"I couldn't agree more." Betsy's gentle grandmotherly features were pinched tight.

Hoping to delay the play and continue the conversation, I pretended to rummage around for something in my purse. "I'm surprised to hear you say that. I thought he was very popular, especially with the opposite sex."

"Yes, he was. But he also filled my Denny's head with non-sense. Running off to Hollywood. Can you imagine?" Betsy's voice shook with anger.

Missy vigorously nodded in agreement.

"Hollywood?" I pretended to be shocked. "Why would they go to Hollywood?"

An angry Missy spoke up. "It was all that troublemaker's fault. Flynn had our Rusty convinced that he should drop out of pre-med. To be what? A photographer? We couldn't talk him out of it."

"Denny was the same way. Saying he was going to ditch his summer job and college and head to California. The four of them were going to surf out there."

"Humppph." Missy commented.

"Surf. Can you imagine?"

Betsy made surfing sound like a criminal act. The two women appeared awfully upset about events that happened over ten years ago, Missy, in particular. Without prompting, Rusty's mother continued the tirade.

"My husband wanted to kill Flynn for putting all those crazy ideas in our Rusty's head. He'd been bragging to all his friends that our son was going to be the third generation of Lieberman doctors. I, for one, was overjoyed when Flynn left town without him." Her hand went to her throat and straightened the collar of her shirtwaist dress.

Our fourth member wisely kept silent.

Betsy started dealing. "Funny you should say your husband was mad at Flynn. So was mine. Ed told me he wanted to knock some sense into the kid."

Missy glanced up from her cards. "Thank goodness both our boys wised up."

That got nods all around. Emotions began to die down.

"I understand congratulations are in order," I said to Missy. "Have your son and his fiancé set a date?"

A withering glance was followed by a noncommittal "We'll see about that."

"One club." Betsy smiled and winked at me.

Missy Lieberman made it clear to all using only body language that she wasn't thrilled with her son's engagement. Was she one of those moms who didn't think anyone was good enough for her little boy? A mom determined to keep her adult son as close as possible? Maybe mommy was the real reason Dr. Rusty Lieberman had moved back to Oak Falls.

As the bids went back and forth I found it hard to concentrate on bridge. That exchange between Betsy and Missy brought up an angle I never thought of. Could one or both husbands have acted on their anger? How crazy was the idea that one of those parents decided to escort Flynn out of town on a permanent basis?

By the end of the evening I'd picked up a couple of recipes, a complaint from one of my clients, and plenty of gossip about who was sleeping with whom. Luke's cousin kept to herself, so there were no updates on his relationship with Dina, and none of my other partners had anything to add about Flynn.

As the Bridge Club members began to file out the door, I hung back to talk to Candy, our brave hostess.

"Thank you for sitting me with Missy and Betsy tonight," I told her as we picked up stray glasses and plates.

"What did you think of Prissy Missy?" Spying a stray score-pad, she reached under the card table and retrieved it, gracefully completing the maneuver despite her high heels.

Prissy Missy. Funny. "I think I would describe her as formidable."

Candy laughed. "Well, if you join any club around here you're bound to run into her. She's vice president of our Bridge Club, a member of the town planning board, and one of the founders of the Hudson Valley Gardening Association, among other things."

I stopped what I was doing. "Gardening?"

"Why, yes. The old bat has a beautiful garden. In the summertime, I deliberately walk past her house just to smell the roses."

Chapter Sixteen

Thanks to the Bridge Club, I now knew that not everyone appreciated Flynn and his Hollywood dreams. After talking to the two moms, my desire to learn more about that turbulent summer became even stronger.

My health insurance had been bugging me to name a local primary care physician. I realized that request provided the perfect opportunity to meet Dr. Rusty Lieberman. To my surprise, when I called his office, I was offered an appointment the following day. To prepare, I waylaid Cindy after work and asked her to update me on Rusty. In a hurry to get home, she briefly recited the facts: he'd gone to medical school, gotten engaged to a local girl, and had recently moved back to Oak Falls to join his father's family medicine practice.

"Rusty's a great guy. Good doctor and easy to talk to," she'd added gathering up her things. "His mom is super thrilled he came back to town."

"Their practice is next to the hospital in Kingston, right?"

"That's the one." We walked together, turning lights out as we went.

"Did you know him growing up?"

She stopped to retrieve her keys. "I was older than him by two years, so we didn't hang out. From what I remember he had a reputation for being smart but shy."

"Not a troublemaker?"

"Never—unless he was hanging out with Flynn and the other guys. That was a different story."

"Did they ever get arrested?" Maybe Luke knew if any of them had a juvenile record. I opened the front door and we stepped out into the parking lot. The gray sky hung over us like a wet blanket.

"Nothing like that." Cindy laughed. "They were pranksters. Putting a bra on the statue of FDR outside the auditorium. Showing up at a basketball game in bathing suits and flip-flops. Nothing serious. Even the principal let them off with warnings most of the time."

"And the townspeople. How did they react?"

Her car door clicked open and she placed her purse and brief-case into the backseat. "Honestly, most of us wished we had the guts to do some of those things when we were in high school."

I felt pretty cold standing out there with no coat, so I wished Cindy a good night.

She rolled down the window and added one last thing.

"You know, Kate. That gang of his would have done anything for him, including committing murder."

Nine the next morning found me in the waiting room of the Mountain Vista Family Practice. Soft-blue walls and big oak chairs gave it a feeling of stability. Professional quality black-and-white photographs of local scenes decorated the walls. A water cooler gurgled when a mom let her daughter fill a paper cup. Calm instrumental music mixed with New Age nature tracks played softly in the background. I wondered if the son was the person responsible for the modern feel of the office. Nate mentioned Rusty loved photography, and the examples on the walls were excellent. In keeping with the gentle theme, the entire staff wore coordinated uniforms in a soothing gray-green. Someone here ran an efficient and very tight ship.

I listened to the receptionist question a patient about her insurance. After a few moments someone else, probably a manager, came in to clarify something. Through the glass separating the receptionist from the waiting patients I noticed a pretty dark-haired woman appear from the back of the clinic. Judging from the behind-the-scene dynamics, the newcomer seemed to be in control.

"Dr. Turner?" Standing in the doorway that said "Employees Only," a middle-aged nurse in scrubs called my name. She held a chart in her hand and asked me to follow her.

After the usual questions concerning my medical history, a weigh-in, temperature- and blood-pressure check, I was left to marinate in the modern, but sterile, exam room. Various posters of anatomical drawings of hearts, kidneys, and ears hung at eye level daring you to study them and imagine the worst.

When the door opened after a quick knock, Dr. Rusty Lieberman caught me checking my phone messages.

The man in the white coat who entered looked about the same as in the old picture—tall, lanky, with a quiet unassuming presence. Only his hairstyle had changed. Now his curly red locks were cropped close to the scalp.

"Dr. Turner. It's nice to finally meet you. Are they working you hard at Doc Anderson's place?"

I shook his cool, dry hand. "Definitely. Although it should die down as winter settles in."

"That's when we get busy. Flu, pneumonia, slipping on the ice, heart attacks from shoveling snow—you name it." He sat down at the desk and consulted the computer screen. "So what can we do for you today?"

I'd rehearsed my story ahead of time. "Because of the move here to Oak Falls I need to designate a local primary care physician for my insurance. I'm pretty healthy, for the most part."

His eyes didn't move from the monitor. "A wellness check?"

"Yes. I suppose you could call it that."

What quickly followed was a review of the paperwork I'd filled out with a few questions detailing my family's health issues. When he noted my brother and mother had died in a car accident, Dr. Rusty accepted it as part of my medical history with no condolences offered. A few basic questions about diet and daily exercise and we were done.

"Can you get up on the table, please?"

The warmth of personality Cindy had described escaped me.

Fully clothed I slipped onto the paper covering and received a brief and, to my mind, perfunctory, checkup. He listened to my heart for about thirty seconds, and lightly palpated my thyroid gland. By contrast, my head-to-toe everyday veterinary exam on my furry patients was a bargain.

"Are you on any medications or supplements?" He gestured to me that I could get off the table and back into my original seat next to the desk.

"Only a multivitamin when I remember to take it. Periodically, ibuprofen as needed." If Dr. Rusty was truly interested in my health, I didn't see it.

"Anything else I can do for you today?" For the first time he looked up from his computer and gave me a brief smile. The vague thought that this was his normal routine with healthy patients crossed my mind.

"If you have a moment I'd like to ask you a few questions about your friend who passed away, Flynn Keegan."

Astonishment was followed by something guarded in his eyes. "And the reason is?"

"His family asked me to look into the last few days of his life. Since you were one of his closest friends, I naturally wanted to hear what you had to say." My instincts told me he was a reluctant witness so I ramped up the pressure. "Flynn's little sister is particularly concerned and upset."

"Fiona?" The professional demeanor began to fade to reveal a tiny glimpse of someone else behind the medical mask.

"Yes. I've already spoken to Nate, who was very helpful."

The change that came over Rusty was remarkable. His body relaxed in front of me and, for the first time, his pale blue eyes held my gaze for longer than a second.

"I'd be glad to help."

I didn't have the luxury or time to mince words. "Do you know anyone who might have wanted to harm Flynn?"

"Harm him?" A broad smile flashed across his face and ten years dropped away. "Everyone loved the guy. Maybe some people were jealous of him, but you couldn't stay mad at him for long."

Nothing new learned, only more of the same old stuff. "What about girls? Did he steal anyone's girlfriend?"

"I vaguely remember that some biker thought so." The memory made him pause for a moment. "This is a bit hard to explain. Flynn liked women, don't get me wrong, but he always made it clear he didn't want to get serious."

I frowned. "A ladies man?"

"No. Not at all." Rusty rolled his chair away from the desk. "A little more complex than that. He knew he wasn't going to stay in Oak Falls. Always knew that from the time we were kids. My gut says Flynn didn't want to be tied down."

"Tied down?"

"Yeah, tied down like all the rest of us." He struggled to explain. "Nate knew if he didn't get off his ass, he'd end up working in his parents' store. Denny, well, Denny was a go-getter, wanted to make money right away. Even in high school he took a job working at his uncle's used car lot after school and on weekends."

"What about you?"

Arms raised, he gestured to the exam room. "My family assumed I'd be following in my father's footsteps. That's all I heard my entire life. You're going to be the third generation of Lieberman doctors."

Something puzzled me. "Someone told me all of you wanted to go out to Hollywood together and strike it rich."

"You know kids," he replied. "Big dreams." A wistful look filled his eyes. "Flynn was destined for stardom, we all knew that. All of us made crazy plans. Who doesn't at that age?" In that moment Rusty came fully alive, his gestures open, emotional, unguarded. "I tell you what," he leaned forward toward me. "Those days were the best days of my life."

"So when was the last time you saw Flynn?"

"I don't really like thinking about this part." His entire demeanor changed from relaxed to slightly agitated.

"I'm sure it's difficult for all of his friends."

He abruptly leaned back in his chair, a look of concentration on his face. "I'm pretty sure I drove past him the afternoon he left, but that's only a vague recollection. My mom had me doing a bunch of errands for her that day."

"Errands? What kind of errands?"

"As best as I can remember she made me drop stuff off at Goodwill, pick up something at the nursery, and I think my last stop was the grocery store. I'm not really positive on that." His right knee unconsciously jiggled up and down.

A quick knock on the door interrupted us. The dark-haired woman I assumed was the manager poked her head in. "I'm so sorry to bother you, Doctor, but there's an important call from Kingston Hospital regarding an admission."

"Thank you, Shiloh. Tell them to hold for a moment."

"Certainly." She hesitated a second before closing the door.

As he stood to leave I said, "I'm surprised you guys remember anything after all this time."

Rusty appeared to have regained his professional manner, all traces of emotion wiped away. "There's a reason for that. We were all so astonished when he left, we compared notes several times, so it stuck in my memory." Abruptly he stopped. "Anyway, it was nice meeting you. Take care." After a quick handshake he was gone.

I didn't know what to make of my interview. On the one hand, Dr. Rusty's professional bedside manner was a bit cool. But then talking about the past, he'd thawed in front of my eyes and become more human and vulnerable. Did I see any anger in him? No. Was he upset and sad about Flynn and his final days? Definitely. Rusty appeared to be a gentle soul who cared deeply about his friend.

Halfway to the truck I heard my name called.

"Dr. Turner."

Someone waved. I recognized Rusty's office manager. When she caught up to me I noticed she hadn't stopped to put on a coat.

"Dr. Turner. You forgot your insurance card."

Sure enough, she handed it to me with a smile.

"Thank you so much…"

"Shiloh Alberts."

That name sounded familiar. "Thank you again, Shiloh." Then it hit me. "You aren't the Shiloh who was Flynn Keegan's date at the prom ten years ago?"

She stared at me as though I were insane. Her arms wrapped around themselves as she attempted to stay warm. "Yes. Why do you ask?"

The parking lot was no place for the kind of conversation I wanted to have with her. "I'm checking into some things for Flynn's family. I've got to get back to my office, but if you don't mind, I'll give you a call."

"Sure." Her lovely face hinted at more questions unasked.

"Thanks again." I held my card up. "Hurry inside. I wouldn't want you to catch a cold on my account."

Her smile showed perfect teeth. "Don't worry. I'm around sick people all the time and never get sick. Born under a lucky star, I guess."

We said our good-byes and I watched her run back into the building. A few moments later, while waiting to pull out into traffic, I glanced at the engraved metal sign in front of the clinic. Mountain Vista Family Practice. It's true that Rusty didn't show much anger about Flynn leaving for L.A. without his gang. But I've learned one thing from my amateur investigations….

Appearances can be deceiving

Chapter Seventeen

On Monday the skies cleared up as if they were welcoming Jeremy to Oak Falls. Yes, the big day had finally arrived. The entire staff of the animal hospital buzzed with anticipation, while I felt a little knot in my stomach. I'd run around all weekend grocery shopping, getting a second set of towels, straightening up the house once more, and even cleaning the inside of the refrigerator. At the last minute I picked up my extra stuff and shoved it in the closet because I remembered how neat Jeremy tended to be when we were students together.

This is supposed to be fun, I kept reminding myself. Don't make it a big deal.

Despite the ruckus around me with the staff staring at every unknown man who came through the door all day, I still had patients to see. Usually I scanned through my appointment list ahead of time but today I'd been too rushed. Which is why I was unprepared for one of my late afternoon appointments.

"Hello, Kate." Luke Gianetti stood up when I came in the exam room. His dark eyes gave me a jolt I didn't expect.

"Uh. Hi." That was the best I could do? We hadn't really been in communication since his unexpected and extremely short Chinese food visit. "What brings you here? Is something wrong with Gatto?" Luke often brought in his grandmother's elderly cat for me to see.

"Yes. Mama G is worried that he's not eating."

Just then Mari poked her head in. "Excuse me, Dr. Kate, but do you need any help?"

"No, we're fine for now." Disappointment flashed all across her face. Mari probably figured she'd be our referee.

Luke bent down and lifted the senior citizen kitty out of his cat carrier and onto the exam table. Sure enough, when I weighed him, I noted he'd lost a pound. That doesn't sound like a lot but when you only weigh twelve pounds to begin with, it is significant. My general physical exam showed no abnormalities until I got to his teeth. It looked like Gatto had a fractured tooth. Since cats resent us poking around in their mouths, owners often don't see this common injury.

"Have you or Mama G noticed him chewing more on one side than the other or drooling?"

Luke shook his head. "Sorry, I didn't ask her too many questions this morning. My job was to bring him over here to you."

"No worries. I'll call your grandmother later and get an updated history from her. I'd like to run some blood tests and take some dental X-rays. His underlying problem might be this tooth." I felt comfortable keeping our conversation clinical. "Animals, like people, can have discomfort from a dental problem that puts them off their food."

"Can you keep him here overnight? I've got to run to work and then tonight there's class." He stroked the cat who responded by head-butting him.

I casually straightened out the stethoscope around my neck. "Maybe your girlfriend could pick him up later?" So much for keeping things clinical.

He frowned, eyebrows knitting together. "She's working all day."

"Oh."

A big awkward moment followed.

"How are you two doing?"

He seemed genuinely surprised. I usually never asked about his personal life.

"I'm helping her deal with some things right now. Dina's

gone through a rough time lately." He bent down and lifted the carrier up onto the exam table. The cat ignored it.

"Well, best of luck to you both." It was all I could do not to ask more questions about his on-again off-again relationship. "Don't worry about Gatto. We'll take good care of him." I texted Mari to come and admit the cat into the hospital. It only took two seconds for her to respond, which made me wonder if she had been glued outside the door.

However, that wasn't why she'd been so close by, as I quickly found out.

"Mari, can you admit Gatto, please? I'll write up a treatment plan for you in a minute."

"Okay." She lifted the cat into the carrier, then turned back into the room, and with a big grin announced, "Jeremy's here."

An unexpected rush of anticipation hit. "Thanks. Tell him I'm almost finished."

"You don't have to wait on my account." Luke abruptly picked up his coat from the back of the chair.

"Jeremy's going to be here for a week or so. I'm sure he won't mind waiting another minute." Not that it was any of his business.

"Okay." In a quick motion he slid his jacket over his broad shoulders.

"Maybe we can all meet for drinks one night?" As soon as I suggested we double date I regretted it—along with the rest of our awkward conversation.

"Great idea." He sounded horribly resigned to it, too.

Another uncomfortable silence occurred before we both reached for the door at the same time almost knocking into each other. Then with a dramatic sweeping gesture he stepped back to let me pass. "Ladies first. Or, rather, doctors first."

Embarrassed, I managed a smile. Once in the hallway I turned and reminded him, "I'll call Mama G as soon as the test results come in."

"Thanks, Kate. I wanted to tell you…" A familiar voice interrupted him.

"There she is." Two strong arms picked me up and lifted me into the air. A hint of musky aftershave tickled my memory before a big bear hug squeezed me tight.

"It's fantastic to see you again, Sweetie."

Jeremy had arrived.

Chapter Eighteen

Seeing an old boyfriend again is a tricky thing.

I met Jeremy my freshman year in college at our Introduction to Anthropology 101 lecture. The class just before Anthropology was on the other side of campus, so Jeremy got in the habit of saving a seat for me. He was gawky, self-conscious, a Midwestern rich boy who wanted to see the world. His passion and enthusiasm for the subject drew me to him. Behind the nerdy glasses lurked a smart and focused guy. We hung out the entire semester, meeting for lunch and studying together. That first summer we both volunteered for a dig with our professor, helping to catalogue a Native American burial site and make coffee runs.

Camped out in the woods our late night chats around the fire turned into something more. We stumbled into a short, but passionate relationship fueled by loneliness on my part. After three months it had run its course. Relieved, I suggested we return to friend-only status. Although Jeremy immediately agreed, I sensed sadness on his part.

At the time I liked everything about him. I just didn't love him.

The following semesters we shared some classes but as my junior year loomed I decided on a pre-vet major, and became immersed in my studies. We hung out less and less frequently, finally keeping up only with quick visits and late night phone calls. Eventually that stopped too. Years went by until a few months ago when we connected up by chance through Facebook.

The older Jeremy I'd seen on Skype looked like he spent most of his time in a hole in the ground—shaggy hair, massive beard, weatherbeaten, dusty clothes.

The man holding me in his muscular arms bore no resemblance to that scruffy guy. In person, a very different, tanned Jeremy flashed a white smile, confident and self-assured, handsome in an offhanded way. Vanished were the thick glasses. His skinny frame had filled out and the battered brown leather jacket he wore fit great on him and looked just worn enough. He had an Indiana Jones thing going, and it surprised the heck out of me in a very, very good way.

It obviously surprised Luke, too, who stared at him, an odd expression on his face.

After a moment I regained my focus and introduced them.

They sized each other up like two bulls in the ring.

Since neither budged, I intervened. "Jeremy, I've still got some treatments to do and cases to write up. Can we meet up later when I get off work?"

He grasped my hand. "I'll wait. Mari's offered to show me around the clinic."

I noticed my assistant animatedly talking to Cindy. "That's perfect. If you get bored, let me know."

Still holding my hand he laughed. "Give me a computer terminal and I'm a happy camper. Besides, do you know how luxurious this place feels to me? I'm usually deep in a smelly pit surrounded by bugs and dirt."

Everyone in the hospital had gathered around us, including the ever-helpful Mari who listened attentively to every word.

"Alright, guys. Jeremy is all yours. Take good care of him for me." My announcement met with a round of applause. "Mari, can you take Luke to the reception area? Cindy has some paperwork for him to sign."

At first reluctant to move, Luke mumbled something and stalked away.

"Glad to have you here." I stood up on my tiptoes and gave Jeremy a big hug, then left it to my staff to sort things out. As I watched Luke and Jeremy walk away I realized I now had two guys in my life sending me two different signals.

This might be fun.

• • ● • •

In about an hour I was done. Jeremy caught up to me as soon as I finished typing my last medical record.

"Hey, Kate. How about showing me around town then going out to dinner?" He looked fresh and alert. I felt sticky and tired.

"Sounds great. After I take a shower. Bulldog slobber." I pointed to my pants and scrub top, which were damp from an enthusiastically happy patient with a major drool issue. If I thought saliva-filled clothes might turn him off, I was mistaken.

"That's nothing. My big problems at work are weird insects, sand fleas, and animal dung all over everything. You never know what you'll encounter on a dig."

He had me beat. "I can't wait to hear all about it when I'm nice and clean."

"Okay." That white smile flashed in his tanned face.

"Why don't you hang out in my apartment while I change? Follow me." We weaved our way to the back of the hospital, then through the connecting door that led directly into the converted garage where I lived.

Jeremy stepped inside. "It's convenient."

"And that's about all you can say for it."

Buddy immediately ran over to sniff the newcomer. After a quick introduction, his rapid tail-wagging indicated canine approval. I let Buddy out to do his business, which he did in record time, while Jeremy tagged along.

Something about my visitor's appearance confused me. I'd been prepared for the Jeremy seen on Skype, not the new, improved version. "Hey, I've got a question for you. How did your face get so tanned when the last time I saw you it was covered by that great big beard?"

He stroked his cheek with the back of his hand, as though still getting used to how smooth it was, then explained. "As soon as the guys heard about the project shutting down, most of them shaved off their beards. You should have seen us—the lower half of our faces didn't match the top part. I looked so weird that I deliberately sat in the sun each day we had left trying to even it out."

"Funny story."

"I'll send you the selfie."

True to his word, he began to work his phone.

"Well, you did a good job. Listen, go ahead and make yourself comfortable. Raid the fridge, if you want. I won't be too long."

I disappeared into the bathroom and turned the shower on. One thing we did have in the hospital was plenty of hot water. I let the steam billow around inside the small enclosure before stepping under the pelting streams of water. My shoulders and neck muscles immediately began to relax. Unfortunately, so did the rest of me. What I desperately yearned for now was a nice nap.

After scrubbing and rinsing the day's remains away, I turned the water off, and wrapped myself in a white terrycloth robe. Fresh out of the shower was the only time I could see any resemblance to a young Meryl Streep. My straight blond hair coupled with a longish nose and high cheekbones were more evident when I was wet, accentuating the Scandinavian blue eyes that were a gift from some long-ago ancestor. Jeremy was right, though. Secretly, I was a little flattered when people noted the similarity, especially since I was a big fan of her work.

After a quick blow-dry and lip gloss I felt ready to face my guest.

Jeremy and Buddy lay sacked out on the sofa together, both lightly snoring and undeniably cute. So much for dinner and a tour of Oak Falls. I let my old college buddy catch up on his jet lag while I cranked back the lounge chair and snuggled into a soft blanket. I fell asleep in a blissful instant.

A persistent faraway ringing noise broke into my consciousness. For a moment I wasn't sure where I was. In the next second everything snapped back into place. It was the ringing of the hospital phone that woke me. Once the office closed, our calls were automatically routed to our answering service. Someone must have been calling again and again, trying to override the system. As suddenly as it had started, it stopped.

I slipped my cell phone out of the robe pocket. No texts from the answering service.

Seeing me move, Buddy became instantly alert and jumped down, pushing Jeremy's arm with his leg. Before I knew it we were all awake.

"Sorry I conked out on you. Did you get some sleep?" Jeremy swung his feet off the sofa, and planted them next to the coffee table.

"Yes, thanks. What time is it?" I'd put my phone away without looking.

"Let's see." He stood and pulled his sleeve up. "It's seven-thirty, and I'm starving."

"Well, if you don't mind casual, I've got just the place."

"Casual is perfect. I'll take Buddy out while you get dressed." Hearing his name, my dog started a little doggie dance.

I hesitated for a moment. "Hey, Jeremy. Do you like pie?"

"Love it." His face broke into a grin. "Haven't had any in six months or more."

"Get your taste buds ready. Tonight I'm taking you to pie heaven."

• • ● • •

Pie heaven, otherwise known as the Oak Falls Diner, had been written up in foodie magazines, filmed for the Food Network, and generally swooned over by critics for its delicious home-made food and scrumptious baked goods. Despite it being late, I stuffed myself to the maximum. How could I help it? The downside was that loose-fitting pants were a thing of the past.

Clinking plates and noisy conversation receded into the background. Jeremy and I sat at a booth by the window, chatting away about old times, our empty plates attesting to our appetites.

He'd begun finishing up his second helping of the pie of the day while I washed down my decadent chocolate raspberry pie with a cup of decaf coffee.

"You don't know how good it feels to be back here in the States. Things were getting a little hairy at the dig." He wiped stray crumbs of pecan pie from the corner of his mouth. After a sip of coffee, a blissful expression blossomed on his face.

"What do you mean, hairy?"

"Oh, thieves, local hoodlums, terrorists threatening us." He paused to enjoy the last forkful on his plate. "Acts of sabotage by day workers happened constantly. You always had to be on your guard. We couldn't even go to the john without our security detail."

"Seriously?" I'd been so caught up in my own situation, I hadn't thought about his at all. "How can you stand working under those circumstances?"

He shrugged. "Those are the facts of life now, depending on where you are in Africa. We anthropologists aren't welcomed anymore."

Our waitress interrupted. "Can I get you folks anything else?"

"Nothing else for me. Jeremy?"

He gestured to the plates surrounding him. "I think I've had enough."

She ripped the check off her pad. "You two have a nice rest of the evening."

Before I could reach over, Jeremy had picked it up.

"My treat, Kate."

"Thanks. I'll get the next one." Something about the way he looked at me just then made my chest ache. Things felt like they were moving a little too fast. "Did you check into your bed-and-breakfast?"

"Yes. It's really a little apartment, with a separate entrance. Very convenient."

"I'm glad you like it. Cindy recommended it."

"Tell her thanks for me." He snuck another of those looks over the rim of his coffee cup.

The room suddenly felt hot.

At that point our conversation dried up. Jeremy paid the bill in cash and we both stood up. As I struggled with my jacket, Jeremy moved behind me, and guided my arm into the sleeve. He left his hands on my shoulders and whispered, "You are still devastating, you know."

My fingers instinctively reached up and touched his. That's what he'd always said so many years ago. Hearing his compliment reminded me of how close we once were.

Our glow didn't last long because someone blocked our way. "Luke?"

Dressed in his policeman's uniform he was carrying a takeout bag and wearing a frown on his face. "Hello, Kate. Jeremy. Taking in the local sights?"

"Absolutely. This place is a gem." Jeremy put his arm around my waist and squeezed me toward him. "Kate and I have been spending time catching up."

I got the feeling these two were in secret competition and I was the door prize. Was catching up a male code? Once again they stared each other down. Luke was back with his girlfriend but I'd swear he was jealous. Good. Maybe now he'll realize what an opportunity he missed.

With my most devastating smile, I maneuvered past him. "Nothing like playing catch up."

"So long," Jeremy said as he scooted past him. "Stay safe out there."

We walked hand in hand toward the exit door. Curiosity made me glance back. Luke stood frozen in place. If looks could kill, Jeremy would be six feet under.

Since we'd left Jeremy's Mercedes in the hospital parking lot, I drove him back in the old F-150, the backseat still stuffed with who knows what. Most of my driving time was spent wondering about inviting him back to the apartment. I'd almost come up with the perfect sentence when he beat me to it.

"You must be exhausted, Kate. You've got dark circles under your eyes."

Great. I snuck a look using the rearview mirror. Sure enough, I resembled a raccoon.

Jeremy continued. "Why don't we both get a good night's sleep, and in the morning, we can plan out the next few days? Especially now that I understand your working situation."

"Thanks, that's very reasonable." My brain and hormones now split in two directions, one happy to have an uncomfortable decision out of the way, while the other was wondering why he didn't want to jump my bones.

We slowed down at the hospital's sign and turned into the parking lot. Maneuvering the truck around the building toward the entrance to my apartment, an idea occurred to me. "Would you like to come along on some house calls tomorrow?"

"Sure." He clicked open his silver Mercedes with the remote. "Sounds like fun. What time?"

"That's the only downside. You'd need to be here by eight." I grabbed my purse and slid down from the driver's seat.

"No problem. Eight, it is." Jeremy opened his car door, leaned in and started the motor. He pulled up the collar on his coat. "I'm not used to this cold. In Africa I'd be wearing shorts."

"So, no camping in the snow for you, like we did that one time?" I teased.

"Not yet. Ask me in a few days." He came over and took my hand. "Listen, I know this is awkward, but nothing's going to happen unless you want it to. No pressure. What was that goofy thing we used to say? I pinky-swear."

Relief swept over me, and I remembered why Jeremy and I had become friends during those stressful college years. He really was a nice guy. I gave him a kiss on the cheek. Was he as wary as I was of repeating old mistakes and jumping into an intimacy we'd both regret? Or were we adult enough now to forge a new and better relationship?

Odd as it might seem, that dumb phrase from our past offered a degree of comfort.

"Okay. I pinky-swear, too."

Chapter Nineteen

Sure enough, at eight the next morning Jeremy popped up, two huge takeout cups of coffee in his hands.

"I hope I got this right. You used to like cappuccinos with a little cocoa on the top." He handed me the cardboard cup marked with a "K."

Astonished he'd remembered, I mumbled a "thank you," then asked him to follow me to the treatment room. Mari was waiting, laptop at hand. Her eyebrows went up when she saw us both drinking Starbucks.

"Anything I should know?" Her curious gaze shifted back and forth between us.

"No." I tried to give her a look that meant pure business. It didn't succeed.

"Jeremy, I understand you'll be riding with us." Mari's voice came out as sweet as maple syrup.

"If it's okay with you. I don't want to be in the way." He focused in on her, checking her reaction.

"I think it will be great." Finished with the morning update, my assistant closed down the computer and fluffed up her hair.

Before the lovefest could get out of hand, I intervened. "So, what's our first appointment?"

Mari reluctantly tore herself away from Jeremy. "Recheck on our pregnant piggy bride."

A quizzical look appeared on his face. "Piggy bride?"

I handed him a white coat.

"Welcome to my world."

• • ● • •

Although our portable ultrasound machine took up a chunk of space in the backseat, Jeremy insisted on sitting in the truck's second row behind Mari and me.

"Are you sure you don't want to move up here next to Kate?" Mari turned almost one hundred and eighty degrees to ask Jeremy again.

"No, I'm fine. I know what it's like to upset a routine. Believe me, this is luxury compared to what I've ridden in. Some of the roads I've driven have more potholes than pavement. One Land Rover we used had springs popping out through the upholstery." Although sort of scrunched up, he did appear to be perfectly content.

I glanced again at his image reflected in the rearview mirror. "What exactly is your average day like?"

"Let me see." He caught my eye and gave me a wink. "When I get up it's hot and dusty. Most of the time I'm enveloped in clouds of mosquitoes despite the massive amounts of bug spray I put on. The food is basic, always presented wrapped in plastic wrap to verify it was prepared in a sanitary manner. My work entails standing in a hole deeper than my head and trying to excavate artifacts that no one seems to care about—except other anthropologists."

"Sounds like fun." My assistant piped up from the passenger seat.

I couldn't help but laugh at Mari's comment. "You do have the thrill of discovery. I remember that from the digs we were on in college."

"Yes. But the real leaps and bounds in the field are being made by DNA analysis. I've been thinking of going back to school, actually, to refocus in that direction."

Mari swiveled around in her seat again. "Funny you should mention going back to school. I've been trying to decide whether or not to go for some technician certifications."

At our turnoff I slowed down and the tires spun on road gravel. "Hold those thoughts everyone, we're almost there. Time to count piglets."

Pulling into the driveway of Nancy Wagner's home, I noticed a rooster standing by the front door. That was par for the course for our animal-loving client who kept quite a menagerie of pets. As I parked, the rooster ducked into the house through a pet door.

"Remember, guys, we're going to be on her web cam, so keep everything PG-rated and politically correct." While I got my bag and started to hoist up the portable ultrasound machine, Mari explained to Jeremy that our potbellied pig bride's owner ran a very popular website and blog. We cautioned him not to react if he noticed anything strange.

"What do you mean—strange?" He pulled his coat around him in the still chill air.

Handing Jeremy a piece of equipment to bring in I said, "Sorry, no hints."

Almost as soon as we knocked, Nancy opened her door. She wore a very pretty Renaissance-style dress in a deep red color, with a faux-fur-trimmed velvet cloak fastened at the throat. On her shoulder perched a big green frog.

"Hi, everyone. Come in."

"Nancy, I'd like to introduce a friend of mine who is riding along with us today. Dr. Jeremy Engels. He's an anthropologist."

"Very pleased to meet you." In keeping with her medieval outfit, she curtsied to him. He responded with a polite bow.

"You look nice today," I commented as we entered the house.

She looked down and blushed. "I'm in costume for a web interview I'm doing in about an hour. Do you think we'll be finished by then?"

"Absolutely, unless the ultrasound machine starts acting up." Mari squeezed past me.

"So where is our princess bride?"

"Oh. Penelope is in her bedroom. Second door on the right."

Jeremy, who was directly behind, me whispered, "I thought Penelope was a pig?"

"And your point?"

"So what's with the frog?"

"He's probably a prince in disguise."

When we rounded the curve in the hallway I spied my pregnant patient in her pink dog bed, lying on her side. I walked over, knelt, and scratched her big tummy. Mari got down on her hands and knees, and searched for a nearby wall outlet. As I squeezed some gel onto Penelope's abdomen Nancy wondered aloud, "That doesn't hurt, right?"

"Not a bit. If she'll lie here nice and still, we'll be done in a few minutes."

Although it was getting crowded on the floor, Nancy got down and began to stroke her potbellied pig's snout. Bored with everything, the frog jumped down her arm and hopped away.

"Okay, showtime." I pointed to the lighted screen and began to move the probe across the taunt skin. "Mari, let's count heads."

"Why heads?" Jeremy asked.

"We count the heads because they're dense and easy to identify. Are you ready?"

Mari enthusiastically said, "Sure am."

Working slowly, and in a specific pattern, the ultrasound soon revealed six little piglets of good size, almost ready to be born.

Nancy immediately announced our findings to the world, her face directed toward the webcam above us. Quickly she added, "I'd like to thank Dr. Kate, her assistant, Mari, and Dr. Kate's boyfriend, Dr. Jeremy, for all their help."

"Dr. Kate's boyfriend, Dr. Jeremy," grinned straight into the camera and waved cheerfully to Nancy's viewing audience.

I wondered how soon I'd see us all on Facebook.

Thankfully, I wouldn't have to explain about the frog.

Chapter Twenty

I was surprised at how much fun it was to have Jeremy around during our house calls. He'd jumped right in to help Mari load the equipment back into the truck, made us laugh with stories of the strange things that happen in the world of anthropology, and had insisted on buying everyone lunch. No doubt about it—he was a big hit.

The next day, knowing Jeremy would be working with us again, I spent a bit more time on my makeup and appearance. Chapstick took a backseat to a colored lip-gloss, and a vigorous brushing left my blond hair looking healthy and happy. My scrubs—well—not much you can do about your scrubs. As a veterinarian, I couldn't risk pins or jewelry or stuff around my neck that might get caught in claws or fangs during an exam. Our profession has horror stories of teeth that slid under wedding rings, breaking colleague's fingers—and much, much, worse. The best I could do was start the day clean and relatively free of fur.

Much to my surprise, when I walked into the treatment room, I found the staff clustered around Jeremy, who was ready to go in a borrowed white coat, that offset his tan perfectly. He must have said something funny because a group laugh erupted before I could get near enough to hear.

"Did I miss something?" I lifted my coffee mug in greeting to my anthropologist buddy.

"Jeremy was telling us about the time a giant dung beetle crawled up his leg." Cindy took a picture of him, looked up from her phone, and smiled. Every moment of her life ended up on social media. I felt torn about it—I enjoyed the posts but I still wanted my private life to stay private.

Most of our morning was taken up with recheck appointments and emergencies. Cindy had also booked two last-minute house call appointments for later in the afternoon, so I expected to be busy all day. After watching me catheterize a dog with bladder stones and remove a bleeding skin tumor, Jeremy took me aside.

"I don't know how you do it, Kate. I'm exhausted and I'm not even working."

"I'm not sure myself. Some days are worse than others."

He kissed me on the top of my head. "Part of me is still on African time. I'm going to go back to my place and take a nap. Don't work too hard."

• • ● • •

Two hours quickly passed and after a particularly complicated recheck on a dog with a broken tail, I was ready for an overdue lunch break. Unfortunately, Mari caught me before I could escape.

"Just a quick question on medication we dispensed in exam room two. The cat is doing much better. I pulled it up on the computer for you."

I rubbed my face. "Tell Cindy I need a fifteen-minute breather after this one." My eyes burned from the fluorescent lights and the waves of hot air that periodically kicked out of the old wall registers. Ignoring a grumbling stomach, I pushed open the exam room door. "Sorry to keep you waiting…"

Luke stood in the middle of the room. I didn't see a cat or cat carrier anywhere.

"Hello, Kate. You look tired."

He didn't, but I didn't want to tell him that. "It's been a long day already. What's up?" Luke had brought in his grandmother's elderly cat to see me a few days ago. After successful dental surgery, the kitty had gone home. "Is Gatto alright?"

"Don't worry. He's fine. Mama G wanted to make sure she was giving him the right amount of medication." Dutifully he pulled out a bottle of pink liquid amoxicillin. "Does she fill it to the top of the line or the bottom of the line?"

This seemed like a question Mari could have answered, but I went along with it anyway. "Fill it on the line, as close as you can get it."

"That's what I told her, but you know how she is." Luke tapped his fingers on the stainless-steel exam table.

I glanced up at the clock over the door. Afternoon appointments would begin in less than an hour.

He shifted his feet. "Did Cindy get a chance to talk to you earlier?"

"Nope. I was off to a flying start as soon as we opened, thanks to a torn toenail that needed to be cauterized."

"I've got an update on the murder for you. At the time of the attack, Flynn was wearing a gold chain with a medallion around his neck, plus an expensive watch he inherited from his father. Both have been recovered with the body."

"So robbery wasn't a motive."

"Doesn't look that way. The lab is also working on the contents of his wallet and a wad of papers found in his pockets. Most of it is in pretty rough condition."

I could only imagine after ten years in the ground. "You know I never asked, but how severe was the blunt-force trauma?"

"There was a skull fracture here, and right here," he demonstrated, pointing to the back of his head and his temple. "But forensics thinks the cause of death was probably a severed spinal cord due to fractured vertebrae above C-five."

Injuries above the fifth cervical vertebrae could shut down the nerves that control breathing. To inflict that kind of trauma didn't require great strength, only the wrong angle of impact. Death would be quick.

I read the distress on his face and impulsively reached over to him. "I'm sorry. I forgot how personal all this is for you."

"Thanks." His warm hand briefly clasped mine. "I wanted to tell you in person."

"Do you think this points to someone local or not?"

"No one wants to commit to that theory. There are more questions than answers at this point, I'm afraid."

"That's how the family and his friends feel, too."

Luke shrugged his shoulders.

I decided to change the subject. "Speaking of friends. You graduated with Flynn. Isn't your class having their tenth reunion soon?"

He looked a bit surprised. "Yes. Dina is on the decorating committee. That's all she talks about lately. She still has her prom dress from that night."

I noticed a slight blush rise on Luke's face. He and Dina had been high school sweethearts. Maybe something other than dancing took place that night.

"It might be helpful to talk to your classmates."

"I really don't think that would do much good." He made motions to leave. "I wouldn't be going to the darned thing if Dina wasn't forcing me."

He took off in such a hurry he forgot to say good-bye. I wondered what it was about the 2007 class reunion coming up that made him so embarrassed and determined to keep me away from it.

• • ● • •

At around four-thirty in the afternoon Jeremy popped up again, his energy now high from an afternoon nap while mine was going down the tubes. The entire staff had heard the update on Flynn through Cindy's connection to Police Chief Garcia, so spirits were a little low and rumors were flying. This time when he came in, Jeremy didn't get any big greeting.

"What's going on? Did I do something wrong?" he asked when we sat down in my office after the last appointment had left.

I desperately wanted to pull off my shoes and put my feet up, but that would have to wait.

"It's got nothing to do with you." My eyes still itched and my head had begun to pound. "Remember I told you about the human remains found a few weeks ago?"

"Right. Is that what this is about?"

"Yes. The victim was a young man named Flynn Keegan. He graduated high school with Luke, the police officer you met the other night."

He straightened up in his chair. "Luke?"

"Mmmmm." The ache in my head had escalated to a dull roar. After rummaging around in my desk I found some ibuprofen and proceeded to scarf it down.

"He came by and told us it definitely wasn't a robbery gone wrong. I'm not sure what that means as far as suspects are concerned." I closed my eyes and gently began to massage my temples.

"Migraine? Like you got in school?"

"Mnnnnnn."

Jeremy stood up. "Come on, Kate. We need to get you to lie down someplace quiet." He took my hand and led me into my apartment. Buddy came running up, circling and jumping for joy. "You lie here on the bed and I'll take care of everything else. Okay?"

He didn't have to convince me. As soon as I put my head on the pillow and closed my eyes, I drifted off to sleep. All I remembered were the lights dimming and a blanket softly covering me.

● ● ● ● ●

The delicious smell of Chinese food penetrated my sleep and woke me up—that and a few sloppy licks on my fingertips.

I saw Jeremy bustling around in my kitchen, trying not to make too much noise. Buddy, on the other hand, thought it might be a good time for me to play.

"That smells good." With an effort I sat up.

"How are you feeling?" He was busy taking bowls and plates down from the cabinet next to the stove.

"Much better, thanks. Headache's gone." No light penetrated my curtains. I wondered how long I'd been asleep. With a big stretch, I stood up. Buddy ran back and forth between Jeremy and me. A plaid dishtowel lay draped over my guest's left shoulder. He looked right at home.

"Go ahead and sit down. I didn't remember what you liked, so I ordered a bunch of things—and of course, wonton soup."

We shared a look. I'd been addicted to wonton soup in college.

He handed me a napkin and a steaming bowl of soup. Suddenly, I felt starved.

"You can't go wrong with soup, I always say." Chinese takeout seemed an integral part of my love life.

"Go ahead and start without me." He had taken the time to pour all the takeout food out of their plastic containers and into bowls. In the middle of the table sat a vase with a single red rose. Everything looked much more civilized than when Luke and I shared dinner.

"This is lovely. Thank you, Jeremy." I took the seat opposite him and picked up my spoon. The hot soup tasted like heaven. When I spied mu shu chicken with pancakes on one of the plates, I couldn't believe my luck. "You hit a home run. All my favorites."

"I cheated a little. The Lucky Garden said you were one of their most frequent customers and fixed me right up." He scooped some shrimp in lobster sauce on his plate next to a pile of fried rice.

Busted, I paused chopsticks in mid-air.

"While I was waiting, I ran into your receptionist, Cindy. We had a nice chat."

"I bet." Okay, the staff and near world would have a bulletin on my personal life by tonight.

"Cindy told me all about Flynn, and how you are investigating what happened to him for his family."

"What?" Hot soup dribbled down my shirt.

"That's very kind of you to try and help a family suffering such a terrible loss."

Then he said the last thing I expected to hear from him.

"Would you like some help?"

Chapter Twenty-one

Jeremy's offer of help caught me by surprise. His visit was the only respite I had from work and thinking about Flynn's murder. Did I really want to sacrifice that?

After dinner, still undecided whether or not to take Jeremy up on his offer of help, I suggested a ride into town. Tourists often drove two or three hours to relax in our picturesque hamlet. Time to show it off. Even though it was cold outside we embarked on my five-dollar tour of Oak Falls.

Starting at Main Street we strolled past historic clapboard houses whose ground floors housed chic specialty shops, their windows arranged to catch your eye. Primarily catering to weekend visitors, the street was fun to window-shop, especially when the weather cooperated. After exploring the old church and graveyard established in 1726, we crossed the street to peek into one of the many art galleries. Local artisans were often featured as well as national and international artists, giving Oak Falls a well-deserved reputation as a nurturing, creative community.

Tonight the Qualog Gallery featured a photography exhibit paired with a grouping of handmade furniture. Several couples milled around inside, some admiring the burled wood dining table and chairs, while others appeared content to simply get warm.

"It's getting chilly out here," I mentioned to Jeremy who peered through the window. When I spoke, my breath turn white. "Want to get some coffee before we continue?"

"Definitely." My friend's teeth had started to chatter.

We scurried over to Judy's Place, a small coffee shop only a few doors down. With no window spaces available, we settled for a small table in the far corner near the server station. Since Judy's was one of the few restaurants open late, it was packed on weekends. Despite the crowd our server quickly took our order. Soon we were peeling off our coats and warming our hands on white china coffee mugs.

"It's a beautiful town. No wonder so many people from New York City buy second homes here," Jeremy noted.

"You'd be amazed at the famous names of some of our residents. The whole Hudson Valley is having a big revival. Even the property values in the smaller towns up toward Hunter Mountain are going up."

"Might be a good time for you to invest, Kate." He took a big sip of his hazelnut coffee and closed his eyes. "We're not getting any younger, you know."

"Dream on," I answered. Jeremy didn't have the stack of student loans to pay off that I had. Why couldn't I have been born rich?

Nice and warm now, we split a Biker Brownie. Noticing that I finished my half way before he did, Jeremy broke off a corner of his and put it on my plate. "Women need chocolate," he reminded me.

"Like Mars needs women." I laughed. Watching the 1967 edition of the cheesy sci-fi movie had been one of our favorite rainy day pastimes.

In the far corner a couple sitting by the window politely argued with each other. My impression was that the woman was winning the argument. We sat too far away to hear anything but not too far away for me to identify both of them. His close-cropped red hair immediately caught my eye.

The woman sitting opposite Dr. Rusty had shoulder-length black hair, doe-shaped brown eyes, and a frown on what normally was a compelling, lovely face. I should know. His companion was Shiloh, the Mountain Vista Family Practice office manager and Flynn's ex-girlfriend. As I watched, he removed his wallet and counted out some bills. I snaked my hand over to Jeremy, interrupting him texting on his phone.

"Remember I told you about Flynn's old girlfriend taking up with one of his friends? They're sitting over there."

"Do you need to talk to them?"

I leaned in and whispered, "Not him. Her."

Unflappable, he didn't question me but instead fished out a twenty-dollar bill and stood up, casually eyeing the room while putting his coat back on. I did the same, keeping the couple in view as Shiloh slipped into her bright red ski jacket.

"Hurry up," I hissed at my companion. "Let's try to meet them at the entrance."

Our server briefly caught our eye, probably alarmed that we might skip out without paying the bill. Jeremy raised the twenty up for her to see before placing it on the table.

"Keep the change," he mouthed. The forty percent tip helped make her suspicions evaporate.

"Have a nice night," she told us, squeezing past, balancing a tray of sandwiches.

We lingered a bit in the double door entry, me pulling on gloves and Jeremy arranging his muffler. No sign yet of Dr. Rusty and company. Trying to look busy, we pretended interest in our phones, although that wasn't a stretch for Jeremy. He was in the middle of a text when our targets came around the corner. Before Dr. Rusty could open the door, I feigned astonishment.

"Why, hello. This is a nice surprise. Jeremy, this is Dr. Lieberman, my new primary care physician. Jeremy is visiting me from Africa."

Out of politeness, Rusty introduced his companion, his fiancée Shiloh Alberts.

"Nice to meet you." Jeremy smiled at the couple and put away his phone. "Kate was showing me around town. Do you have any favorite spots you can recommend?"

Rusty checked with Shiloh before answering. "There are a

few historic homes worth seeing, including my parents' home. It's a bit late, though."

"Tonight is only a quick tour. We're going to come back this weekend and spend more time here." I made a show of buttoning my coat. "Maybe we can tag along with you for a few minutes?"

That was probably the last thing Rusty wanted to do, but he continued to be polite. "If you like. It's only five minutes from here. We're temporarily staying with my parents in their guest house."

It sounded like a little too much togetherness.

Thankfully, Jeremy began chattering away with Rusty. "When was your father's house built? I'm a sucker for old homes. So many details on them you don't see on modern places these days. Like that one." He gestured to a place across the street. "They were designed for a more gracious, less hectic lifestyle, don't you think?"

"Not necessarily. Those houses often held numerous members of the extended family, such as spinsters, various cousins, relatives down on their luck, plus various servants," Rusty explained, and moved ahead next to Jeremy. The width of the sidewalk forced Shiloh and me to follow behind, perfect for my purpose.

"We meet again. Butterscotch?" Shiloh reached into her pocket and offered me a candy wrapped in gold foil. "I'm afraid Rusty and I are addicted to these things."

"Thanks." Her engaging smile was as charming as could be. No wonder Flynn asked her out.

"Have you lived here in Oak Falls for a while?" We'd fallen behind the men, who busily talked architecture.

"Well, my mom and I moved here in 2006, so I became the new girl in town."

"And you met Flynn…"

"On the baseball field. I played on the women's softball team."

I pressed harder. "Did you know Flynn was planning to leave?"

Her breath smelled like butterscotch when she answered. "He always talked about traveling, but my mom and I left in late

July to go to Colorado to be with my aunt. I didn't hear about him going to California until I got back."

"I'm surprised you ended up back here in Oak Falls."

The candy crunched on her teeth. "After I obtained my degree in business from Albany, I started looking for jobs in the medical field. Finding one near my old hometown was appealing. That was two years ago and I've been office manager at the clinic ever since."

This was turning out to be the easiest interview ever. "So you're the brain behind that well-run office." I was starting to get the picture. "Wonderful for both of you."

She shrugged her shoulders. "Thanks, although balancing staff and doctors' egos can be a challenge. You must know all about that, Dr. Turner."

"Please call me Kate." Maybe she suspected that my innocent questions weren't so innocent after all. "Did Rusty mention I'm looking into Flynn's death for the family?"

"Yes. He's taken Flynn's death very hard." Shiloh popped another butterscotch candy in her mouth. From her casual attitude, I suspected her grief didn't run that deep.

"And you? How is it affecting you to know he was murdered?"

She lowered her head against a particularly brutal blast of wind. "I'm much more fatalistic, I think, than Rusty is. Flynn and I only dated a few months, but Rusty has known Flynn his whole life."

"What do you think happened?" Shiloh represented a more impersonal point of view. It made me curious as to what she would say.

Her calm dark eyes looked into mine. "Truthfully, I have no idea." She pulled her hands out of her pockets and rubbed them together to warm them up. "I don't see how it matters that much after all this time."

My fingertips felt frozen. "Sorry but the family wants to know."

"No problem," she took out another candy. "Maybe next time we meet we can talk about normal things."

"I'd like that." We picked up our pace. I made a mental note to ask her where she'd purchased her staff's uniforms.

The guys had stopped in front of a huge white clapboard home with a wraparound deck, widow's walk and turret, and several tacked-on additions. Whatever shrubs lined the iron front railing were covered with mulch and soil and wrapped with garden fabric, probably in anticipation of winter storms.

"We're here," she said, putting an end to my questions.

"This is my parents' place." Rusty announced. "As you can see from the historical marker, it was built in 1789. What they don't tell you is it was partially destroyed by fire in 1851 and rebuilt over the next year." Rusty pointed out the iron sign attached to the side of the house. "Shiloh and I live there." He gestured to a building with two Grecian columns attached to the main structure by an enclosed walkway.

"That's convenient for you." I squeezed in between Jeremy and Rusty.

"Sometimes too convenient," joked Shiloh who took her fiancé's hand.

"Your place is lovely, too. Does it have a rose garden?" I tried to delay them for a moment, trying to think of a way to bring Flynn into the conversation.

"The addition has no garden at all. The entire backyard was paved for off-street parking." Rusty's fiancée spoke up, a frown on her pretty face. "Missy is the only plant person in the family. Anyway, it was nice to see you both." She nodded to Jeremy and me, firmly grasped Rusty's arm, and almost dragged him through their gate.

• • ● • •

"Was that helpful?" Jeremy laced his arm through mine on our way back to his car.

"Not really. I confirmed Shiloh was in Colorado the day Flynn left so she's not a suspect. Maybe there was some kind of jealousy thing going on I don't know about." We continued together along the cold sidewalk, our breaths created white puffs. Once we reached the car I slid into the passenger seat while Jeremy started the ignition and adjusted the heat.

"You'll be warm soon." He must have noticed me shivering. Barely lukewarm air blasted out of the vents.

"A love triangle doesn't seem that likely anymore." I let my frustration pour out. "You know, I feel like I'm never going to solve this thing."

Jeremy didn't reply, his eyes focused on the road.

"So where's the pep talk?" I turned and faced him. "'Don't worry, Kate, you can do it if you set your mind to it. You'll figure it out, you always do.'" A hint of sarcasm laced my voice. "Please, you offered to help."

We drove for a few minutes before he answered.

"No pep talk from me." His eyes never strayed from the road "Truth of the matter is a cold case like this is difficult. You're not superwoman after all."

"Hey, I'm so far from being superwoman it's not funny."

His response surprised me. "Your staff would probably disagree with you."

I laughed. "How would you know? You haven't been here that long."

After downshifting he briefly squeezed my hand. "I know from the way they talk about you and admire you. You've made quite an impression on them."

For some warped reason I felt he was describing someone else, not me.

"As far as helping, as an anthropologist I'd be tempted to focus in on the grave and how the body was positioned and buried."

I was thunderstruck. In all the times I'd talked to Luke he never revealed any of those details, nor did I ask. "Do you mean…?"

"Was the corpse wrapped and what was it wrapped in? That could be a hint of premeditation or not. Did they notice a particular positioning of the body, folding of the arms, etc. Even though the grave was disturbed, a forensic anthropologist can usually figure those things out."

Impulsively I leaned over and kissed him. "Thank you so much. This is really helpful."

He kissed me back. "Glad to be of service. Want to continue this at your place?"

"Absolutely."

• • ● • •

Fate had other plans. Before we got on the highway, I received an emergency call from the answering service. A good client's dog had cut his pad and needed stitches. With our evening plans sideswiped, Jeremy dropped me off at the animal hospital and we reluctantly called it a night.

Before he left, though, he cautioned me: "Without access to the state labs and testing facilities, Kate, you're at a disadvantage. All the forensic information those investigators are compiling is going to be an unknown to you. But in my opinion, you're doing the right thing by speaking to anyone who was around when Flynn disappeared. Those memories are the only evidence left, and memories are bound to fade."

"It's been ten years already."

"Exactly. Comparing stories and formulating a timeline can't hurt. I'm a big believer in the kind of old-fashioned detective work you're doing."

His advice made a lot of sense. But I had something else to ask him.

"Jeremy. You've known me for a long time. Why do you think I'm compelled to get involved in this case?"

A frown wrinkled his forehead. "I'll have to think about that. But as long as I've known you you've always needed to right any wrong. Oak Falls' own personal caped crusader," he joked before I opened the passenger door.

My emergency hadn't arrived yet.

"Next time, let's hope we aren't interrupted." His implication was clear.

"Looking forward to it."

I'd made my decision. It was time to give our relationship another chance.

When he pulled out of the parking lot, I waved good-bye, wishing some other caped crusader was available to swoop in and save the day.

By nine-thirty my happy-go-lucky spaniel patient with the cut pad was given a long-acting antibiotic shot, sutured up, and ready to go home. A high-energy kind of guy, he wiggled and jumped around as if nothing had happened. I released him with strict orders—do not let him take his bandage off, keep the cone collar on, and only take him outside for quick walks on the leash. Footpads are notoriously easy bleeders and I didn't want him getting rambunctious and pulling out the stitches. After a final reminder to come in for a quick bandage check tomorrow and arming them with a few emergency doggie tranquilizer tablets, I sent the entire family home. I'd let the kids pick the bandage color so Wags now had one neon green foot.

It took me about twenty minutes to clean up the treatment room and exam room I'd used. Wags had managed to leave bloody footprints on the floor, walls, and exam table before his anesthesia kicked in.

I checked to make sure the front door was locked and then went around turning off all the lights and setting the alarm system. On my way to the apartment I thought about Dr. Rusty and his fiancée and wondered if they ever privately talked about Flynn.

Energized from the emergency, after walking Buddy, I poured a glass of white wine and faced the murder board. I picked up a few notes I'd jotted down. One said "angry parents" and on the other I'd simply drawn a triangle with the name Shiloh in the middle.

Still curious about the Rusty/Shiloh connection I called Mari to get all the gossipy details.

"Yep, Rusty is engaged to one of Flynn's old girlfriends, the girl he took to the senior prom, but they got together way after Flynn left town."

"Sure?"

"Positive. Rusty didn't date much in high school."

"Okay." That shot down a romantic triangle theory for murder.

Mari continued her Oak Falls gossip update. "Shiloh left town right after high school graduation. Her mother died and she went to live with an aunt or something. Truthfully, I completely lost track of her until she came back and got a job working at Rusty's dad's place."

"Any idea why she came back?"

"You'd have to ask her. Even in high school she flew pretty much under everyone's radar."

While she talked I wrote down a few thoughts. "It sounds like Oak Falls is one big happy family."

Mari laughed at that. "We're a small town…how happy we are, who knows? People do talk, that's for sure. Moms brag about what their kid is doing to another mom, or better yet, complains. It's crazy what women will share about members of their families."

That caught my attention. "Such as?"

"Oh, all kinds of things. Like their son is a secret online gambler, or their daughter is hiding from a stalker—stuff you think happens only on television."

"Gramps always reminded me that still water runs deep."

"That's the truth. It's the quiet ones who surprise you."

After we hung up, the image of still water stayed with me. Standing in front of the murder board, I paged through more notes. One of them said Alessa Foxley.

• • ● • •

There's an old saying that you can run but you cannot hide. Thanks to the Internet, the saying is truer than ever. A Goggle search on the name Alessa Foxley gave me insight into why she might need a fortress.

The stories dated over a five-year period. They started with Alessa signing a modeling contract and being called the "new face of the century." Multiple pictures showed her walking the runway in Milan, New York, and Paris. One year later she had a huge diamond on her finger and a rich and powerful husband, Mark Evans. A multibillionaire real-estate mogul, Evans also ran a successful international investment company. His name was vaguely familiar to me, but I didn't remember why.

After scrolling through dozens of movie premieres, restaurant openings, and society events their storybook tale darkened. Tabloids caught them on camera fighting in a parking lot one week and the next week snuggling on a beach in Mexico. Canceled modeling engagements followed. A makeup assistant whispered to the press about camouflaging bruises with makeup and tear-swollen eyes. They were seen less and less frequently together in public. Just a matter of time before the big breakup, headlines predicted.

What no one predicted was the depth of Mark's anger. One night in their Park Avenue apartment he beat Alessa mercilessly, concentrating on that glorious "face of the century." He left her lying on the bloodstained carpet and vanished with billions of his investors' money.

It took twenty surgeries and three years for plastic surgeons to put her together again. Their skill reconstructed most but not all of her former beauty.

Mark brilliantly planned his escape. Although police received reports of sightings from all over the planet, he remained a free and very rich man.

Scrolling by date, I read one of the last published interviews. Alessa told the *New York Magazine* reporter her last memory of the night she was attacked was of Mark whispering in her ear. He warned her to keep looking over her shoulder because he planned to return—return one night when she'd let her guard down. Then he'd kill her and kill any man she loved.

Did Alessa's horrifying story have anything to do with Flynn's disappearance?

That black-and-white photo of those four teenage boys kept haunting me.

If I could see all the way to the bottom of the quarry Flynn and his gang dove into, whose face would stare back at me?

Chapter Twenty-two

Alone in my apartment Friday night I restlessly began folding up old newspapers, rescued one of several blankets crumpled up on the sofa and picked up a veterinary article to read. Jeremy had driven into the city to meet up with a professor friend for drinks and dinner. He planned on staying the night and coming back in the morning. I already missed him.

My choice to be aggressively single for these past months had been deliberate. Over six months ago, in a mind-baffling move, Jared, my boss/boyfriend, dumped me for a nineteen-year-old airhead with big boobs who constantly flattered him—the polar opposite of me. That deep wound to my heart and my pride had barely scabbed over.

Now I realize she gave him something he needed. With my anger finally burned out, I could see how ill suited we were as a couple. Too bad hindsight comes after the fact. Being hurt by the person you love is a paralyzing blow. My solution—not a great one, I understood in retrospect—had been to run away. You would think I'd know that ignoring painful problems doesn't make them go away.

My feelings for Jeremy were growing as Luke deliberately faded into the background. Back with Dina, he should be entirely out of the picture, like Mari reminded me. So why did he keep popping up everywhere Jeremy and I went and with that concerned look on his face?

Good sense ordered me to put Luke on the shelf, but my silly heart couldn't quite let go.

The veterinary article I'd begun reading lost my interest. Looking around for something to do, I folded more laundry. Sorting the pile of cargo pants, button-down shirts, sweatpants, and giant sweaters that made up my depressing wardrobe didn't improve my state of mind. I needed to talk this out.

A handful of corn chips and the last inch of salsa in my refrigerator later, I was ready. I called the only steady man in my life, the guy who had rescued me after my mom and brother had died. I'd gotten into the habit of sparing my Gramps any bad news or problems I thought would upset him. Maybe that was selfish in a different way.

He answered on the third ring.

"Hi, Gramps. Hope this isn't too late to call. How's everything going?" Since moving to an independent living situation he'd been busier than I'd ever seen him. "If you're on your way out, I can call you later."

"Everything's fine and much better now that I'm talking to you, Sweetheart."

"Good. Just wanted to hear your voice." Each time I spoke to him on the phone I secretly assessed his lungs. Although his voice was husky from long-ago smoke damage, I didn't notice any shortness of breath tonight.

The phone became still. "Is something wrong, Katie?"

He was the only one left who ever called me Katie.

"Not really. Nothing to worry about."

"I know that sound in your voice. Here, let me get into my chair and then you can tell me all about it."

He'd brought his favorite old recliner chair to his new place. If I closed my eyes I could see him in it; that shock of white hair, kind blue eyes, and ruddy complexion—a big rough guy who filled up a room. When I was young it seemed like everyone in our neighborhood knew my Gramps and would shake his hand or give him a hug when he walked by. At fifteen I found it totally embarrassing, but when I came home from vet school at age twenty-four I was proud to learn he was the most popular guy around.

"Gramps, I'm not sure what's going on." I sunk into the sofa. A few seconds later Buddy jumped up and lay by my side.

"Tell me what you mean. Is there something at work?"

"Work? No nothing to do with work."

"Is it that cold case you told me about? I warned you…"

I interrupted him. "No, it isn't that. This is hard to talk about." In his wisdom he didn't prompt me but simply waited.

"Do you remember my friend Jeremy from college?"

"Sure. Nice kid. A little awkward back then."

"Well, he's up for a visit and we are really hitting it off."

His laugh erupted through the receiver. "So you're thinking about jumping into the swim again. Welcome back to life, Katie. Messy, unpredictable wonderful life."

Without pausing, he plunged into it.

"I've been worried about you, Honey. After that last disaster of a boyfriend, you walled yourself off from everyone except your clients. Your only, shall I say, romantic contact in the last six months was with Luke, who conveniently came lugging plenty of baggage of his own."

"But Gramps…"

"You're too young to hide away from life and love. Listen to me. Forty years ago I'd broken up with my girlfriend and vowed off women. Then my friend Mike made me go to a dance with him. I saw your grandmother across the room—a white gardenia in her hair—and I was lost. Completely lost and completely found. We'd never have been married for thirty years and had your mom if I'd told Mike to go to that dance by himself."

I'd listened to this story a thousand times but for some reason tonight it sounded brand new.

"I guess I'm afraid of being hurt again." My confession embarrassed me.

"Katie, if I could protect you from everything in the world that could hurt you, I would. I'd wrap you up in bubble paper so tightly that nothing would harm you. But that's not how it works."

His words reminded me of what I already knew.

"My last word to you, little girl, is take the leap. Take a chance on life. It's time to follow your heart. But remember, the sadness and the joy go hand in hand."

Chapter Twenty-three

My Gramps' advice rang in my head the next day as I got ready for a double date—Jeremy would be here any minute to pick me up and then we were meeting Luke and his girlfriend, Dina, at a local restaurant for drinks and dinner.

I hoped the two guys would get along. At least I'd finally meet the elusive Dina.

Competing with those random thoughts were worries about what the Keegan family expected of me. Three weeks had passed and I had nothing new to tell them. Flynn's ten-year high school reunion was only a week away. My instincts told me that the best way to understand who Flynn was would be to talk to the people who knew him best. But did I want to crash the class of 2007's big event?

Hair finished into a high sleek ponytail, I stepped into my new dress. Simple, black, with a scalloped neckline and hem, it looked flirty and carefree—two adjectives that normally didn't apply to me. I loved it. Eyelashes bristling with mascara and lipstick in hand, I was applying the final touch to my makeup when the doorbell rang. Buddy immediately barked until I gave him a hand signal to stop. Shrugging on a wool coat and clutching a small black purse, I glanced around the apartment feeling as though I'd forgotten something. Then I looked down.

Oops. My toes were still nestled in fuzzy purple slippers. With a tug I slipped on the fancy pair of black leather boots I'd left next to the sofa. Finally put together, I opened the door.

Jeremy's eyes widened. He smelled good, and looked great in a Brooks Brothers-style camelhair coat, a thin gray cashmere muffler draped around his neck.

"Hello, beautiful." He held me at arm's length like we had all the time in the world.

"Hello, yourself." Our soft kiss knocked the temperature up a notch.

We stood close for a moment until a gust of cold wind reminded us where we were. Together we scuttled over to his Mercedes. Like the gentleman he was, he held my door open. The inside of the car immediately hugged me in a toasty embrace.

"Where exactly are we going? Do I need to put the address into the GPS?"

Amused, I settled in and straightened out my dress and coat. "Oak Falls is a pretty small town. Don't worry, I'll be your guide."

He strapped in his seat belt. "I'm at your mercy then. Guide away."

During the car ride, to my surprise, I started having fun, all nervousness dissolving. We spent the time talking about college days and friends I hadn't thought about in years. Late nights cramming to get our term papers done and long breakfasts at IHOP. The day I dropped Professor Tatum's notebook into one of the anthropology dig holes after a rainstorm, and desperately tried to scrape the dirt and mud out from between the pages. Once again I was glad Jeremy had come for a visit. He wasn't a stranger anymore.

"Tell me how you got into investigating murders." He sounded a little bewildered at my exploits.

I started by explaining about life in Oak Falls and how I'd been pulled into crime investigations through the suspicious deaths of some of my veterinary clients.

"That's a strange thing for you to be doing," he commented. "And now there's this cold case."

Seen from someone else's perspective I'd have to agree. "I'm not sure you can understand, but in an odd way, I find it a challenge to try and solve the mystery of Flynn's disappearance and death. The situation has been especially hard on his sister, Fiona, not knowing what happened. There's a lot of unresolved anger in her and I sympathize with that."

"So you've solved two crimes up here? Very interesting."

"I didn't do it alone. Luke helped quite a bit." We turned off Main Street, now only a few blocks from our destination.

He downshifted, before casually asking, "Anything between you and Luke I should know about?"

I thought carefully about my answer. "Nope. Only friends."

"Murder in common, I suppose?"

"Hey, plenty of other people gave me leads, too. Ultimately, I'm persistent—a lot like my Gramps."

He slowed down, looking for a space. "Wasn't your grandfather an investigator or something?"

"Fire department. Arson cases mostly."

"Remember you asked me why I thought you felt compelled to investigate Flynn's murder?" He pulled in between a big truck and a tiny Smart Car and put the Mercedes in park. "Maybe it has something to do with your past—not knowing who the hit-and-run driver was who killed your mom and brother."

His words startled me.

I'd never given much thought to why I kept trying to solve crimes. It was only recently, with this cold case, that I'd questioned my motives.

Uncomfortable with his perceptive analysis, I came up with a lame response. "I don't know. Like I told you, it feels like the right thing to do."

"I'm sure it is." He turned off the car and faced me.

We sat for a moment before I picked up my purse and buttoned my coat. All the while I pondered his conclusion. Maybe Jeremy was right.

I was searching for the justice my mom and brother never got.

We strolled, arm in arm, in silence across the blacktopped parking lot. Stars lit the dark sky above us. The cold crisp air felt invigorating after the warm car. Many a night on campus we'd walked like this in the cold, chatting all the way to the dorm.

I'd forgotten how many times the two of us had stayed up till midnight talking about our families, his rich and demanding, mine distant and disinterested, except for Gramps. Jeremy knew all my secrets back then and I knew all of his.

The pungent smell of Italian cooking and my demanding stomach drew me abruptly back to the present.

A laughing couple rushed past hoping to sneak ahead of us. We followed in their wake and almost immediately saw Luke signaling to us from one of the small tables next to the bar. At least ten people milled around in front of the reservation desk. Snaking our way through the crowd we arrived at their table after only one minor accident when my purse smacked someone in the head.

Luke stood up. "It's going to be another half-hour wait, but we saved you seats."

"Good to see you again." The two men shook hands.

"Likewise. Let me introduce you both to Dina." In the chair next to him sat a women, her back to us. All I registered was a fluffy mane of streaked blond hair. Then she turned around.

"Everyone, this is Dina Chassen."

I'd heard Dina was pretty, that she'd been a cheerleader in school, but we'd never met. Big blue eyes with lots of black mascara stared at us from a babyish round face. Her perfect pink lips reminded me of a kewpie doll, but a doll built with an eye-catching rise of bosom that filled out her fuzzy peach sweater.

"Nice to finally meet you, Kate." Her voice stayed pleasant but her expression suggested something else.

"Nice meeting you, too." Now I understood why Luke kept breaking up with, then going back to, his high-school sweetheart.

"And who is this handsome man with you?" Her lake blue eyes zeroed in on Jeremy, a little half-smile on her face. Damned if she didn't have dimples, too.

"This is Jeremy Engels. He's an anthropologist friend of mine visiting from Africa." My introduction sounded lame but no one appeared to be listening that closely. Luke nervously gestured for us to sit down. I slipped off my coat and hung it on the back of the chair. Glancing demurely through her long lashes, Dina gave my little black dress the once-over.

"This place is pretty busy." Jeremy took in the full bar and the crowd waiting to be seated.

Luke explained that the owners, transplants from New York City, had tried to create a Tuscan country atmosphere in upstate New York.

I added, "Trattoria Toscano got mentioned in the *New York Times* food section a couple of days ago. Nothing like a little publicity to bring people in." Again, no one seemed very interested in my news update. Jeremy craned his neck to glance at the beamed ceilings, Dina stared at Jeremy's Rolex, and Luke observed it all.

I made another lame comment on the weather while Luke signaled for our server. The waiter must have gotten the message because thirty seconds later he squeezed out of the crowd like toothpaste from the tube.

Will, our young red-haired server for the evening, introduced himself then earnestly recited the evening's specials and their preparation, and asked for our drink orders.

"Champagne cocktail for me." Dina gazed up from the menu and giggled. "I like the way the bubbles tickle the inside of my mouth."

All three men smiled.

I could have puked.

Jeremy was still studying the drinks list, so Luke added, "I'll have a glass of Zinfandel."

The waiter caught my eye next. "The house Chardonnay for me, please."

Will's attention turned back to Jeremy, the last holdout. His order was surprisingly sophisticated. "Rémy Martin. No ice." The server nodded and took off. My college buddy gently clasped my hand and made a surprise announcement. "By the way, everyone. I insist that drinks and dinner are on me. You have no idea how much I've missed evenings like this. It's so kind of all of you to include me."

"Are you sure?" Luke tried to catch my eye as if to double-check.

"Absolutely. You can thank my family trust fund. I certainly do."

Dina narrowed her eyes. A pink fingernail lightly caressed a loose curl. Her focus tightened, like a lioness on the Serengeti Plain noticing an antelope separated from the herd.

"That's so sweet of you, Jeremy." She scrunched up her nose and squeezed his hand.

He leaned into her perfumed space. "Anytime."

What the heck was going on? Did Jeremy have an ulterior motive for paying for dinner? My lengthy list of possible justifications ended when our drinks arrived along with a basket of crusty bread and a small plate of unfiltered olive oil for dipping.

Almost immediately Dina monopolized the conversation with little stories about how someone hurt her feelings at work, how getting her nails done in a new salon turned out to be a disaster—basically, endless prattle.

My mind wandered while she chattered away. Suddenly something Dina was saying resonated in my brain.

"...so I've decided to wear my original prom dress. Don't you think that would be fun? It still fits but it's a little tight around... *the girls*, if you know what I mean." All the men's eyes followed as she gestured to her cleavage.

"Lukey, you just have to wear your tux, too," she added, a little petulantly, explaining to Jeremy and me why what good old Lukey wore was so important. "We both are members of the King and Queen's court."

"In case you forgot, I rented my tux, Honey. Remember? I barely got it back on time."

A quick memory-sharing look passed between the two of them.

Then I had a crazy idea.

"You know, I'd love to see the two of you in your prom outfits. It would be so much fun!" I held my glass up in a toast and tried to sound super enthusiastic.

A slight scowl swept over Luke's face but before he could say anything, Jeremy chimed in.

"I missed my high school prom. Had a bad case of mononucleosis. Always regretted it." He directed his comments to Dina.

I held my breath.

"You know," Dina paused dramatically, "if I took Jeremy as my date and Luke took you, Kate, we could get you both in." She clapped her hands with excitement. "Jeremy would finally have his prom. But you have to promise at least one dance to me, you silly boy."

Luke's hand tightened around his glass.

Dina continued, oblivious. "I know they've got room because we've had a couple of last-minute cancellations. Did I mention I'm on the prom committee?"

Jeremy and I shook our heads in unison.

"There shouldn't be a problem. I'll just say Lukey and I had a last-minute fight." She stopped to giggle, laid her hand on his arm, and lowered her voice. "Believe me, it wouldn't surprise anyone."

Luke stared at her like she'd lost her mind. "Dina, I don't…"

Before he could finish, our server popped out of the crowd and announced, "Your table is ready. Would you please follow me?"

We picked up our glasses, Luke and Dina leading the way.

As I squeezed past Jeremy, drink in hand, I hissed, "Was all that prom stuff for real?"

He maneuvered around a column then snuck a kiss behind my ear. "Hardly," he whispered. "I went to both my junior and senior proms with my friend, Sarah. Just helping you out, like I promised. Dina fell right into my trap."

I squeezed his arm in thanks—except Dina wasn't the only person who'd fallen into his trap.

Jeremy had fooled me too.

Chapter Twenty-four

The following morning at the animal hospital before appointments started, I inadvertently dropped what turned out to be a big bombshell.

"You're going to the Oak Falls High School reunion?" Disbelief in her voice, Mari stopped what she was doing.

My casual announcement to the staff got quite a reaction. You'd think I had just told them I was going to the moon.

Cindy came right to the point as she edged closer to me. "Who's taking you? Jeremy?"

"No. I'm going with Luke." I heard a gasp.

"Luke?" Although Mari was across the room, she was able to shout Luke's name so loudly, it reverberated. "How could you be going with Luke? He's with Dina now."

Even Mr. Katt put his four cents in by catapulting past and glaring at me from behind the IV stand. I explained how the idea came up last night at dinner. My only reason for going, I told them, was to help investigate Flynn's death. Finally everyone calmed down.

I expected someone to ask me about investigative strategy, but instead there was only one unanimous question.

"So, what are you going to wear?"

Okay. I have to admit that a part of me I don't let out much was excited about picking a dress to wear to the tenth-year reunion prom. Intellectually, I knew it wasn't really a prom, but the lonely seventeen-year-old who sat in front of the television eating fudge ripple ice cream on her prom night was psyched. My inner geek never expected to get a second chance.

That afternoon, over my half-hearted protests, Cindy hijacked me to go shopping, even as I insisted once again that I was going to this reunion to gather information, not to party. Together we drove to one of her favorite stores, a vintage/secondhand shop in Rhinebeck. Since arguing proved futile, I decided to put myself in Cindy's fashion-savvy hands.

"This is the store I was telling you about. I figured a vintage piece would be perfect. Get it? Vintage reunion, vintage threads." We pulled over to the curb in front of a building that said *Jillian's Old and New.*

I don't know what I expected but to my surprise it looked like a regular women's store. Right away I noticed how organized and busy it seemed. Shoppers intently perused the racks searching for something out of the ordinary.

Almost immediately a woman in her fifties greeted us at the front door. She was impeccably dressed in shades of silver and gray that complemented her dramatic white hair.

"Good afternoon, ladies. I'm Jillian. How can I help you today?"

My fashion consultant immediately spoke up. "Kate here needs an evening look."

Jillian gave me the once-over. I had no doubt she'd instantly nailed my dress size and everything else size. "That will be in the back and against the wall. We've got some fabulous dresses in stock. Let me know if you need any help."

Cindy immediately headed to the formal wear section. I trailed behind, curious to see the wide variety of styles, from the forties to the nineties. By the time I got there, she had started without me.

"Look at all these gorgeous dresses," she said while zipping through the rack at warp speed. "Too bad I don't need anything."

"This one's nice." I picked out a poof of a dress with layers of overskirt that reached the floor. The princess dress made my inner teen smile.

"Wrong color for you, puff sleeves, prominent darts on the bodice—absolutely not." With that, she almost ripped it out of my hands and shoved it back where I'd found it.

Reluctant to confess I wasn't sure what was appropriate for the occasion, I pulled out another one. The pale green color was pretty. "What about this?"

My office manager eyed the dress and me. "Absolutely not. Look at the ruffle at the neckline." She flipped it up and down. "It looks like a clown costume. We're going to find something that makes you look fantastic."

"I'd like to look fantastic."

"You will, believe me." Cindy happily smiled and dove back into the sea of satin, chiffon, and rhinestones. So did I.

With Cindy starting at one end of the rack and me at the other, we worked toward the middle, my friend pointing out the pros and cons of each piece. Ever since my college and vet school days I'd chosen utilitarian clothes over flattering ones. After all, when you spend most of your time in scrubs, you get used to loose pants and shirts that don't require much attention. In a way, I think I started hiding myself even back then, daring a man to work for what was underneath. I knew what looked good on other women but never got the hang of it for myself. Gramps had been both mom and dad to me from fifteen on, but a fashion buff he wasn't.

"Find anything?"

"Not really." I glanced over to see Cindy holding three dresses.

"Let's try these on." Cindy steered me into the back, past a raised platform surrounded by a huge three-piece mirror. "Dressing rooms are in there. What kind of bra do you have on?"

Bewildered I said, "Uh. White."

That answer didn't earn me any fashion points. "You might need to buy a strapless," she cautioned before shooing me into the back.

Sure enough, behind a long curtain were five separate dressing rooms. I heard two women arguing in the one closest to me before the door flung open and a teenager pushed past.

A few seconds later an older woman with a scowl on her face came out of the same dressing room, a pile of dresses slung over her arm. "Kill me now," she said to no one in particular. I put an empty dressing room between us and entered the one on the far right.

I had to admit Cindy had made some interesting choices. Not necessarily what I would have chosen, but I was getting used to that. All my female friends except Mari were always advising me on what to wear.

"Yuck," I muttered when I looked in the mirror wearing Cindy's first pick, a shiny blush-colored satin dress with a tight bottom and a slit on the side. It reminded me of a weird bridesmaid dress you wear once and then try to give away.

My appearance in the dress was met with stony silence. Cindy and the store's owner had positioned two chairs in front of the viewing area like Project Runway judges.

Cindy shook her head. "Nice color for you, but the wrong silhouette."

"We can do better, I'm sure." Jillian got up and disappeared down one of the aisles.

"Let's see the next one," my friend ordered.

I was hurriedly sent back into the dressing room. The next two were also disasters, one bunching up around my hips while the other, although pretty, hung off my shoulders in a very depressing way. I was about to put my own clothes on and hit the racks again when someone knocked on the dressing room door.

"Go ahead and try this one on." Jillian anchored a hanger over the top of the dressing room door.

Her pick wasn't like the others I'd tried on. The strapless sweetheart top was fitted and embroidered with a silky lavender thread slightly darker than the rest of the dress. An ombre lilac chiffon skirt flowed to just below the knee finished by a beaded lace sash that sparkled at the waist. When I gazed in the mirror I was astonished at how sophisticated I looked.

I waltzed out to the judges who greeted me with applause.

"Beautiful." Jillian popped up out of her chair and carefully checked the fit and hem length. "We don't have to change a thing."

"Gorgeous, Kate. Elegant but still young. Jeremy is going to be floored when he sees you."

"We're going to the prom. We're going to the prom." I whispered to my seventeen-year-old self. Three versions of me smiled in the mirror.

"Twirl around so I can see how it moves."

I happily complied, watching the swirling skirt twinkle under the lights.

Jillian walked back over to Cindy. "What prom is she going to?" The implication in her voice made it clear she thought I was a little old to be celebrating graduating from high school.

"Kate is going to the Oak Falls High School class of 2007 reunion next week. The decorating committee is recreating prom night. It should be a blast."

A skeptical look crossed Jillian's face. "I remember that year. I'd just taken a job at Fabulous Formal Wear in Saugerties. My boss wouldn't keep his hands off me so I left in July, right after most of the local high schools graduated. Hopefully, there won't be any fights this time."

"What do you mean fights?" I stopped in mid-twirl.

"Three girls were in the store trying on dresses when a high school boy sort of burst in and demanded to see one of them."

"What happened?"

"He asked to talk to her in private, so I let her stand right outside the front door. I had to stay just inside watching because she was still wearing one of our dresses. It was pale yellow that set off her blond hair. Later on my boss chewed me out about it, which is why it stuck in my memory."

"Do you remember the girl's name?"

Jillian gave me a look. "After all this time? No. But she did run back in the store crying her eyes out. I had to follow her around with a box of Kleenex so her tears wouldn't stain the fabric."

"What about the guy?"

This time Jillian nodded. "Him, I remember because his picture was just in the paper. The police say he was murdered. A really handsome guy."

I held my breath. "Can you—"

"Flynn," she interrupted. "She called him Flynn."

• • ● ● •

With my beautiful new dress safely tucked away in my closet, encased in plastic, I decided to call Mari and see if she remembered any drama surrounding that year's prom.

Much to my surprise, she knew exactly what I was talking about.

"I'd forgotten that stuff until you mentioned it. Flynn was between girlfriends then, and everyone was surprised when he asked Shiloh Alberts to the prom. You wouldn't believe what a big deal it was. Shiloh was a new student. Most of the kids didn't know her. She certainly wasn't considered part of the popular crowd. I guess it floored everyone, especially Angelica Landon, since she expected to be Flynn's date."

"What do you know about an argument, just before prom night?"

Mari didn't say anything right away. I gave her time to think. When she finally answered she dropped another bombshell. "What I heard was that Angelica had been spreading all kinds of rumors."

"Rumors?"

"You know… that Shiloh was a tramp…that she'd been kicked out of her old school for cheating on a test. Anything Angelica could think of to turn her classmates against this newcomer who'd stolen her boyfriend. She was furious and let everyone know it. Especially Flynn."

Emotions run hot and deep in high school.

"What did he do?"

She scrunched her face up. "I think he found Shiloh crying and confronted Angelica about it. Or at least, that's my impression."

"That must have been awkward. Wasn't Flynn Prom King? Who ended up being his Queen?"

"The student body had already elected Flynn as King and Angelica as Queen. By the time the prom rolled around they were barely speaking to each other. Let's see—Dina and Luke were part of the court...I can't remember the rest. I'll have to look in my yearbook."

"Do you think you could bring it in to work so I can see it? Having some kind of familiarity with the graduating class would make everything easier."

"Okay. I bought one every year. That ought to keep you busy."

"Great. And try to remember as much gossip as you can."

Mari didn't sound that comfortable with the idea. "You want me to take a trip down memory lane? I'm ecstatic my teenage years are over." There was a sad finality in her voice. "I barely made it out alive."

"Me, too." Only relentless studying had relieved my agony.

After we hung up I thought about all the angst of high school, and the crazy meaningless ups and downs that enveloped students every day. Between classes, wave after wave of raw emotion flowed like lava down the halls. Imagined slights. Painful encounters. Bottled up feelings. They all added up. Some of us carried those slights around for years and others never put them down.

I'd assumed the handsome and popular Flynn had had it easy in high school.

Maybe I assumed wrong.

● ● ● ● ●

I had one more surprise that night. Perhaps Shiloh's ears were burning because she phoned me right after I hung up with Mari. "Hi. I hope I'm not calling too late."

"No, of course not. I'm glad to hear from you." I settled into my lounge chair ready to put my feet up and relax. Dress shopping was exhausting.

Shiloh sounded a little embarrassed. "You said you wanted to talk. Well, I'm very close to your hospital and I have some free time. Only an hour, though."

"I'm sure it won't take that long. Where would you like to meet?"

"How about your place? Just one thing though, I'm allergic to cats."

Oops. Where would you find a cat in an animal hospital?

"We can talk in my apartment, if you like. Just go to the back entrance of the hospital. You'll see a Ford pickup parked outside my door."

"Alright."

"Are dogs okay?"

She laughed. "Yes, dogs are fine. See you in about ten minutes."

Ten minutes later almost to the second, I heard a knock. Buddy sprang into action, barking up a storm. With a hand signal I told him to quiet down.

Shiloh stood outside, her pale cheeks flushed pink from the cold.

"Come in," I told her. "This is Buddy." My dog did his doggy duty by wagging his tail and sniffing at her shoes.

After hanging up her coat and pouring us both cups of tea I got down to it. "What I was curious about were the dynamics of your high school that last year, as far as Flynn was concerned."

"Normal, I guess." She thought for a moment. "We were all excited about graduating, that's for sure. Flynn always talked about going to California, so when I heard he left I wasn't that surprised. Most of the other kids were focused on finals and their SAT scores. I remember Rusty had been accepted to pre-med and Denny was, well, being Denny."

"What do you mean?"

"Denny was all about money. Always hustling."

"Still is, I guess." I stopped to take a sip of Earl Gray tea.

"So I hear," Shiloh said diplomatically.

"Any enemies or problems with Flynn in those last few months?"

"Not really. Unless you count his stepfather, but you probably know all about that."

"They were on bad terms is what I've been told. Bruce had been abusive with Flynn's mom and sister."

She took a sip of her tea before answering. "That's all I know, too. We didn't hang out with his family much."

"What about Angelica?"

"What about her?" Now my guest blotted her lips with the napkin.

"Wasn't there some bad blood between you and her and Flynn?"

Her steady brown eyes looked directly into mine. "By that summer we had all made up. You see…my mom died suddenly and…everything changed. That prom stuff all seemed petty."

"I'm so sorry," I told her. "My mom died when I was fifteen. Losing your mother turns your world upside down."

Her brow furrowed. She nodded in agreement.

"Mostly, I remember talking about where to go to college and how to pay for it."

It didn't appear that Shiloh could be of much help. I felt bad bothering her with all of this, raking up a painful time in her life.

"Now I've got a question for you. Are you finished talking to Rusty?" she asked. "I'm afraid he's taking this whole investigation very hard. Truthfully, I'm worried about him."

"I think so." Remembering how her fiancé almost came to tears thinking about his murdered friend, I understood her concern. "At this point I'm verifying where everyone was on that Friday in August when Flynn left town. You know, what cars were seen in the vicinity, any eyewitnesses who saw him hitchhiking—all the silly little details of that afternoon. I'm coordinating everything, then I'll turn it over to the family and the police."

"That's a lot of work."

"It is. I wish I could say I have something to show for it."

Shiloh murmured sympathetically. I shrugged my shoulders. "Well, after the reunion is over, if I don't get any new clues, I'm going to call it quits. I'm afraid too much time has passed for me to be of much help."

She glanced at her phone and stood up. "Maybe we can have lunch sometime and talk about more pleasant subjects."

"I'd like that." Buddy rose from his bed and watched us walk to the door. For once he didn't dance around like a maniac.

I'm curious," Shiloh said. "How often are cold cases solved?"

"No idea. Not that often, I would say. Now if the investigators had found some old DNA evidence, that would have been another story." I opened the door for her.

"Yes, that would be another story," she agreed while buttoning her coat. "One I'm sure the entire town would like to hear."

Chapter Twenty-five

Monday I had appointments all day so Jeremy decided to drive up to Cornell to meet some colleagues and tour their new laboratory facilities. With his dig now closed down indefinitely he felt it might be time to reassess his academic future. Anthropology had always been his true passion in life. With so many changes taking place in the field he wanted to discuss his options with other professionals who were dealing with the same issues.

We walked out into the hospital parking lot, an autumn chill in the bright air.

"I'll miss you."

"I'll miss you, too."

"When will you be back?" He looked particularly attractive in his old bomber jacket. I watched him load a suitcase into the trunk of the car. A little pang of regret he'd be gone pinged in my chest.

"I'm not sure. I'll call you."

"Hey, don't forget our prom date on Saturday night. You and Dina, and me and Luke."

"How could I? Sorry I'm so preoccupied. One great thing, though, this time we don't have to worry about a curfew." He winked at me.

That got a laugh.

"Did you hear any more about your project re-opening?"

"No. I'm not counting on it." After adjusting his bags he slammed the trunk door closed.

A thought occurred to me. "Jeremy, you never told me why they closed down your dig."

He walked over to me, an odd restlessness in his movements as though he was already miles away. "One of the porters was murdered." With a quick kiss and hug he bid me good-bye, slid into the driver's seat, and drove off.

I waved.

He didn't wave back.

As soon as I got inside the hospital we received an emergency call that immediately took up all my attention.

When the clients arrived I hurried into the exam room. One look and I knew we were in trouble. A handsome French bulldog puppy lay motionless on the exam table, his breathing shallow.

"What happened?" I asked his owners while I started my exam.

A distraught young couple stood in front of me. "Baby seemed fine this morning. Acting normal. I had to shoo him away from the pantry because he raided it and made a mess."

"Can you tell me what he ate? Any chocolate or raisins, grapes, onions or garlic?"

Some seemingly innocent products on pantry shelves can be deadly to pets. "What about medications?"

"No. We keep those things away from him." The husband turned to the wife, panic in his eyes. "Honey, what did you find on the floor?"

His worry reflected in her face. For a moment she froze.

"Take a deep breath and think about what you picked up."

Mari poked her head in to see if I needed help. I had her set up for an IV and some preliminary blood tests and continued my exam.

The client stared at her quiet pet. "He tore open a box of cheese crackers. Pieces were scattered all over the tile. I also swept up some chewed plastic and a few gum wrappers."

"Sugarless gum?"

"Yes. It's the only kind we buy. That can't hurt him, can it?"

I scooped the puppy up in my arms. "Wait here. I'm going to take him to the treatment room."

As soon as I shut the door I picked up speed and flung open the swinging door to the back of the hospital.

"Glucose drip," I yelled to Mari.

Without putting the dog down, I opened the lower cabinet next to the sink and grabbed the Karo syrup.

Mari rushed over to the treatment table with a bag of five percent glucose and hung it on the IV stand.

I handed Baby to her. "Let's get a catheter in him and draw a quick glucose and preliminary panel. I suspect hypoglycemia." As fast as I could, I twisted off the top of the Karo syrup, poured some in my hand and then rubbed it under the puppy's tongue and along the gums. The mucous membranes of the mouth would be quick to absorb the sugar, like a person with a heart condition putting a nitroglycerin pill under their tongue.

Baby swallowed at the taste, a very good sign. Together we inserted the IV, drew the pre-treatment blood sample, then hooked him up to the IV drip.

Next we induced vomiting and were soon rewarded with a sticky mess of plastic, clumps of half-digested food, and a small wad of gum. After a few more dry heaves it appeared the puppy had barfed everything up.

Using the in-house lab equipment, we had our diagnosis in minutes. Baby had severe and potentially life-threatening low blood sugar. The cause—something as innocuous as sugar-free gum.

"Look, Doc." Mari's excited voice came from over my shoulder.

We watched as Baby slowly held his head up, his eyes focused on us. A quizzical look on his face, I expected he wanted to ask us what all the fuss was about.

Since I knew this puppy's owners were stressed to the max, I called Cindy at the front desk and told her to escort them to the treatment room.

The puppy turned, ears up, when he heard his human parents say his name.

"Let me tell you the good news," I explained as they kissed their puppy. "Baby had hypoglycemia, that's low blood sugar, from eating the sugarless gum. There's an ingredient in some of the sugarless gums called Xylitol that causes a drop in blood sugar in dogs. The severity of the symptoms depends on the pet's weight and how much gum they ingest. Because Baby is still a puppy, and only fifteen pounds, that gum he swallowed overwhelmed his system."

On hearing his name again, the puppy wagged his little tail.

"This chemical can also affect the liver. He's very lucky you brought him over to the hospital right away."

The couple, whose names I still didn't know, hugged each other.

"By the way, I'm Dr. Kate Turner."

"Phil and Lisa Simonson. Thank you so much, Doctor." Mari located a box of Kleenex for Lisa, who had started to cry with relief.

"Put a note on the treatment board to repeat the blood glucose and liver values," I told my technician, then turned to the ecstatic couple. "Why don't you fill out the hospital paperwork at the reception area while we let Baby rest for a while? I'm anticipating keeping him here under observation for twenty-four hours. He's not out of the woods yet. If all his blood tests, including a liver-function profile are within normal ranges, he can go home tomorrow with a recheck in one week."

After pointing them in the right direction, I helped Mari put Baby in an upper cage and attached his automatic IV pump next to it. We placed a soft collar around his neck that prevented him from chewing his catheter out and gave him a tablespoon of canned food. He wolfed it down.

While I made my notes in the computer, Mari started the cleanup. "That's one lucky puppy," she said.

"He sure is. If he'd been alone when this happened the outcome might not have been so good."

"Woof."

We both stopped what we were doing to check out the source of the noise.

Baby was standing up in the cage smiling a French bulldoggy smile, ready to get into more trouble.

• • ● • •

At the end of my stressful day I decided to relax in front of the computer in my office, idly surfing the news and watching cute animal videos. While reading about a funny-faced cat with its own website, a thought occurred to me. Flynn had disappeared ten years ago. Maybe there were still postings from him on social media sites. I made a note to find out from his family. After their initial enthusiasm, now only Flynn's grandmother, Sophia, promptly replied to my e-mails and texts. The downside was she hadn't known many of Flynn's high school friends. As he got older, her grandson only shared happy news with her.

Swiveling in the office chair, I reached behind me and removed a bright red notebook off the crowded bookshelf. I'd dedicated it to the random thoughts and gossip accumulating about Flynn and events in Oak Falls ten years ago. Mari and Cindy contributed what they remembered too.

Maybe it was a combination of stress and sleep-deprivation, but for some reason I felt unsettled. I had to face the fact that Flynn's murder no longer elicited outrage in those who knew him, probably because time worked to soften the impact. His family and friends had moved on. Shrouded in the past, the events and motives that might have led to Flynn's death were proving distant and difficult to uncover.

I resolved to back off after the reunion and start enjoying myself.

Little did I know the past and the present were set to butt heads and surprise us all.

Chapter Twenty-six

It felt like the end of the week was galloping along at warp speed. Baby, the French bulldog, went home with no damage to his liver or kidneys. A tiny miniature pincher came in suffering from minor frostbitten pads after trying to keep up with her bigger and hairier dog pals. Thank goodness the rest of my appointments during the next few days were uneventful.

The looming prom night reunion this Saturday became more complicated the closer it got. Luke texted me he'd rented us all a limo. The dry cleaner forgot to give me back my belt and Jeremy called with a head's-up that he couldn't get back much earlier than Saturday afternoon with tux in hand. By that time, hopefully, Dina would have successfully stuffed "the girls" back into her dress. Thanks to Cindy's help, I now was fully fashionably accessorized and ready to rock and roll.

My personal plans were to do a little sleuthing, have a fun night with Jeremy, and explore taking our relationship to a more romantic level.

● ● ● ● ●

Late afternoon on Thursday, when we got back from our house calls and started unloading the truck, Mari asked again about my high school prom.

"Didn't go." I made a show of checking to make sure I had my favorite stethoscope and doctor's bag. Although Mari and

I were close friends, I still felt uncomfortable revealing certain parts of my past. While dumping some trash from the backseat, I got a whiff of rotten fruit.

"Why not?" Mari's curiosity where I was concerned had no boundaries.

It was a subject I strenuously wanted to avoid. "Yuk. There's a loose banana or apple somewhere back here." Maybe a forgotten food search would steer her away from this touchy subject. All kinds of stray objects often slid under the seats.

A white-tailed deer stuck its head out of the woods, saw us, and darted off.

"Hey, look what I found." Clutched in her hand was a shriveled up black banana.

"Finder's keepers," I grinned. "So, Mari. What was the theme of your prom?"

"Our theme was *Shangri La*. Not very original, I suppose, but it sounded exotic to us. I helped build a jungle set that we hung with lights and fake flowers."

"Sounds nice." One last check of the backseat and we were done.

"What kind of theme did you have at your senior prom, Kate?"

"Honestly, I'm not sure. Long story." I didn't elaborate.

My assistant leaned up against the truck's front fender. "Well, I went with four members of the women's track team. None of us had dates so we decided to rent a limo and go together. We had a blast."

"I'll bet you did. I'm envious."

For a moment I thought about telling her how pathetic senior prom day had been for me. No one asked me out, and I didn't have enough confidence at that time to do what Mari did. Instead I picked a fight with Gramps and locked myself in my room with a pepperoni pizza and a gallon of my go-to favorite ice cream—fudge ripple.

After I locked the truck, I noticed one of the tires seemed low and bent down to check it. Mari waited for me on the walkway.

"I told you. High school wasn't that easy for me," my assistant confessed.

"Me either."

"It's a love/hate thing, I guess. People say you remember your high school experiences forever. You know, I still have my prom dress in the back of the closet somewhere." Mari shouldered the computer bag and started walking up the pathway to the animal hospital.

As I followed, I wondered how many old prom dresses were hidden in closets across the USA and what kind of stories they could tell.

Later that night, after hours fighting an irrational craving for a piece of pie, I gave in and took the quick drive to the Oak Falls Diner.

I'm not that easy to find in a crowd but my truck is, since it has Oak Falls Animal Hospital written on the driver and passenger side doors. That must have given Bruce, Flynn's stepfather, the idea to wait for me in the parking lot so we could "have a little chat." His words.

"I think we need to have a little chat," Bruce said to me for the second time.

"Fine." No way this was turning into a long debate, not with me holding a takeout bag in my hands.

Bruce didn't seem to know where to start. His short staccato breaths turned frosty in the cold like the trail of a steam engine. "So, I hear you want to talk to me about Flynn?" After what Evelyn and Fiona said about Bruce I knew I didn't like this guy. I certainly didn't want to stand around in the parking lot arguing.

"Sure."

Stoked up now, he went into a long rambling story about meeting Lizette and Flynn and immediately falling in love with both of them. It sounded like a soap opera. Blah, Blah, Blah he went on and on until I heard words that sharpened my focus.

"So don't listen to that ungrateful little daughter of mine," he said. "Fiona lives in some fantasy world. She'll lie about anything and everything."

What was he talking about? I wondered. Fiona had barely said twenty sentences to me. Her descriptions of Flynn's friends and confession of how much she wanted to leave Oak Falls were the sum of her statements. I decided to see if he'd expand on the topic. "Fiona had a lot to say…"

Bruce's already pink face turned blotchy red. "She's always lied. Both of those kids lied, accusing me of all kinds of things. Lizette used to fall a lot, because of her MS. But Flynn had to go and make a big deal out of it, claimed that I hit her. I show my own daughter a father's natural affection and Flynn went and put a sliding bolt on the inside of Fiona's bedroom. If I didn't…" He suddenly stopped, maybe aware he was revealing too much to me.

"If you didn't what?"

Not so eager to talk now, he shifted his weight and rubbed his hands together. "Listen, Lizette knows I'd never do anything to either one of the children. Ever since Fiona hit her teenage years we've had trouble with her—sneaking out, creepy boyfriends, acting out in school. You name it."

Yeah, I thought. I'll name it. Those can all be signs of abuse.

The tirade slowed down. "Anyway," Bruce said, "we're getting off the subject. My wife and I are grateful you offered to help find out what happened to Flynn, but we're ready for closure now."

I wondered how many times he'd rehearsed that little speech.

"Consider yourself free to move on," he continued. "We're leaving everything up to the police cold case investigators, so, like I said, you're free to move on." This time Bruce tried to look solemn and super sincere.

"So I'm free to move on." I repeated.

He nodded his head. "Yes."

I clicked open the truck and placed the takeout on the floor behind the front seat. "That's good to know. I'll give Lizette and Fiona a ring tomorrow to confirm."

That got a reaction. He inched away from the fender he'd been leaning on. "Uh, don't bother. That's not necessary. Better not bring up a painful subject again. That goes for Sophia too."

Interesting. He didn't want me to contact any of Flynn's family. I found it funny that he'd slipped Sophia, Flynn's grandmother, into the mix, since she made no secret of the fact that she hated his guts. No way that feisty woman would let Bruce speak for her.

He stared at me as if trying to read my mind. What was going on behind those puffy eyes?

I put a smile on my face and played my final card. "I understand your position. But for my own records, where were you on Friday, August 10, around three in the afternoon when Flynn disappeared?"

His jaw and fists clenched. Bulky shoulders moved forward and reminded me this guy was bigger than I thought. "No more questions, do you hear me?"

A burst of laughter sounded behind us as a large group came out of the diner and headed toward their cars.

When Bruce saw them he hesitated, kicked my tire with his boot, and stalked away. Before I got into the truck he turned back, a nasty expression on his face.

"Stay away from my family, Doc, or you're going to regret it." His petulant face gave him a sulky toddler look.

"I'll take that under advisement, Bruce."

• • ● • •

"Bruce is a world-class jerk," Mari said the next day. I'd told her about my late-night chat with Fiona's dad and, like the high school drama teacher, she had nothing good to say about him.

"So why does anyone put up with him?" I asked. We'd just pulled into a gas station to top off the tank before Cindy called and told us our last appointment of the day had canceled. The rest of our day was free.

Mari wiped a big streak of something off the fender. "From what I heard, Bruce got a big cash settlement after an accident at his job six years ago."

The gas pump clicked off. "That doesn't seem like a reason to stay with the guy and be miserable the rest of your life."

"People do weird things," Mari answered with her brand of wisdom.

Done fueling up, I got in the truck, put my hands on the wheel, and asked, "So, where to? Want to head back?"

She offered me some trail mix before coming up with a different suggestion.

"We're almost at Sheckter's Hill. Want to check on that bear situation?

"Sure." I'd spoken to someone at the New York State Department of Environmental Conservation a few days ago. They were crazy busy because of budget cutbacks and hunting season. Whoever I spoke to said their latest information indicated there never was a bear on the property. I figured it wouldn't do any harm to follow up on the rumor—but only if Mari knew Crazy Carl. I didn't want to trespass on some trigger-happy guy's property.

"You definitely know him?"

"Absolutely. He's crazy as a bedbug."

That didn't sound promising. "Do we have to be worried about a confrontation, Mari?"

Sounding nonchalant, my assistant replied, "Nope. If you see a bedbug, you step on it."

Sheckter's Hill boasted some of the most scenic property around Oak Falls. On our drive over Mari pointed out the vast national park land that bordered many of the homes we saw.

While she chattered away, I remembered wild stories I'd heard from fellow veterinarians over the years about people with raccoons in their apartments, tigers in their basements, and chimpanzees raised like human babies. Most of these owners meant well, but a wild animal is just that—wild—and when they become sexually mature adults, those loving baby characteristics tend to fade away. What is often left is an animal confused and unpredictable, that can't be successfully returned to its natural habitat to live the life Nature intended for them.

The scenery started to look familiar.

"This is pretty close to where Flynn's grave was found, isn't it?" I still was getting my bearings in some of the rural areas.

"Yep. It's the next ridge over." She pointed off to the left. "Okay, slow down, we're almost there."

Forest Road 27 was set on at least twenty acres with one of those trailers you sometimes see in the distance as you drive by on your way to somewhere else. Located off the main road, the front acreage was strewn with the remains of three rusty vehicles that had seen better days, along with several tires, a washing machine, and an old sink. The tattered remnants of a striped awning flapped in the wind. Nailed to trees bordering the dirt driveway were multiple signs: Private Property Keep Out, Trespassers Will Be Shot, Beware of Dogs and a faded and incongruous Home Sweet Home.

Three cinder blocks served as the front steps. Several outbuildings dotted the property most with rusted sheet-metal roofs. I could faintly see the outline of a barn through some pine trees behind the doublewide.

Mari got out of the truck then uttered an expletive when her hiking shoe sunk into the mud.

Forewarned, I reached behind the driver's seat and grabbed my knee-high green rubber boots.

After scraping her sole against a stepping stone several times Mari reached the trailer's front door and knocked.

I jumped out and stretched a bit, waiting for some kind of response. After all of Mari's stories, I was curious to meet Crazy Carl.

"Looks like he's not here," she said after yelling out his name and banging on the door a few times.

"No harm in looking out back, I guess." My nose had picked up a musky animal smell. "Maybe he's in the barn."

"You go ahead," Mari called out, not willing to venture through the muck.

"Okay." The back of the place looked worse than the front. Engine parts and random old pieces of furniture were scattered haphazardly around. An outbuilding that listed to the side in the damp ground appeared stuffed with junk and moldy mattresses. You could see daylight through the gaps in the pine board walls. Somewhere an unlatched gate slammed in the wind.

Several large trees blocked my view of the corral, but I detected no familiar smell of horses or cattle. Once I ventured past a few overgrown shrubs I saw something that tore my heart out.

An almost fully grown black bear stared at me from inside a large steel cage, a pile of dirty hay serving as bedding. One narrow metal door attached to the enclosure led to a smaller capture cage. As I approached I noticed the bear's left rear leg was chained with an iron shackle, the kind they used in old prison movies. When he saw me the animal got up and lumbered toward a half-filled metal bowl in the far end of the enclosure.

The taut chain stopped him about six feet from the food.

With a massive arm the bear attempted to swipe the bowl closer, his curved claws scraping ridges in the dirt. Our eyes met.

I knew hungry when I saw it.

"Hold on, big guy," I told the animal. Since it was vital to document the abuse I took several pictures and immediately texted them to our local wildlife office. Then I lifted the latch on the barn door and searched for food. Bags of dog kibble were stacked just inside. A bucket of wilted vegetables and bruised fruit lay on the dusty floor.

I lugged the bucket outside and tossed the contents next to the bear, all the while telling him things would be okay. My phone chimed, confirming that wildlife had received the messages and a team would be sent out today. While the bear greedily ate, I threaded the garden hose through the bars to fill up an old horse trough with water.

Out of the corner of my eye I realized someone was walking toward me, a smallish man in his thirties with greasy brown hair dressed in a red ski jacket and jeans. A shotgun swung from his hand.

"What are you, one of those animal rights ladies? You're trespassing, you know. I could shoot you right now." Strangely enough his breath smelled like Butterfingers mixed with tobacco.

"Stop being an ass, Carl." Mari appeared behind us, a frown on her face and mud caking both of her shoes.

Carl's ferret-like face scrunched up. "This ain't cruelty. I've had him since he was a cub. Look how nice he's grown." The hand with the shotgun gestured toward the bear. "I've been teaching him how to dance like they do in Russia. Got a rich guy in Texas who wants to buy him."

"I don't think so."

His eyes squinted in a sly look. "Who's gonna stop me, blondie?"

I stretched myself to my full height and moved directly in front of him. "That would be me."

His reaction was to spit a wad of chew at my feet. The brown drops splattered my rubber boots.

"Don't mess with her," Mari advised him. Her eyes drifted to the figure of the bear in the corral in front of her. "Holy cow."

I realized the bear had stopped eating for a moment to raise its massive head and stare at us.

Outraged about this capture situation, I continued. "I suggest you call your lawyer, Carl. I've already texted pictures of the corral, the bear, and your address to the Environmental Conservation Police officers. They should be here any minute."

"Tell the government to stay out of my business." He raised the shotgun and scratched his crotch.

"Don't point that at her." Mari raised her voice.

Our potential standoff was interrupted by the chime of a text message. My assistant glanced down at her cell phone. "Sorry, Kate, we have to go."

Satisfied the authorities would now handle Crazy Carl and take possession of the bear, I started to walk away.

Of course, that provoked a response. "Keep your nose out of my business, girly. That goes for you too, Mari. Come back here and you'll both be sorry."

He yelled something else at us but that final threat was swallowed up by the wind.

My contact at Fish and Wildlife called me two hours later.

"No bear found on the property, Kate," she told me. "At first Mr. Sheckter denied everything but between your pictures and our investigation there's plenty of evidence one was here. We found bear scat in the corral and all around the barn. This guy tried to clean up but he didn't do a very good job. I uncovered a shackle that had been recently cut hidden in the hay with fur still stuck on it. There also was a store of illegal tranquilizer darts, which is probably how he managed the animal.

That surprised me. "Where did he get those?"

"The Internet, Craigslist, who knows? Anyway, we issued him a citation. Just wanted to tell you how it went."

"Any idea where the bear is?"

"We're hoping he's wandered up into state park land by now. Sheckter got him in the small capture cage, cut the leg restraint off and let him go."

I heard the frustration in her voice.

"We've got an alert posted for any sightings and a team searching the area now."

The idea of a large bear loose in a populated area worried me. It might take this animal a while to get its bearings.

"Let's hope he's made it back into the woods on his own," I said, "for everyone's sake. Especially the bear's."

Chapter Twenty-seven

Prom night finally arrived.

My date picked me up in his Mercedes. Jeremy looked fantastic in a classic tuxedo, obviously not rented for the evening. Our plan was to have the limo pick us up at his place. Mari graciously agreed to walk Buddy for me.

My feet were jammed into four-inch heels with serious attitude. Cindy had loaned me a small shiny evening purse that barely held keys and a lipstick. My dress fit perfectly in all the right spots and shimmered under the lights. Bundled in a fun faux fur coat, also borrowed from Cindy, I waited with Jeremy in the lobby of the Stanton Inn. A crackling fire burned in the massive old fireplace of the main building, a farmhouse built in the 1800s. We were ensconced in a pair of wing chairs separated by a small inlaid mahogany table. My date ordered white wine and a plain iced tea for me.

"I'm so glad I went up to Cornell," he said as he sipped his drink. "The faculty members I met gave me great advice."

Ever since he'd gotten back earlier in the day Jeremy had been a ball of energy. Since the news about his dig in Africa didn't look good he'd concentrated on weighing his options. Scheduled to be on sabbatical at the dig for another year meant his university had no classes for him to teach. A big chunk of empty time loomed ahead of him.

"What do you think of me going back to school?"

He looked more animated than I'd seen him in a long time. More like the student I'd known.

"Great idea," I told him and toasted him with my iced tea. "All the intrigue you work under was pretty disturbing."

"Dangerous, too. DNA advances have changed the profession so much. I'm excited to jump back into it." He pulled out his phone and started texting. Even though I was right across from him, I might as well have been on the moon. We both were super dedicated to our work. A tiny feeling of doubt wormed into my soul.

"I've got a great idea, Jeremy. No electronics this evening. I'd like to concentrate on us tonight."

He immediately powered off his screen. "I thought you'd never ask."

Due to some last-minute issues with the limo, the four of us arrived later than we'd planned. The party was in full swing and the music was super loud. We all dutifully pinned on our printed name badges and signed the guest book before entering the Lakeside Hotel Ballroom.

A giant Eiffel Tower fabricated from PVC pipe and sprayed with metallic paint dominated the room. Blinking blue and white lights woven in and out of the structure gave it a surprisingly realistic look.

Directly opposite the entrance, taking up most of the wall, a giant screen displayed candid photos featuring members of the graduating class paired with old video footage of various high school events. In another corner, red velvet curtains hid what appeared to be a small stage. Chandeliers refracted the light while a bevy of silver metallic stars suspended on wires glittered and gently swayed whenever anyone passed by.

"Doesn't it look fantastic?" Dina twirled around checking out every detail. Her prom dress, originally down to the floor in the old pictures she'd shown us in the limo, had mysteriously shrunk to alarmingly micro proportion. A cluster of guys hanging out at the bar didn't hide their admiration of what showed under her flirty now short, short skirt.

For once I agreed with something Dina said. From what I could see, the decorating committee had done an outstanding job. Round tables clustered around the dance floor, decorated in silver and white. Miniature Eiffel Towers festooned with flowers served as centerpieces. Additionally, each table had a schedule of events for the night firmly encased in a Lucite holder.

Our enthusiasm didn't match the moods of our dates. Luke and Jeremy were like two horses ready to bolt out of their stalls and take off.

A server in black pants and a white shirt moved past with a tray of canapés.

Lifting a tiny spear of shrimp by a toothpick I popped it into my mouth. The food tasted delicious. "I'm impressed, Dina. Aren't you guys?"

Both of them nodded their lackluster approval while helping themselves to the appetizers.

"My friend Robin Daniels designed it. She works for an event planner in New York City. We rented most of this stuff. Denny helped cut the stars in the shop room and I anchored most of the Eiffel Tower lights to the frame."

Luke commandeered Dina's arm and began to plow through the crowd. "Let's find our table. We're at number six." Jeremy and I followed closely behind.

"I feel a little out of place." I tried to whisper in his ear but ended up almost shouting.

"At least you know some of these people. I only know the dynamic duo in front of us." He deftly steered me away from a near-collision with a somewhat tipsy guy balancing two martinis. "I'd rather be alone with you."

"Ditto." I squeezed his hand. "I've come to the conclusion this was a dumb idea. How am I supposed to talk to anyone with all this noise going on?" As if to prove my point, the DJ raised the music volume. All the videos projected on the screen had their own sound track so that noise summated along with the boisterous classmates who were laughing, drinking, and making up for lost time.

"Well, maybe it will quiet down," Jeremy commented when we arrived at a table located not too far from the exit door. "Shall we dance?

Our bodies fit together easily. The smell of his aftershave and the angle of his shoulder as we swayed to the music were familiar but new at the same time. This Jeremy was handsome, decisive, and looking at me with a longing that touched my heart.

The slow dance melody, like honey with a beat, made it easy for us. Dressed in my party outfit I felt like a princess who had found her prince. Jeremy pressed his cheek next to mine and twirled me around, glints of light sparkling in the chiffon skirt.

When the song ended we stood for a moment, wrapped in each other's arms. Then he led me back to our table and the real world. Dina was already busy gabbing with a couple at the next table while Luke had a bored look on his face.

After we sat, our eyes drifted to the huge screen.

"Look. That's me on the wrestling team." The bored look disappeared from Luke's face. A video of two guys on a gymnasium floor, one in a headlock, played overhead. With only parts of faces showing under the helmets I didn't recognize anything.

Jeremy gave Luke a mock punch on the arm. "I wrestled in high school, too."

That started a lengthy conversation about weight groups and diets that I could barely hear. Sharing similar stories did allow them both to visibly relax a bit. While they talked, I couldn't help but compare the two men.

Luke had opted for a dark suit tonight instead of a tux. Perfectly appropriate, he looked handsome, but in the limo Dina complained bitterly about it, which set off a major argument and subsequent hissy fit. Their pattern of fighting and making up was exhausting to watch. Jeremy, on the other hand, seemed like an oasis of calm and wore a tux that fit him perfectly.

Both guys turned to me at that moment in the midst of a sentence.

"Sorry, I can't hear you." I cupped my ear.

"Anyone want a drink?" Jeremy stood up and made a drinking gesture with his hand.

Luke laughed and gave him a thumbs-up.

Dina had finished visiting by that time and grabbed hold of Jeremy's arm in a playful manner. "Hey, don't forget, you're actually my date." Then she looped her other hand around Luke, basically sandwiching herself between the two men while strongly working the slutty prom look.

Since I didn't want a drink, I opted out. "Go ahead, everyone. I'm going to freshen up. Meet you back here."

The troika moved away and was quickly swallowed up by the crowd. If I nosed around now I could relax with Jeremy later. Using Dina's fluffy shawl to mark our table, I headed for the ladies room in search of gossip and respite from the noise. After losing my way in the lookalike hallways I finally stopped one of the servers and asked for directions. He sweetly took me on some kind of short cut, then pointed to a corridor lined with potted plants.

The women's bathroom line snaked out the door and down the adjacent long hallway. Thankfully, the music level here was tolerable. I quickly took my place at the back of the line, barely beating out two women wearing men's tuxedo pants, red waistbands, and sneakers.

In front of me a short blonde with dark roots, abruptly turned to the woman in green beside her. "Did you see Angelica?"

I pulled out my phone and pretended not to listen.

A bark-like laugh exploded from the green lady's very thin lips. "How could you miss her? She's got on her tiara, for goodness sake. How tacky."

"Tacky is the word, alright. Is that her original prom dress?" Blondie tossed down the rest of her drink as we inched along.

"Think so. My memory is gone from the point where Denny spiked the punch." That set off another wave of laughter.

We all moved forward.

Blondie abandoned her empty glass in one of the artificial palm trees lining the hallway. "Didn't he get into trouble with the principal? I kind of remember he got suspended for a week."

Thin Lips nodded before sarcastically commenting with a slurred voice, "I wonder how many girls got knocked up that night?"

"Half the cheer squad, that's for sure." The braying laugh was joined by a high-pitched giggle.

"Too bad Flynn isn't here. I heard he had one heck of a mess to clean up that night, what with that fight in the men's room, and his date and Angelica trying to scratch each other's eyes out. I don't know what possessed him to take Shiloh to the prom. Didn't someone spill Hawaiian Punch all over her dress that night?" The Lady in Green lowered her voice as we entered the tiled bathroom.

Blondie didn't seem to care who heard what she said. "Those evil twins, Dina and Angelica, probably cooked that whole thing up. I heard Angelica was the one…"

Just then two stalls opened up and the classmates disappeared.

The bits and pieces of gossip I'd gathered sounded like more petty high school stuff. Hissy fits and Hawaiian Punch. I'd hoped for something more substantial. Before returning to our table I decided to look for Angelica Landon, the 2007 Prom Queen. It didn't take long to find her. As the ladies had said, no one else was wearing a tiara.

I cornered her on the edge of the dance floor. "Excuse me." I pointed to her head. "Were you the 2007 Queen of the prom?"

"Yes, I was." She involuntarily touched the crown with her left hand. The right held a large glass of white wine. "Isn't this party awesome? Uh, I'm so sorry but I don't recognize you. Can you refresh my memory?"

With a big white smile lighting up her face she looked like Central Casting's idea of an American high school Prom Queen—blond, built, and bubbly. I wondered if there had been any rivalry between her and the other blond bombshell, Dina, or had they joined forces and ruled their little high school empire together as the evil platinum twins?

"I didn't go to high school with you but we have a bunch of friends in common. I'm Kate." With all the noise I wasn't sure she heard me since a puzzled look replaced her smile.

Just then a picture of Flynn looking extra handsome, his Prom King crown perched rakishly on his head, flashed on the big screen. The audience began to clap and cheer.

When Angelica saw his image her eyes filled with tears. "I can't believe he's gone. Who could have done such a thing?"

"Do you have a moment to talk?" I gestured for her to follow me and pointed to an empty table in the back of the ballroom.

She nodded consent. Not able to navigate between the tables without lifting her poufy skirt, she impressively gulped down her entire glass of wine then picked up her skirt with both hands and followed me. Once seated, she found a clean napkin and carefully patted her eyes.

"Angelica, you knew Flynn better than almost anyone else. Luke Gianetti and I are trying to figure out who could have killed him."

"Who killed him?" Finished blotting her eyes, she pushed a stray curl back into place. "No idea. Maybe someone snapped— got mad and lost control. My husband, Norman, used to lose control all the time."

This unexpected answer threw me off. I moved my chair closer. "Excuse me?"

Her big blue eyes opened wide. No signs of any tears now. "He's a doctor, you know. A surgeon. A very important surgeon." She smoothed out the ballerina-like layers of her skirt. "He liked to accuse me of cheating then chuck things at me, especially after a few drinks. The third time he did it, I called the cops and got a restraining order. After I threw him out and got a divorce lawyer, he begged me to forgive him."

"And did you?"

"Yes," she leaned closer, "because I still love him to death. Norman and I are in couples counseling and I think it's working. In fact, we're planning a second honeymoon."

Her frank confession surprised me, especially telling such intimate details to me, a total stranger. I wondered what she might reveal about her former high school boyfriend if I approached it from a different angle. "Angelica, you seem very perceptive. Can you help me understand why someone would kill Flynn?"

A canny look came into her eyes. "Flynn was a popular guy. But he also could make people really mad. Especially when he ignored you."

"Who did he ignore?"

The former Prom Queen smoothed her skirt again. "He ignored the people who loved him. We'd dated on and off for three years and suddenly—it was over. I never knew why. Don't get me wrong, we still talked, he was nice and all, but it wasn't the same." The blue and white blinking lights cast elongated shadows on the wall behind her that appeared and disappeared like ghosts.

The DJ began to play a Beyonce tune and urged the audience to get up and dance. Angelica started to sway with the music.

I pressed on. "Was there anyone in particular you knew who held a grudge against him or threatened him?"

"No, of course not." Surprise and disbelief colored her voice. "At least, I don't remember. Besides, it was so long ago. My life is completely different now." She stood up, eager to get away from me. "Nice meeting you."

"Someone told me there was a fight between you and Shiloh at the prom."

Her spine straightened and a frown pulled her perfect brows together. "Beauty queens don't fight. Shiloh and I had a little disagreement."

"You spilled Hawaiian Punch all over her dress."

"That was an accident." Her voice became indignant. "I apologized but I don't think forgiveness is in that bitch's vocabulary."

Quite a cheap shot on Angelica's part, but I let it pass. Instead, I tried one last time to get some real information. "Were you in town on the day Flynn left? About three o'clock on August tenth. That was a Friday."

"What?" She stared at me, mouth open.

"Did you notice him getting into a car? He might have been hitchhiking."

"A car?" Her pretty face registered nothing except interest in the music playing. Her feet started to tap. "I'm supposed to remember something like that? From ten years ago?"

Someone yelled her name across the room pointing to another glass of white wine. She immediately waved and nodded.

I got up. "Thanks for your time."

"No problem. Listen, you've got to stay for the King and Queen and their Court reveal. The committee decided to honor Flynn and drape his empty chair in black. That was my idea."

Before I could comment, she smiled her Prom Queen smile and drifted away in a cloud of pale yellow chiffon headed for the dance floor.

• • ● • •

So far, the evening had been a bust. I'd heard little else but gossip that got me nowhere. On the dance floor Jeremy waved to me while twisting away near the Prom Queen, her tiara listing at an angle on her blond tresses. Not ready to join in the fun yet, I waved back.

While I weighed my options Dina pushed past me making a beeline in what seemed like the direction of the restroom. On an impulse I followed, hoping to corner her and uncover more about the Hawaiian Punch episode I'd overheard.

Sure enough, she led me straight there. Staking out a spot in front of the mirror I waited until she came out of the bathroom stall, then ambushed her.

"Isn't this fun?" I tried to duplicate Angelica's Prom Queen smile.

"Not at the moment. My feet are killing me." The attitude she gave me said it all. Without the men around, Dina cut out all the cutesy crap.

A gander at the stilettos she wore explained her discomfort. Since the bathroom had a temporary lull in customers, I continued. Even in her towering heels, I had the diminutive diva by six inches.

"Dina, do you remember someone spilling Hawaiian Punch on Shiloh Albert's dress the night of the prom?"

She frowned, her cupid bow lips settled into a pout. "Vaguely. Luke told me you were looking into Flynn's murder. Why are you sticking your nose into things that you shouldn't?"

"Because the family asked me to. Now, are you going to help me or not?" We both had become too tired to care about being polite.

Her patented pout got bigger. "Alright. I'm sure you'll rat everything to the guys if I don't cooperate."

Of course that wasn't true but I held my tongue.

She glanced around before answering. "Angelica is a big phony. She was so pissed at Flynn for dumping her that she tried to punch him out in the men's room. I think she was behind that Hawaiian Punch thing too."

"Really?"

"Pretty sure. Anyway, the girl was bawling in the bathroom."

"Shiloh. His prom date?"

"Yeah. Whatever."

"Anything else you can think of?"

Dina's left eyebrow arched up slightly. "Not really. Luke and I were a little busy that night." Her knowing smirk said it all.

I kept my expression blank and fought to give nothing away.

Not getting the reaction she anticipated, Dina continued. "Denny spiked the punch that night so some memories are a little hazy. And some aren't."

Subtle, she wasn't. "What can you tell me about Flynn's high school posse? The guys he hung out with?"

"A bunch of losers. Always catering to him like he was a god or something." Her voice sounded particularly annoyed.

"They weren't all losers," I countered. "Didn't Rusty become a doctor? And I hear Denny is a very successful real estate agent."

She raised that left eyebrow again. "Yeah, Rusty barely got into medical school. We think his dad pulled some strings. And Denny—he's a fast-talking con artist. Word is his real estate empire is going to crash and burn if the banks call in his loans."

I'd underestimated Dina. She was smarter than she let on. "What about Nate?"

A nasty little sound escaped her pink lips. "Yeah, he went really far—as far as Main Street."

"So, who do you think killed the Prom King?"

This time both eyebrows rose up as far as they could go. "How the heck would I know? Some creep he ran into. Luke thinks Flynn hitched a ride with one of those serial killers." She blotted the tip of her nose. "I don't know why you both are so riled up. I'm sure the murderer is long gone by now."

Her words struck a chord. If that ended up being true, we would be at a complete dead end. No justice for anyone.

"Now I've got a couple of questions for you." She checked her lips in a pocket mirror nestled at the bottom of her sequined evening bag.

"Sure."

"How tight are you with Jeremy?" Astute blue eyes bored into mine. "Does he really have a trust fund? I've never met anyone with a trust fund. How does that work?"

What was Dina up to now?

"The answer to Question One is: none of your business. Answer to Question Two: none of your business. As far as Question Three is concerned—go ask a financial advisor."

She squinted her eyes a bit. The possibility she might be scheming something was most likely one hundred percent.

"Aren't you forgetting about Luke?"

"A girl always needs a backup plan."

With that, Dina slipped under my arm and sashayed back to the party.

An hour later the noise made any meaningful conversation impossible. I'd given up trying to catch Denny alone, and although Luke said Rusty was somewhere in the room, I didn't have the energy to go searching for him. I considered the night a bust. Ten-year-old petty gossip didn't lead anywhere.

Jeremy and Dina got up to dance again. Where they got their energy from, I don't know. I begged off and told them I was going to step outside for some air.

"Want some company?" he asked. A party hat with Class of 2007 sat firmly on his head.

"No, I'm fine. Go enjoy yourself. I'll be right back." With two fingers I blew a kiss at him. With a big gesture he threw one back at me.

Temperatures had started to drop but with no wind, a short walk would be bearable, especially if I kept up a brisk pace. I slipped my gloves out of my coat pocket and put them on. The cold air started to energize me. Truthfully, I wasn't much of a party animal.

Several couples clustered at the exit door chatting and smoking. Passing between them I followed the scenic walkway out the main door toward the water. By the service entrance of the hotel I could see hotel staff, all dressed in black pants and white shirts sneaking cigarettes, swirls of smoke mixing with the scent of the pine trees. Low-voltage lights lined the bluestone walkway while spotlights dramatically lit up the trees from below.

Quick steps behind alarmed me.

"Hi." Luke appeared slightly out of breath.

"Hi, yourself." I continued walking, happy for the company. "Where are our dates?"

He stuck his hands in his pockets. "Inside, dancing up a storm."

"The noise in there was driving me crazy," I explained as we passed a gazebo perched by the water's edge. "I needed a break."

"Me, too. Any idea how many people asked me to fix their traffic tickets?"

I turned toward him, his face silhouetted in the moonlight. "Let me guess. About as many as wanted me to magically cure their cat from peeing outside the litter box."

We both laughed. Rounding a bend I noticed two cars leaving the parking lot. "There go some lucky people who got to ditch the party early."

He briefly glanced over then pointed to the roof of the hotel. "My cousin and I patched those shingles my senior year in high school."

"That's pretty high up." The gabled roof had several peaks with almost vertical slopes of slate shingles leading down to more gradual overhangs.

"We worked on the overhang, not the gables. I'd have to be crazy to do that." We both paused to admire the historic hotel ablaze with lights. "Back then I did all kinds of odd jobs to make extra money."

"I know what you mean. During high school I worked for a company in Brooklyn that scooped dog poop from million-dollar backyards."

"That must have looked great on your resume." We started walking again. "How's the sleuthing going?"

"It isn't. The noise isn't conducive for conversation and what little I did find out falls under the heading of ancient gossip. By the way, your Prom Queen, Angelica, is tossing down the drinks so fast I'll be surprised if she's standing by the end of the night."

"She's recreating history."

"Funny." I had no doubt that was true. "No one I spoke to admitted seeing Flynn in town the afternoon he disappeared and I still haven't confirmed where Denny or Rusty were that day. Frankly, even the family wants me to cease and desist."

"You're not the only one. From what I've heard the investigators haven't got anything either. Nothing came of the moldy paper they found in Flynn's pockets. Word is they're scaling back." He took my arm as we hit a spot of uneven pavement.

"By the way, Officer Gianetti…" I paused for effect. "…in the interest of being thorough, where were you the day Flynn went missing?"

"Are you kidding me? I confess." He threw his head back and raised his hands to the sky. "My dad and two cousins and I were on a camping trip."

"Prove it," I said.

"That's the problem, isn't it? Proving anything after all this time."

The hotel and its bright lights were reflected in the calm dark lake, a shimmering mirror image. Pinecones clustered under the trees. We walked a bit more until the faint strains of "The Hokey Pokey" drifted across the water.

"Shall we turn back?" he asked.

"Sure. I'm ready to have some fun. After all, this is my first prom."

"Then let's party, by all means," he replied as we quickened the pace. "Only another two hours before Dina will let us out of here."

• • ● • •

Over the next half hour, the DJ dimmed the overhead lighting even further and it became hard to recognize anyone. The blinking blue and white lights from the Eiffel Tower created a strobe effect that made my eyes burn and washed out colors. Between the noise and the pulsing lights I could feel a migraine coming on. Jeremy sweetly offered to take me home but I figured I could last two more hours. Ice water and Advil helped but didn't make me feel less like a big party pooper.

Luke pointed out Nate Porter to me. Dressed in an ill-fitting suit and tie, he stood alone at the bar, a bunch of empty beer bottles lined up in front of him. I briefly spied Denny Alantonio, the real estate agent, who appeared to have come to the party solo. Always moving, he busied himself by chatting away with group after group of partygoers, probably trying to sell them something.

"Denny had a crush on Angelica," Dina informed me when she saw me watching him. "She shot him down but good."

Before I could question her, she popped up and headed for the dance floor.

Hoping to escape the music for a moment, Jeremy escorted me into the lobby. No one manned the greeting table and only a few pre-printed badges remained, none of the names familiar to me. The busy uniformed cleaning staff hustled around us trying to keep up with all the half-empty plates and glasses.

"I'm officially danced out," my date admitted.

"Can you believe how packed the ballroom is?" The deserted space felt like heaven.

"Do you think some of the locals crashed the party?" Jeremy asked. "I saw some guys who looked suspiciously younger than they should."

He had a good point. Security was nonexistent.

We hung out chatting for a while until hunger drove us to the buffet table again. After absentmindedly stuffing myself with greasy fried food, I wanted to forget all about murder and go home. Unfortunately, we had to wait for the big King and Queen and their Court thing to happen. Part of me was surprised they'd even decided to go through with it.

Jeremy had gone to get us both some decaf coffee when Angelica appeared behind me.

"Are you sh'tay-ing for the Royal Court reveal?" She seemed pretty pleased with herself and more than a little bit loaded.

"Yes, we are," I replied, my body language radiating zero enthusiasm. "We're sharing a limo with Luke and Dina and they're part of the Court." I slipped my high-heeled shoes off under the table and hoped I'd be able to squeeze them back on my swollen feet. Noting her intoxication, I said, "Maybe you shouldn't be driving tonight. We'll be glad to give you a ride if you need one."

"Me, need a ride? Duh." The look Angelica gave me implied that Prom Queens always had rides.

Music blared as the DJ loudly encouraged the crowd to join a twisting congo line. The Prom Queen began to sway more or less to the beat.

I was about to turn away when Angelica leaned in and whispered, "I did remember something about the day Flynn left. Maybe I know who could have snapped, after all. Just like a big old rubber band." She mimicked pulling something with her fingers and hiccuped.

Alarmed, I urged her to tell me.

"Nope. First one to know will be Offis'sher Lukey, because he's a member of my Court. Get it? Court?" She hiccupped again. "Bye-bye." With another small hiccup she took off, vanishing into the thick crowd before I could locate my shoes and follow.

To my right, I spied Luke deep in conversation with Evelyn Vandersmitt, Flynn's old drama teacher, famous for her red lips and eccentric ways. Unsure of what to do, I interrupted them.

"Excuse me, Luke. I think this is our dance?"

Without waiting for a reply, I pulled him onto the dance floor. The singer crooned about love gone wrong.

"Do you want to tell me what this is about?" Although our respective dates had been dancing up a storm together, we'd been otherwise occupied. He placed his arm around my waist.

"Angelica thinks she remembers someone who was angry at Flynn."

Luke pressed me close. "Kate, our Prom Queen loves attention—and has a great imagination. I wouldn't put a lot of stock in it if I were you." Then somehow he twirled me around and brought me back into his arms in perfect time to the beat.

My astonishment temporarily wiped away Angelica's revelation. "Where did you learn to dance like this?"

"My sisters and all my girl cousins. They made me practice with them." He punctuated that revelation with a confident dip.

I felt like I was in a forties black-and-white movie.

"If you want, we can talk to her after the whole Court thing," he continued, "which is in about fifteen minutes."

Sure enough, I saw Dina waving frantically on the sidelines to get Luke's attention. The singer hit a high note, the music finished, and he dipped me again, slowly, smoothly, my hair touching the floor. Decades old ballet classes kicked in and I extended my hand and one foot out as gracefully as I could. The couples dancing around us broke out in a round of applause. Expertly, he carefully brought me to my feet.

"That was fun. Sorry, but I've got to go." Luke released my waist and took Dina's hand. The two of them disappeared backstage leaving me standing alone under the tin stars.

• • ● • •

Half an hour later the audience was still waiting for the big finale. Jeremy returned to the table after ducking outside to check on our limo. He glared at his watch.

"They should be starting any second now. It's almost midnight," I said.

"It was fun, but I'm more than ready to leave." He took my hand and kissed it. "Are we getting too old for this?"

"Absolutely not." I stood up and took his arm. "How about one last dance?"

With my headache almost gone and two glasses of wine soothing my sore feet, Jeremy and I walked onto the dance floor and sang along to the true love lyrics. Pressed up against his chest I relaxed and looked forward to the rest of our evening together. His witty observations on the other dancers soon had me in giggles.

Abruptly, the music stopped and we went back to our seats. The DJ then called a few teachers up to the mike and what seemed like an endless parade of past student council presidents and band leaders, none of whom we knew.

"Oh, by the way, I saw that Dr. Rusty guy leave while you were talking to the Prom Queen." Jeremy gestured toward the ballroom exit door.

"Lucky dog," I rested my head on Jeremy's shoulder and prayed for the reunion to end.

Luke and Dina and several other couples had slipped off behind the stage what seemed like ages ago to find their props and get into place. A server sped by, accidentally banging the back of my chair and knocking my borrowed purse to the ground. The clasp popped open and most of the contents spilled on the floor. By the time I lifted my head to protest, all I saw was a waiter's familiar back, and a pair of black pants hurrying toward the door.

"Great." My keys, lipstick, and a half-empty roll of mints lay strewn under the chairs and table.

Jeremy offered to help but I told him I'd get it.

When I moved my chair back to retrieve my stuff, I barely avoided another collision with a different server. Annoyed and stressed he muttered his opinion of me, and our entire table. A creative description of what I could do with myself sizzled in the air. Embarrassed, I kept my head down until he was out of sight, before stuffing everything back into my purse. Tempers were wearing thin. A metallic screech of static caught the audience's attention. Someone tapped on the microphone.

"Ladies and gentlemen, fellow classmates…" The DJ with the booming voice attempted to quiet the audience down.

"Show time." Jeremy moved his chair to face the stage and helped twist mine toward the main attraction. The remaining lights darkened all the way down.

A lone spotlight focused on the announcer. "Please take your seats. It's time to greet your 2007 Prom King and Queen and their Court."

Oh good, I thought. Let's wrap this up.

The red velvet curtains lifted, revealing two backlit thrones—one empty and one with a silhouetted figure. Draped above them, barely visible in the dim light, a black banner with glittery gold lettering read "RIP Flynn Keegan, 2007 Prom King."

The DJ continued, but amped up his voice a notch for dramatic effect. "We salute in memoriam Prom King Flynn Keegan and encourage you to greet the members of the Royal Court. Please stand and give them all a round of applause." Spotlights flitted back and forth over the Royal Court who carefully descended access stairs on opposite ends of the stage, to form a semi-circle facing the audience. As each couple was announced, applause welled up from the crowd.

Dina made goofy faces to one of her friends while Luke stared off to the side.

A drum roll sounded.

"Now, ladies and gentlemen, put your hands together and greet Her Royal Highness, our lovely 2007 Prom Queen, Angelica Landon."

The Court turned to face the stage and in a cheesy choreo-graphed moment bowed and curtsied to their Queen.

Center stage lights came up dramatically, bathing the stage in rose and gold. Two spotlights focused on the thrones.

Those closest to the stage realized it first. The Prom Queen didn't rise and wave to her adoring crowd. Something metallic was twisted impossibly tightly around her neck, cutting into her flesh. Unblinking eyes like colored glass stared at the audience.

A woman screamed.

Angelica's dark purple face clashed horribly with her pale yellow dress.

Chapter Twenty-eight

It was two-fifteen in the morning by the time we left the reunion from Hell. A silent Luke stayed behind with the rest of the police force while Jeremy, Dina, and I gratefully crawled into our limo. After dropping her off, we went back to my place.

Once Buddy was settled, I poured us two ice-cold glasses of white wine and joined Jeremy on the sofa. Our faces reflected a certain numbness from the night's events.

"Do you mind staying here tonight?" I asked Jeremy. "Your place is more romantic but I'm way too tired to care."

"Wherever you are is romantic enough for me." He opened his arms and I gladly leaned against him. Just being held felt comforting.

"Poor Angelica." My words were muffled by his chest.

"I know." He stroked my hair and kissed my ear. "Do you think you'll be able to sleep?"

Sleep wasn't what I needed now. I leaned over and kissed him. Jeremy's lips were soft and warm and took their time. Clasping his hand in mine, I turned the light off and led him to my bed.

● ● ● ● ●

I woke up to the delicious smell of bacon and coffee.

"Breakfast." Jeremy stood in front of the stove in boxers and a tuxedo shirt with a very attentive Buddy directly below. With his hair all ruffled up he looked like the morning-after in a sexy

European movie. Waking up to food by Jeremy was getting to be a delightful habit.

I, on the other hand, felt like I'd been run over by a tractor-trailer. In jagged pieces the events of last night intruded on the new day. Not wanting to go there, I sat up, grabbed my robe, and headed toward the bathroom. After putting myself together, I ventured into the kitchen. A vase filled with sunflowers and a glass of orange juice greeted me. I stared at them in astonishment.

"Did you go to the store this morning?"

"Yes, and in my tux, believe it or not. You were down to a bottle of mayo and a can of dog food." He kissed the top of my head and pointed me into a kitchen chair. Before I'd settled in, a steaming cup of coffee appeared.

"I remember you weren't much of a morning person."

"That hasn't changed. You're spoiling me," I said as I took my first sip.

"Honey, you deserve to be spoiled." He turned back to the stove and began flipping something.

Thinking of Jeremy buying orange juice in his tuxedo made a great image. Even the weather cooperated, as sunshine streamed through the curtains. Sunshine? I looked around for my phone but must have left it in my purse. "Jeremy, what time is it?"

"A little past noon. You slept almost eight hours." With a flourish he divided up a professional-looking omelet and slipped it onto my plate.

Eight hours of sleep and no crazy dreams. Maybe my body was telling me something. "This looks good." I tried a forkful of eggs. Delicious. "When did you learn to cook?"

"Sheer necessity. You figure out how to make meals for yourself pretty quickly on a dig. Otherwise you starve to death. We had an Italian archeologist join us on an expedition in the Yucatan peninsula a couple of years ago and I got a crash course from her." He slid the rest of the omelet onto his plate, brought over some bacon, and refilled our two mugs of coffee before sitting down opposite me.

A sigh of contentment escaped. "This is such a luxury. I nor-mally chug a burnt-tasting cup of coffee standing up and grab whatever is hanging around for breakfast."

"I noticed." He lifted his glass of orange juice. "You need to take better care of yourself."

My fork speared the remaining piece of bacon. "Now you sound like Gramps."

"That's a good thing, 'cause if I remember correctly, your Gramps is usually right."

I stuck my tongue out at him.

When he quit laughing he said, "Why don't we take today to chill? Let's have a lazy Sunday at home. With what we've been through, we deserve it."

"Agreed."

"Then maybe after breakfast we could go back to bed." His grin was inviting and a bit lascivious.

Grinning back, I said, "It's a date." Getting reacquainted last night had been very satisfying. I was looking forward to more of the same.

Buddy stood up, walked over to the door and growled. A moment later the doorbell rang.

"Oh, no," I muttered.

"Who's that?" Jeremy asked.

I reluctantly got up and wrapped my bathrobe more tightly around me. "It's probably one of the staff doing Sunday morning treatments. Sometimes they forget their keys." Hushing Buddy, I pushed away the blinds and curtain and peeked out the window into the parking lot.

"Shoot." At any other time I would have welcomed Luke, but not now. Hiding was out of the question since he'd already seen me.

I slipped the chain lock and deadbolt and opened the door.

"Good morning." When he came in he brought in a blast of cold air in more ways than one. As soon as he saw Jeremy at the kitchen table with his boxer shorts peeking out from under his tuxedo shirt he stopped, unsure of what to do.

"Hey, Luke. Want some coffee?" Jeremy lifted his mug and gestured toward an extra chair.

Luke's head swiveled between me, then Jeremy, the messy bed, and back again.

I noticed his left hand had a death grip on a paper bag. Seeing that I had a romantic life of my own obviously affected him. "Is that for us?"

"Uh, I brought you some bagels."

Jeremy had a bemused look on his face. "Kate, Honey, come back and sit down. Your coffee is getting cold."

Buddy enthusiastically wagged his tail and followed everyone to the kitchen table. Jeremy sliced up a few bagels, put out cream cheese, and poured our visitor a cup of coffee.

Seeing Luke unfortunately reminded me of last night and Angelica's murder. "Have you had any sleep yet?" I asked him. Gray shadows lurked under his dark brown eyes.

He held the coffee mug with both hands. "I caught a few hours on the cot at the station." The grim expression didn't leave his face.

Jeremy joined us at the table, then asked, "What brings you here this morning?"

Luke stared into his mug as though the answer were floating there. "The murder last night. Remember the stars hanging from the ceiling?"

I nodded.

"Well, the killer used one of those wires to strangle Angelica."

A beautiful image of the sparkling stars gently twirling above us now morphed into something sinister. I heard a quick intake of breath from Jeremy before Luke continued.

"It was a murder of opportunity."

Jeremy and I exchanged glances.

"And I'm sorry to say all of us are considered suspects. Including me."

"You've got to be kidding," Jeremy said for the millionth time. Talking about murder definitely had spoiled our romantic mood.

The three of us moved to the living room and since Luke was off duty and it technically was past lunchtime, the guys had progressed from coffee to ice cold beer.

"Tell me about it." Luke sat in the lounge chair, a happy dog pressed up against him. He patted Buddy on the head and continued his explanation. "They took me off the case."

"Any other officers at the reunion?"

"No. Just me. But the Chief has a major problem on his hands. No witnesses, no surveillance video, and a zillion fingerprints and trace evidence from practically everybody in town is scattered throughout the entire venue."

"Doesn't the hotel have security cameras?"

"Yes, but the system was down that night. They were so busy with the reunion no one called in their tech guy."

"Does that happen often?" I asked him.

"More often than you'd think. Management updated their reservation software and individual room security in the hotel area but never got around to the separate ballroom systems. Plus, half the outdoor cameras, including the ones in the parking lots, aren't working because of the ice storms."

I made myself a mental note to check the animal hospital's security system.

"How can I be a suspect? I didn't even know Angelica." Jeremy's angry voice rose in protest.

"That only puts you into the category of crazy-ass killers who don't need a motive." Luke pointed at him. "Didn't you tell us they shut down your dig because one of your porters was murdered? Maybe you are a secret psycho."

Jeremy glared at him. "That's not funny."

"I'm sorry, but you are under arrest."

Before this got any further, I jumped in. "Come on, guys. We've got a real crime here. What other motives does the Chief have at this point?" I raised my sore feet in their fuzzy purple slippers up onto the coffee table.

Luke shrugged his shoulders. "Take your pick. There's jealousy, greed, anger, money, you name it."

"Has anyone questioned Angelica's estranged husband?" I looked at him for confirmation but didn't get any.

"That's one direction they're looking into. It did occur to the Chief that maybe someone at the reunion killed her because Flynn's body was found, but that was as far as it went."

"Some kind of revenge?" My thoughts went back to all the gossip I'd heard.

Our conversation was interrupted by Luke's cell phone ringing.

Jeremy and I huddled in silence as Luke stood up and deliberately walked away from us. Although he'd turned his back, I caught a few noncommittal words before he hung up.

"Good news, of a sort. That was a friend at the station, who will remain anonymous." He came back and picked up his beer. "It seems Angelica was going through a bitter divorce with her orthopaedic surgeon hubby. We've got two eyewitnesses who saw him at the reunion, even though he wasn't on the guest list."

That got my attention. "So he's a suspect? Have they interviewed him?"

Luke took another sip before he answered. "No interviews. He crashed his car into a tree this morning a little before one a.m. Right now he's in intensive care with massive head trauma in an induced coma."

I remembered a vibrantly alive Angelica confiding in me last night that she and her husband might go on a second honeymoon.

"So what's the deal?" Jeremy asked. "Husband kills her then is overcome with remorse and tries to commit suicide?"

"That's what Chief Garcia suspects happened—a crime of passion. The husband certainly had enough medical knowledge to strangle her."

That information made me shift in my seat. "Luke, she did mention to me that her husband, Norman, had a temper."

"I don't think it was any secret. You probably need to go down to the station, though, and give them a statement to that effect."

Jeremy lifted his bottle. "Now you sound like a cop, Luke."

Luke waited a moment before raising his own bottle. "Well, that's because I am a cop. Don't forget it, Jeremy."

It sounded like a warning.

• • ● • •

A steady icy rain fell for the next hour. Every ten or fifteen minutes Luke's cell phone would ring and he'd walk off into some corner. I expected Jeremy to get annoyed that our lazy Sunday had been hijacked, but he appeared to be fascinated by the ongoing investigation.

I took advantage of a break and asked what the husband's prognosis was. Head trauma could go either way. Since Luke wasn't officially on the case, he was more forthcoming than usual. Whoever his sources were had no ethical problem keeping him up-to-date.

"Not good. Maybe that's for the best."

More questions occurred to me as I thought about the couple. "Any children?"

"Nope, and no relatives close by. Angelica's parents moved to Florida. Her husband's sister lives in Manhattan and she's on her way to the hospital. That's all I know."

"I've got a great idea," Jeremy suggested from the depths of the sofa. "Let's change the subject."

The guys started to talk about wrestling while I excused myself to get out of my pajamas and into some clothes. Maybe the police weren't concerned, but it seemed odd that two members of the Class of 2007 had been murdered. Who was it that said there is no such thing as coincidence? I'd spoken to Angelica the second time that night only minutes before her murder and she hadn't seemed upset at all. By the time we talked she must have encountered her husband, but her manner was bubbly and vibrant, like she was in her element that night.

Veterinarians are trained to remember details. When Angelica admitted her husband had a violent temper, she made it sound as though that problem was in the past. Certainly planning a second honeymoon would indicate that.

If he was there at the reunion and she was afraid of him why was she hiccupping and happy only a few minutes before going backstage? Our table was near the ballroom exit door. The only people who scurried past us during that critical time frame were the waiters.

Maybe the police force was convinced her husband stalked her, then killed her, but my women's intuition told me it was more complicated than it seemed.

Chapter Twenty-nine

My women's intuition appeared to be on vacation because in the next few days damaging information surfaced about Angelica and her doctor husband, Norman. Three restraining orders had been filed against him over the last two years. Their divorce turned contentious when Angelica's lawyer fought to overturn the prenup agreement for a bigger slice of the couple's combined assets. The doctor, known for his temper at the hospital where he worked, had threatened to "kill the bitch" in front of witnesses. Operating room nurses and staff confessed that the volatile surgeon often threw scalpel blades and other surgical instruments at the walls during medical procedures and had been verbally abusive on numerous occasions. The head of the hospital noted diplomatically that Norman was currently on an administrative leave of absence.

The only contradictory statements came from Angelica's sister-in-law. In an interview Norman's sister insisted that her brother had worked on his anger management issues with a therapist. He'd called her the night of the reunion and told her he was meeting Angelica after the prom, and then the two were leaving for a second honeymoon. On further questioning, however, she admitted Norman was taking several different medications after being diagnosed as bipolar and currently struggled with bouts of acute depression.

Hopes of obtaining a confession were dashed when the doctor died from his injuries the following day without regaining consciousness. After obtaining results of trace evidence from Angelica's gown and confirming that the DNA matched her husband, Chief Garcia announced the investigation closed.

Life in Oak Falls went on. No one asked me about Flynn anymore. Even his family stopped calling me.

• • ● • •

Four days later I went from having two guys around, to zero guys. An excited Jeremy left for an interview at Harvard while Luke went back to his old routine—police work during the day and classwork at night. I assumed the demanding Dina took up the rest of his time.

I'd complained about my personal life being too complicated and now it had gone back to being deadly dull. Jeremy's romantic goodnight calls were no substitute for the real thing.

That evening restless dreams took over my sleep, one dream after another. In the deep, dark woods Flynn appeared being pulled in all directions by people with animal masks covering their faces, screaming, "He's mine, he's mine." My client, Daffy, and her Chihuahua floated by wearing floral crowns, her hands sprouting roses and thorns instead of fingernails. I stood at the top of a cliff staring down at a quarry filled with water. The sun was blazing hot. Flynn stood beside me and grasped my hand. He wore swim trunks exactly the same as in the old picture scotch-taped to his bedroom wall. "Don't be afraid," he told me. I felt myself falling backwards as we plunged together, toward the rocks below. At the top of the cliff stood Luke, sadly waving good-bye.

I awoke with a start, still feeling as if I were falling. My nightgown was drenched with sweat. Buddy jumped onto the foot of the bed and woofed at me. The alarm clock read three in the morning, way too early for the night to be over. I got out of bed and paced around for a while before deciding to make myself a cup of chamomile tea in the microwave.

Ever since my mom's accident, I'd been plagued with vivid dreams. The therapists I'd gone to in my teen years told me my subconscious was trying to sort things out. In veterinary school they'd receded into the background and been replaced by normal anxiety dreams—forgetting your locker combination or missing a test. But now, since I'd moved to Oak Falls and started investigating murders, they'd come back full force, as though they'd been lurking in the shadows of my mind all along—waiting for a chance to come out and play.

Determined to go back to sleep, I opened an old organic chemistry textbook and brought it into bed with me. It had put me to sleep many times when I was studying. I hoped tonight wouldn't be any different.

While my drowsy eyes wandered over the Krebs cycle, I considered the latest dream.

How did Daffy fit into this whole thing?

And why didn't Luke try to save me as I fell into the gorge?

Chapter Thirty

Coincidentally, the following day Mari and I paid a return visit to the client who had appeared in my latest dream. As we drove up, I noticed her beautiful garden now was completely winterized. Mounds of hay protected the hundreds of bulbs that would appear next spring. The white picket perimeter fence gleamed with a fresh coat of paint. Everything appeared tidy and neat, just the way she liked it. Daffy didn't feel comfortable unless she had absolute control over her tiny bit of the universe.

We waited on the porch and listened once more to her custom doorbell ring. The familiar tune "How Much is That Doggy in the Window?" echoed around us and inside the house.

"What do you think they'll be wearing this time?" Mari shifted back and forth in the cold.

"Something spectacular."

When the door opened we both laughed. Daffy and her Chihuahua, Little Man, were dressed as gypsies. Not real gypsies, but make believe gypsies out of a 1950s Hollywood movie. What made us laugh the most was the big false moustache Little Man wore.

"That doesn't bother him?" We walked into the house, Mari closing the door behind us. "By the way, I don't think a fake moustache is a good thing to put on his skin."

Little Man seemed to understand what I said because he gave his owner a dirty look.

Daffy immediately removed the offending bit of hair and offered her pet a kiss. "I confess. That was for your benefit only. I put it on him just before I opened the door."

"Well, I think he's pretty happy that it's gone."

Little Man growled at me in agreement.

Since we saw them every two weeks, our visits with Little Man and Daffy usually proceeded like clockwork. Mari and I glided into position to outmaneuver the grumpy dog and put a small muzzle on him before we trimmed his nails. I think the mustache might have demoralized him because today he barely put up a fuss.

"Daffy," I said as I began my exam, "I hope your boy isn't wearing clothes all day long. That's also not good for his skin."

Little Man must have recovered his dignity because he bared his teeth as best he could when we finished his front paw.

To my discomfort his owner satisfied my curiosity a little too candidly. "Silly, we dress up only for company. Normally, he doesn't wear any clothes around the house—and neither do I."

The appointment over, Mari and I sat at the kitchen table in front of the usual array of brownies, cookies, and pie. I tried hard to get over the image of Daffy blissfully putting out the spread for us as naked as the day she was born, except for a pristinely ironed Laura Ashley-style apron. However, pie is pie, and for the sake of my appetite, I put all thoughts of her private nudity aside and helped myself to a second slice of delicious strawberry-rhubarb pie from the Oak Falls Diner.

Daffy smiled benignly at both of us wolfing down way too much sugar before she brought up the cold case.

"The grapevine tells me you are still investigating poor Flynn's murder."

"Daffy, is there anything that happens in this town that you don't know about?" The napkin caught the remaining crumbs decorating my mouth.

She pursed her lip. "Oh, there might be a few things."

With an effort, I tore away from devouring another cookie to keep up my end of the conversation. "Anyway, you're right, although it's winding down. I've got a few more interviews to do, but after that..."

"Cold cases are just that—cold," Mari interjected before wrapping up a huge oatmeal raisin cookie for later.

Little Man growled out the doggy opinion.

"Be nice," Daffy cooed.

The Chihuahua turned to look at his owner, his bat ears translucent. A bulbous head, big dark eyes and thin skin gave him a baby-like quality, until he growled.

Ignoring her pet, Daffy asked us a question. "Have you checked to see when Mr. Cassidy got out of jail?"

I stopped mid bite. "Who is Mr. Cassidy?"

"The teacher Flynn turned in to the police."

"What?" This was news to me. "Can you tell me about it?"

She picked up Little Man, gave him a treat, and tucked him into his bed before sitting down with us. I suspected Daffy enjoyed a little drama with her revelations.

"Homer Cassidy was a well-respected Oak Falls High School gym teacher, that is until Flynn saw him take money from the carwash fundraiser receipts."

"The gym teacher was a thief?"

"Yes. Well, Flynn thought so. He told the principal and, sure enough, Cassidy had been embezzling money from the school for years. Money for uniforms, equipment, student fundraisers—anything he could get his hands on. But he was smart. He'd only take small amounts each time, but they sure added up. They calculated he stole over twenty thousand dollars."

"Did the school prosecute?"

"Absolutely. I believe he was sentenced to four or five years in prison. It was quite a scandal. Turned out he had a gambling problem."

"So when did he get out of jail?" I took a sip of coffee.

"That, I don't know."

"Perhaps he came back looking for revenge." Mari pushed away her plate.

"Was Bobby Garcia the Police Chief then?"

"No. It was Chief Pollack, who passed away in 2010. Heart attack."

That meant I had to ask Luke.

• • ● • •

During our good-byes to the pair in their gypsy outfits, I thought about Flynn and the courage it took to turn in a popular teacher.

When I got back to the hospital, I called the only person I knew who could do a trace.

Luke did me a favor and said he'd check on Homer Cassidy and get back to me.

Ten minutes later the phone rang. In the background I heard multiple people talking followed by laughter. "Sorry, Kate. It's the Chief's birthday today and someone gave him one of those gag books for old guys." This time Luke's laugh joined the others.

I waited until the noise level dropped. "Wish Garcia a happy birthday from me."

"Not a good idea. I think he's still annoyed at you for bypassing law enforcement on that last murder case you solved."

To keep the peace, my succinct response to that statement remained under wraps. "Did you find out anything about Cassidy?"

"Yes."

"Any idea where he is now?"

"Yeah, he's doing pretty good for himself. He's outside of Albany."

Albany was an easy two-hour car ride. "Has he got a job?"

"You might say that. He's the minister of one of those drive-in-and-get-blessed churches. Cassidy landed on his feet, alright. Just Google him."

"Google him?"

"He found God in prison. From what I gather, he's now Reverend Cassidy, a multi-millionaire from faith healing and Bible thumping as the founder of The Righteous Church of the Lord. You can see him every Sunday on cable TV."

"That's a big life-change."

Luke continued. "Sorry to tell you this, but he's not your killer. Records show he was still incarcerated on the day Flynn disappeared."

"Really?"

"As God is my witness."

Amen didn't feel like an appropriate response.

Chapter Thirty-one

With the born-again gym teacher out of the picture, I ignored Bruce's ultimatum once again. I was determined to interview the one remaining member of Flynn's gang. The last of the three, Denny Alantonio, sold real estate up and down the Hudson Valley. According to his advertisements plastered around town and in the newspaper, his niche was the second-home market, targeting rich city-dwellers yearning to breathe fresh, country air on the weekends.

It was Jeremy's idea to contact Denny about purchasing a home near Oak Falls.

"Remember, I offered to help you investigate." Some of his statement was muffled because he'd stuck his head in my fridge.

My boyfriend had been gone for the last five days. Determined to explore the newest avenues in his field, he'd scheduled multiple interviews with molecular anthropologists on the East Coast. Now that he was back in Oak Falls, we took up where we'd left off.

"Are you suggesting we play house?" I threw a shirt at him from the mound of laundry I was folding.

"Of course not. We should stick to our real stories, otherwise it gets confusing. This is a little too small for me, don't you think?" He wadded my clean shirt up into a ball and lobbed it back at me.

"Good. I don't need any more confusion in my life." With the last scrub top folded and ready to be put away, I plopped down next to him on the sofa.

"It isn't that bad an idea, Kate. We can look at houses and interview him all at the same time."

A ball whizzed by as he and Buddy began an indoor fetch game. My ecstatic pet zipped past the sofa, focused on the chase.

To prevent damage to my toes, I scooted my feet up out of danger.

"So I've got it all planned out. I'll tell him that Oak Falls is about an hour and forty-five minutes from my parents and I've been thinking about making a real estate investment. Something close to the city that I could rent out if necessary. The Hudson Valley area is perfect." He moved closer and put his arm around me.

"Well, don't do this for me."

"Hey, I'm always looking at property. You can quiz him to your heart's content about Flynn and I can evaluate the real estate market. I'll handle all the arrangements." He squeezed a little closer.

"Okay. You're on," I told him.

"That's not the only thing I hope to be on."

We were interrupted by Buddy jumping on the sofa between us with the forgotten toy in his mouth. His dark brown spaniel eyes begged us to continue his game. His partner in crime gladly tossed it across the room.

"So what's been happening while I was gone? Any more news about Angelica's murder?" Jeremy asked as he helped me carry the laundry over to the closet.

"Nope. Looks like her husband did her in."

"No surprise there," he said. "Sometimes we kill the ones we love."

Surprised by his statement, I frowned, puzzled by what he meant.

"Metaphorically speaking, I mean," he clarified to me. "Strictly metaphorically."

Since my only days off were on the weekends, Jeremy arranged to meet Denny on Sunday at nine o'clock in the morning to look at houses. To save time, instead of driving to his real estate office in Rhinebeck, we were meeting at the first of several properties he'd lined up.

Bright and early, at fifteen minutes past eight, my doorbell rang.

"Ready?" A big smile on Jeremy's face promised a fun day, as did the chocolate croissant and coffee cup in his hand.

"I am so ready now," I told him after taking a big bite of the pastry. "You are shamelessly bribing me, you realize."

Careful not to get any crumbs in the car, I eased into passenger seat. As soon as I had settled in, the big car took off.

"What kind of house did you tell him you wanted?" Once inside the car my attention became focused on directing some heat on my feet to keep them nice and toasty and drinking the coffee Jeremy had picked up for me. He'd put the address into the GPS before we left the animal hospital, so I wasn't exactly paying attention to where we were headed.

It was a beautiful day, clear but cold. The sun tried to warm things up a bit, but so far with no success. His Mercedes downshifted effortlessly as we climbed a hill, not rattling like the old truck I drove, making the drive very smooth.

"I told him I wanted something dramatic, open floor plan, stone fireplace, a couple of acres—river view—the usual."

"The usual? This is a first for me." Trees flashed by before we crested the hill and rounded a curve.

Jeremy slowed down. "What do you mean?"

"I've never looked at houses before." My confession embarrassed me a little. "Even in school I was always the one who answered the ad for a roommate. I'm only in this converted garage apartment because it came as part of the employment package."

"My little vagabond. Consider this a dry run." The GPS indicated a turn in one quarter of a mile.

"For you, maybe. I've got piles of student debt and no real credit rating to brag about."

"Hey, you've got your degree to bank on." He put his signal light on.

"Right. That's what I keep telling myself. Kate, eventually you will make money."

"Well, stick with me, then. All this could be yours, too." His tone was mocking but I wondered how much truth lay buried below the surface.

As the Mercedes glided cleanly around the curves in the road, I realized how different our lives and futures were. Did my college buddy ever worry about money or have to count coins to fill the gas tank? No. That part of his world was as smooth as the ride.

And the ride was smooth, indeed. Jeremy and the lifestyle he offered were a seductive package. The question was could I picture myself riding alongside him on a permanent basis?

As we pulled into the first property on the list, Denny got out of his Lexus to greet us. Close up, he turned out to be an older more sophisticated version of the teenager in the picture. Well-groomed, hair slicked back in a vaguely euro look, he exuded confidence. When Jeremy climbed out of the car, I noticed the real estate agent's eyes register the Rolex on his wrist, polished Italian leather boots, and of course, the Mercedes. After a brief glance at my Sears jacket, purchased on deep discount, and seven-year-old scuffed Frye boots, he focused his attention on the person with the money. Before showing us the house, though, he whipped out a broker representation agreement for Jeremy to sign. Once that was nailed down, Denny launched into his sales pitch.

While the two men went over all the features this first house had to offer, I lagged behind until their conversation became only background noise. No doubt about it, the house was gorgeous. I'd zoned out the outrageous asking price. Each room's high ceilings were defined by layers of thick crown molding. Elegant long windows at the front of the house framed strategically placed walkways and trees. As I caught up to Jeremy and Denny, I overheard snippets of sentences—former estate, small gatehouse, pool—until Jeremy gestured to me. Obediently, I took my place by his side, feigning interest in the wall colors.

"I've saved the best for last. Take a look." With a flourish Denny raised the floor-to-ceiling drapes in front of us to reveal an expansive bluestone patio with a slice of Hudson River-view.

"Spectacular." Jeremy opened the double French doors and we followed him outside to a welcome spot of unexpected sunshine. "Is there a survey that shows how far the property extends?"

"Certainly. I've got it in the information packet."

Being outdoors reminded me of the real reason we were here—not to buy a house, but to talk about Flynn. I interrupted the guys in the middle of a spirited discussion of current interest rates.

"Did you grow up around here, Mr. Alantonio?"

He blinked for a moment. I think he'd forgotten I was here.

"Please…call me Denny. Yes, indeed. Let's see, I was born on the other side of the river in Oak Falls, kind of that way." His finger pointed in a northwestern direction. "Lived along the river most of my life. Went away to college but came back because my roots are here." He made a dramatic gesture with his hands. "Deep roots."

"Deep roots," I repeated but without the hand movements. "When did you go off to college?"

"You're making me show my age." He appeared amused at my questions. "Graduated Oak Falls High School in June 2007. Entered the State University at New Paltz that September."

"Those were the days." Jeremy finally stopped running mortgage numbers and picked up the slack. "You can't beat old high school memories."

"That's true. Except when the deranged husband of one of your classmates kills his wife right in front of you," he chuckled. "No joke."

Why did it sound to me like he was boasting about Angelica's death?

Jeremy kept going. "It's been a bad couple of months for Oak Falls. You probably knew the fellow whose body was found in the woods."

For the first time, Denny didn't have a quick comeback.

"I'm sorry. We didn't mean to pry," I fibbed.

"Flynn Keegan was one of my closest friends." Denny paused, lowered his head somewhat dramatically, and continued. "He called me at my uncle's used car lot the day he disappeared to ask for a ride. I remember I was getting ready to test drive a Mustang convertible just brought in for a trade." His eyes shone as he described the car. "Cherry red metallic paint, white leather seats, a 1999 GT convertible. That thing flew down the road."

His best friend's death seemed to take a backseat to the memory of the Mustang.

"So what happened then?" Denny's alibi was the last one of the gang's I needed and I was anxious to hear it.

"Oh, yeah. I didn't have time to drive him all the way to Kingston. My uncle kept pretty close tabs on me back then."

"Not to mention the Mustang."

"That too. I'm embarrassed to say I got really pissed at him."

"You turned down his request for a ride," Jeremy said, unbuttoning his coat, "and you were pissed at him? That doesn't make any sense."

"I got pissed because all four of us, our gang, made this stupid pact to leave town together. Set out for the adventure of our lives." He laughed. "That's what Flynn called it—the adventure of our lives. Only it didn't turn out that way."

"What do you mean?" We sat down on the cold stone benches arranged in a semi-circle that looked out onto the river.

Denny stared out at the sun-speckled water. "Flynn decided to fly solo."

"Did you fellows blame him?" I really had no idea what Denny's answer would be.

"You bet we did. After he left, we cussed him out left and right, especially Nate. It wasn't just us, you know. He abandoned everyone—his family, his ex-girlfriend, the old ladies he did errands for. Everyone was furious that he didn't care enough to say a proper good-bye."

Looking out at the peaceful garden, something occurred to me. "Maybe Flynn thought you'd all try to stop him."

Anger spilled out this time, spoiling the agent's cool euro vibe.

"He would have been right. If the three of us could have kidnapped him and chained him up until we talked some sense into him, we would have." Suddenly he stopped and looked embarrassed at revealing so much to clients. Denny rose from the bench and made a big show of carefully brushing off his pants. "It's strange how important it seemed back then."

"High school days. What can you say?" Jeremy took my arm and together we strolled to the end of the patio and lingered for one last look at the view.

"Too bad the garden isn't in bloom." Denny gestured at a metal arbor walkway that led to a nearby fountain. "The flowers are gorgeous. By the end of the summer the arbor is covered with white roses."

Roses again, white roses for remembrance. Was the whole Hudson Valley full of roses?

The benches must not have been cleaned recently because our coats were covered with debris.

"So, Denny, how did you get into the real estate business?" Jeremy asked while I busied myself helping brush the dust off the back of his coat and trousers.

"That's a crazy story. The summer of my last year in college, I met a very pretty girl who was enrolled in real estate school, so I signed up for a six-week course to be near her. Long story short—I dumped the girl and landed a career."

"You're obviously successful," Jeremy commented. "What happened to the girl?"

"Oh, she married a friend of mine. Now they're living happily ever after. Not." He smiled at his own joke before playfully tapping Jeremy on the shoulder. Mr. Real Estate was back in control. "Let me show you the six-car garage. It's going to blow your mind."

The two guys started talking about cars. I followed behind again, thinking of what Denny had said.

A red Mustang convertible may have cost Flynn his life.

Chapter Thirty-two

House-hunting with Jeremy had been an eye-opener into a luxurious lifestyle I could only imagine. After seeing several homes, he whisked me away to dinner at a five-star restaurant on the river followed by a romantic interlude at his suite in the Stanton Inn. For someone like me who counted each dollar, it was a heady experience—like two planets colliding.

Predictably, on Monday morning I needed a jumpstart beginning with a strong cup of coffee. Jeremy begged off joining me on my house call appointments to get some additional sleep and catch up with his paperwork, so Mari and I again had the truck to ourselves. When my stethoscope, which was hanging off the rearview mirror hit me in the nose, I knew I was in for one of those days.

"So how was your weekend?" Mari waited for all the details but I wasn't playing that game.

"Dreamy." My off-the-top-of-my-head description surprised me because in so many ways that's exactly what it seemed like. A warm fuzzy dream that you don't want to end.

By the end of our shift I could also describe my workday as dreamy—in a bad dream way. At three o'clock when we started back to the hospital we'd been spit at multiple times by an annoyed llama; Mari sported a long scratch courtesy of an angry cat; and a nervous dog had taken a pee on my leg. In addition, I'd been unsuccessful in convincing a new client to run some much-needed blood work on her dog, and the truck got a flat tire. Our hopes for a short day evaporated when Cindy called us with an emergency.

"Guys, this owner called and is pretty sure her dog has popped a hernia. The condo complex she's in is on your way back. I'll text you the info."

A hernia can be fairly benign or a big deal, depending on what's inside it. Sometimes loops of intestines become trapped in the hernia pouch, requiring surgery. I wiped the thought of a nice hot bath out of my mind and told Cindy to call the client and tell her we were on our way. Mari entered the address in our GPS and pulled out a bag of potato chips to tide her over.

The address turned out to be in one of the buildings closest to the road. Before we got out of the truck, a ground-floor unit door flung open and an expensively dressed young woman with a fluffy white dog ran frantically down the walkway.

"Are you the vet?" As Mari and I gathered our equipment, I noticed she'd been in such a hurry, she hadn't even put on a coat.

"Yes, I'm Dr. Turner and this is my assistant, Mari. Come on, let's get both of you inside." We hustled out of the cold and stepped into a small entryway. The girl shut and locked the door, indicating for us to wipe our feet before gathering in the stylish living room. Our client definitely had modern tastes, evidenced by her choice of a sleek black leather sofa on stainless-steel legs paired with two pod-like armchairs. The semi-shag area rug sprouted like grass under our feet.

"Do you have a table we can use for the exam, Ms....?" I realized I didn't know her name.

"Faith Snyder. And this is my sweet little Princess." The cute dog in her arms stuck a pink tongue out at us as it wiggled with excitement. Her loving owner covered her with kisses.

Mari must have spied something to use because her question came right on the heels of Faith's doggie introduction. "There's a table in the next room. If you get a sheet or blanket, we can use that."

"Is it going to be messy?" The owner's eyes darted back and forth between us.

I tried to reassure her. "It shouldn't be. This is only a preliminary exam. Princess looks quite comfortable at the moment."

The patient wagged her tail and entertained us with a series of sharp yips. "Alright, let me get something." Faith and Princess disappeared for a short while and when they returned the dog was under one arm and a folded pad was under the other.

"Will this do?" We had now moved into a small dining room with a glass-topped table and four Lucite chairs. A blue folder lay on one of the seats. "Here's her shot record from when I adopted her."

I took a quick look to make sure the dog was up-to-date on everything. "Great. We'll enter all of this into our computer at the end of the exam."

Mari made room and placed the pad down to protect the table and give Princess a non-slip surface to stand on while I opened my veterinary bag. The general exam was unremarkable until I asked Faith where the hernia was.

"On her tummy."

We gently turned Princess on her side and separated her long fluffy hair.

"I Googled all her symptoms and Google said she had an umbilical hernia," Faith's voice rang out confidently. "Umbilical means where her belly button is."

Mari rolled her eyes.

One quick glance confirmed my diagnosis. "Well, the good new is Princess doesn't have a hernia."

"Are you sure?" This time her owner's tone sounded more belligerent. With a beautifully manicured finger she pointed at her dog. "Then what's that?"

Mari's eyes rolled again. Thankfully, Faith's attention was focused elsewhere.

"That," I explained, "is completely normal. Princess is a boy."

"What?" Faith continued pointing at her now obviously excited pet.

"Princess is a boy dog, not a girl dog."

"What?"

"She's a dude." Mari's blunt explanation didn't help. "Definitely a dude."

We rolled Princess back on his four feet. Faith protectively scooped her baby back into her arms.

"Someone made a mistake when Princess was a puppy and wrote down female in the records instead of male," I explained, as gently as possible. "It happens more frequently than you might think. He was neutered before you adopted him so you never saw any testicles. What you think is a hernia is his penis coming out of the sheath."

Faith looked horrified. "But she can't be a boy. She doesn't lift her leg."

Mari busied cleaning up while I broke the news. "Some young male dogs don't lift their legs right away."

A wistful expression shone in Faith's eyes when she gazed at the two pink polka-dot bows clipped behind the ears of her little Princess. "But I bought her a tutu for Christmas."

"Is it pink?"

"Yes."

"Well…" I thought for a moment. "I'm sure he will look beautiful in it."

"Dr. Google strikes again." Mari slammed the passenger side door and stowed away my bag. The truck engine roared to life. I set the heat on high and wiped off the film of humidity that had built up on the windows.

"Now, Mari, you can't fault people for trying to understand a problem. The Internet is a great information source." Finished with my lecture, I added, "However, at least in veterinary medicine, nothing beats experience and a hands-on exam."

After waiting for a car to pass, we carefully pulled away from the curb and started back toward the animal hospital.

A minute later, though, I couldn't help but laugh. "By the way, thanks."

"For what?" Mari looked up from her keyboard.

"She's a dude. When you said that, I thought I'd crack up." Our much-needed laughter rang in the enclosed cab. "That was classic, Mari. Simply classic."

● ● ● ● ●

Alone in the apartment after the staff had gone, I found myself staring once again at the picture of Flynn and his buddies. I'd now spoken to all three members of Flynn's gang: Nate, Denny, and Rusty. In the quarry photograph, Rusty stood next to Flynn, same general build and height. However, as in my dream, one of them shone as bright as the sun while the other paled in comparison like the moon. Side by side, they stood. Red hair and faded blue eyes in an ordinary face contrasted with Flynn's streaky blond hair and azure eyes in a movie-star face you couldn't forget.

Rusty had stayed the course and become the third generation of Lieberman doctors, arguably the most successful of the group.

Nate had fared the worst—overweight, possibly alcoholic, he reminded me of someone who had given up. Did he see a lonely future of stocking shelves and hitting the bars stretching endlessly before him?

And what about real estate mogul Denny Alantonio? To all appearances, he was the least affected by his friend's death. Flynn's tragic tale was eagerly told to us to create sympathy in the buyer. Was he willing to use anything, however personal, as a sales ploy to ingratiate himself? Perhaps, but from what I saw, the anger he tried to hide appeared real.

The good old high school gang. If you asked them if they were happy, what would they say? Did they regret their life choices? Flynn was their catalyst. Without him, California had faded into the distance.

Only Flynn had shown the courage to throw everything aside and follow his dreams—and look what it got him.

Chapter Thirty-three

It was Friday afternoon at the Oak Falls Animal Hospital and the smell of hot cheese and tomato sauce overpowered all other odors. Massive quantities of free pizza served as the big incentive not to miss our once-a-month staff meeting.

Like everyone else, I'd hit the pizza and hit it hard. Our office meetings always managed to be a welcome diversion.

"Okay, everyone. Quiet down, please." Cindy, our unflappable office manager, had an agenda in her hand and she was going to read it, whether we liked it or not.

"First, I'd like to remind all of you to park in the back parking lot, please, and leave the front parking for clients." Cindy tried hard not to look at any one person when she made her pronouncement, but all eyes in the room became glued on Nick Pappadopolis. Our weekend tech was notorious for pulling his car as close to the main door as possible.

Nick responded by standing up and bowing to everyone. "Hey, sometimes I forget."

I could attest to that since one Saturday I watched him tear into the parking lot only seconds before his shift started, looking like he'd been out partying all night. Our popular college student had an enviable and active social life yet still managed to stay in the top ten percent of his class.

Mr. Katt briefly jumped up on one of the chairs to sniff the pepperoni pizza. Every meeting he did the same thing and always ended up disappointed. Pepperoni was too spicy for his tastes.

In a huff he sauntered across the floor, tail high, implying that he was the only true gourmet in the whole place.

Meanwhile, Cindy reported some esoteric problems she'd found in our veterinary software program that no one cared about. When she finished, Mari raised her hand.

"Did you order the new uniforms yet?"

An audible groan rose from the group. This was an ongoing discussion among the staff. Trying to decide what color to order had taken months. A fierce debate had broken out on whether part-time employee votes counted the same as full-time and the fight got down and dirty. I wondered if Dr. Rusty's color-coordinated staff members were given any choice of uniform colors or if that decision went directly to management. Maybe I could ask Shiloh the next time I saw her.

As always, Cindy remained an oasis of calm. "Thank you, Mari, for bringing that up. It's on today's agenda. I've gotten the okay from Doc Anderson, who sends his greetings from Easter Island, by the way. He's approved the expenditure. Now," she looked down at her notes, "the majority of you chose the stone-gray color."

Heads nodded. So far, so good.

"I just need to know if you want the poly blend or the new comfy cotton blend that breathes better but might wrinkle a little more."

I groaned and put my hands over my face.

Fifteen minutes later, Cindy halted the heated argument that had erupted. "Sorry, everyone, but we don't have time to discuss this further. I'll get samples of both types in our chosen color and put them in the break room for you try on."

A sort of huff of approval greeted her solution.

Mari raised her hand again. No surprise. Mari raised her hand at every meeting.

Cindy still managed a smile. "Yes, Mari?"

"Are we still trying to find a home for Spider-Guy?"

This was another ongoing issue. Our in-house tarantula and his gigantic wood-and-glass habitat needed to find a good home.

When his owner moved out of state, the staff accepted him for adoption and assumed it would be easy to place him. That was nine months ago.

Feeling it was my duty, I offered some thoughts. "I was going to suggest we contact the local schools. Also, we could put something up in the waiting room for clients to see."

"Already did that. No go." Cindy seemed resigned to being foster mommy to a spider.

I tried again. "What about contacting the media and asking them to run a story about him?"

"Didn't we do that six months ago?" Mari stopped, deep in thought. "I guess it wouldn't hurt to try again."

"Good job. I've some names in my public relations file." Cindy beamed at all of us as though we were kindergarteners who had finally stopped wiggling around and were sitting up straight. "I think we got a lot done this time. Congratulations."

Sensing the meeting was about to end, Nick hastened over to the stack of pizza boxes and piled three more pieces on his plate.

"Well, if that's—" Cindy's comment was interrupted by Eugene, our kennel helper, who raised his arm and pointed straight upwards.

All eyes lifted, including Mr. Katt's wary cat eyes. Strolling on the ceiling in a leisurely tarantula style was Spider-Guy. This was the second time he'd escaped during a meeting. Captivated, we watched him crawl over the automatic sprinkler in the ceiling.

Nick began to snicker. Mari cast him a suspicious look.

I could see what struck Nick as funny. By some optical illusion it appeared Spider-Guy was giving the staff a rather rude gesture with three of his eight hairy legs.

Chapter Thirty-four

After another long and stressful workday on Friday, Mari and I decided to run into town for brownies and hot chocolate. Jeremy was stuck in the city for the next few days so it was easy for me to justify a sugary frenzy. Since I needed to change clothes and walk Buddy, Mari left a few minutes before me. We'd decided the perfect rendezvous was at Judy's Place in the village.

By the time I got there Mari, firmly ensconced at a table by the window, was busy people-watching.

"I'm so ready for this," she told me.

"Me too," I confessed.

After a few minutes, our server appeared. Mari decided to go crazy and opted for extra whipped cream and sprinkles on both her hot chocolate and brownie. "Thank goodness this week is over. I'm planning to sleep for the next two days. What are you doing this weekend?"

The waitress came with our drinks, which prevented me from answering her right away. One sip made everything all right. Sometimes a girl needs a bucketful of chocolate to smooth the way.

"Paperwork." After another blissful sip, I explained, "Everyone wants me to wrap up this whole Flynn investigation and put it away. After talking to Luke and Gramps, I realize it was probably hopeless right from the get-go."

"Mmmmm." My technician nodded in agreement and started in on the brownie.

As we ate, I gazed out the window. The village was moderately busy for a winter Friday, with scattered groups of tourists strolling past. Across from us, a few cars were stopped, waiting for a coveted parking space right on Main Street. Relaxed at last, I secretly felt relieved to put the investigation aside. Maybe Jeremy might want to go on a ski weekend when he got back.

Mari scooped the last bit of whipped cream off her drink. "You know, I had high hopes in the beginning, but now…now I guess I feel like you. But, Kate, don't feel bad because I know you did your best."

"Thanks." I glanced out the window again. "Nobody likes to fail, although I'm coming to terms with it. Don't think I'm crazy, Mari, but I got so desperate, I asked Flynn to help me."

She looked up from her plate, a puffball of whipped cream on her upper lip. "Didn't Mrs. Vandersmitt tell you she channeled Flynn's spirit and his spirit didn't care if the murderer ever was caught?"

"Yes."

She drew a circle around the side of her head with her fork. "And you think you're the crazy one?"

Feeling slightly guilty and a little nauseous after my chocolate indulgence, I waved good-bye to Mari and walked to the truck. On the way, I passed a group of teenagers huddled together laughing and smoking outside a mini-mart. It was easy to spot Fiona in her Goth get-up. When she saw me, I nodded and kept going. To my surprise, she called my name.

We walked together several feet away from her friends before she spoke.

"Bruce ordered us not to talk to you." She kept her head down, mumbling, shuffling her feet back and forth.

"I thought he might do that. Don't worry about it." This kid had enough guilt to deal with. I wasn't going to add to it.

"Right." Anger came off her like heat waves, almost scorching me.

"Fiona…"

"Flynn was the brave one," she suddenly cried out. "I'm not brave like him. He always watched out for me. When they teased me in school, he came to the rescue. I miss my big brother." Tears, long held back, streaked down her face. "He at least tried to get away, but I can't. I'm such a coward. *A stupid coward*," she whispered.

I reached out to comfort her but she pulled away.

• • ● • •

Pockets of mist hung over the road as I drove out of town and got thicker the closer I got to home. My heart ached for Fiona. I knew how it felt to be alone in the world.

By the time I got to the turn-in to the animal hospital parking lot, the truck was barely crawling. The beams from my headlights bounced right back at me. With visibility so limited, I missed seeing a late-night visitor until I opened the truck door and stepped onto the asphalt.

Startled, I stopped, before taking a step backwards, my keys tight in my hand.

Someone dressed in black waited in the mist near my apartment door. I noticed the glow of a cigarette and faint reflections from the chrome of a motorcycle.

"Can I help you?" I didn't see any animal with him so I doubted this was a business call. Acrid smoke drifted over his head. I slipped my left hand into my jacket pocket. No pepper spray.

He tossed the cigarette down and stomped it out using the steel-tipped toe of his leather boot. "You the vet who's been asking questions about Flynn?"

"Yes." I moved slightly to the right to activate the automatic light mounted high on the hospital wall.

The sudden brightness made him squint.

For the first time I got a good look at him. The distinctive do-rag and his general appearance gave him away. "Weren't you at Flynn's memorial service?" This was the sickly older man who had been at our table talking to Flynn's grandmother. "I'm sorry, but I didn't catch your name that day."

"People used to call me 'D.'"

"Diablo?" The name slipped out. From the past, he'd materialized into the now. That story Henry James, my baking biker client, had told me of a monster named Diablo almost kicking his friend to death reverberated in my memory. Except this frail man was a far cry from any nightmare. Was I in danger? Should I jump back into my truck and take off?

His gruff voice, hoarse from decades of smoking, broke the silence. "Please don't be afraid. I've got some information for you about Flynn Keegan."

"Okay." I kept my distance, still weighing my options.

He coughed in the dampness, the rattle coming from deep in his lungs. The spasm went on for at least a minute, with Diablo doubled over, a tissue pressed to his mouth. When he caught his breath, he explained. "Between the cancer and being on dialysis, I barely have the energy to get on my bike these days. Henry James told me where I could find you. Said you were good folks, said you'd listen to me, which is more than the cops would."

Diablo's eyes were tired and even in the dim light the whites glowed yellow with jaundice. Leather pants that appeared two or three sizes too big drooped on his thin frame. Bony wrists exposed by his jacket sleeves glistened as pale as my sheets.

Curiosity got the best of me. "Alright. But let's make this quick." I tried to sound business-like and hoped I wasn't making a big mistake.

Too weak to take off his coat, Diablo sat at my kitchen table, a cup of coffee in one hand, the other hand stroking Buddy's fur. As I poured myself some water, he told me his story.

"Back in 2007, I was raging at the world. Living on the loose, high on meth and pills and anything else I could get. I'd beat you up if you looked at me wrong."

So far, so bad.

"Someone told me Flynn had messed with my girlfriend, so I got him alone one night in town after he left his shift at that Chinese restaurant."

"Go on."

"Funny thing, though. The kid wasn't afraid of me—told me flat-out I was wrong about the woman, then asked me if I'd served in Afghanistan. Talked about his dad and how he died. Told me I needed to get my life back in shape for myself, my family, and all the troops who hadn't made it home."

He took a long sip from his mug.

"Reminded me of a buddy I served with."

I noticed the hands that held the coffee trembled. While I watched, he reached into his pocket and pulled out an amber medication bottle. He shook out two pills before using the coffee to wash them down.

"When was this?"

He grimaced for a moment, like the pills tasted bitter. "Best I can remember, we talked back in late February, early March some time in 2007."

That corresponded with Flynn's senior year in high school. How did Diablo's story fit in with the victim's disappearance in August?

"What happened next?"

"I checked myself into the V.A. and got help. This time rehab worked but only because other medical stuff had caught up with me. The doctors diagnosed me with hepatitis C. My blood pressure also read crazy-high, and that had affected my kidneys. Anyway, I went home to Rhinebeck, cleaned up my act, and started working at a friend's garage. I've been mostly straight ever since, except for a little weed."

I nodded along, not sure what this confession had to do with Flynn.

"Last month I got diagnosed with liver cancer—already spread into my lungs and lymph nodes." His face looked resigned, like he'd come to terms with his fate.

"I'm so sorry." Socially correct words but always inadequate.

He cracked his knuckles, then continued. "Just want to live out what time I have in peace, which brings me to Flynn. After I got out of rehab, I decided to look him up and thank the kid. See if he needed anything. That was in August 2007. I was in

Judy's Place eating lunch when out of the corner of my eye I saw him get into a car."

His words startled me. Had Diablo seen Flynn's murderer?

"What kind of car was it?"

"Don't remember. Something sporty, I think."

Sporty? Denny was driving a red Mustang convertible that afternoon.

"Then I saw him again."

That confused me. "What do you mean you saw him again?"

He shifted in his seat. "There was a big bike rally near Saugerties that weekend. On my way out of town, I passed someone on the side of the road by the traffic circle. He had a backpack on and looked like he was hitching."

"So the first car must have dropped him off."

"Must have. Didn't realize it was the kid standing there until I passed by, so I doubled back, you know, to talk to him."

My mind played the scene in my head.

"But before I got there, some guy with an SUV pulled up."

All my senses went on high alert. "Can you describe him?"

"A white guy, maybe in his twenties or early thirties, with sunglasses and a baseball cap. He lifted the tailgate and put Flynn's backpack next to a suitcase, then slammed it closed. I veered off since they were on the road toward Kingston and I needed to go in the other direction."

"Do you recall what time that happened?"

"Friday, August 10, mid-afternoon. I remember because after I said hi to some buddies at the rally, I met up with my old lady at the Forever Flowers shop in Rhinebeck, where she works. I surprised her as she was closing up around five, and asked her to marry me. Figured I could skip buying her flowers that way."

He punctuated his joke with a weak chuckle.

"Next time I drove into Oak Falls, I asked the kid in the Country Store where I could find Flynn and he told me he'd up and gone to California. I ate some ice cream and headed back home to Rhinebeck. That's it until I read about his remains being found."

"Okay. Can you remember the make of the car he got into or the color?"

"Sorry." His voice had faded a bit. "Before I came over here, I wracked what little brain I have left and the only image is a vague impression of an SUV of some kind."

"Could it have been a Jeep?"

"Maybe. I don't rightly know. The whole thing lasted maybe a minute or two."

My mind started putting everything together. Diablo saw an SUV driven by a young guy. Rusty drove a Jeep that summer. What about the sporty car picking Flynn up outside of Judy's Restaurant? Denny told us he test-drove a Mustang that day.

Did they both lie to me? Could the quiet doctor and the real estate agent have killed their best friend?

After Diablo left I went back to my murder board, reenergized. Sure enough, it all fit. Restaurant owner Judy had mentioned to Luke about the weekend motorcycle rally and noticed bikers cruising along Main Street the last time she'd seen Flynn. Rusty drove that famous sweet ride, the Jeep from his parents, so it would be natural for Flynn to ask either him or Denny for a lift to the bus stop in Kingston.

Piecing together what happened next would be the hardest thing to do. Rusty wasn't the only person in the Hudson Valley who drove a Jeep back then and there were always plenty of sport cars and SUVs cruising along country roads in the summertime. Going back over Diablo's story, I realized I'd forgotten an important item. As far as I knew, no backpack had been recovered at the burial site. What did the killer do with it?

And there was another thing. Diablo said he saw a suitcase in the back of the SUV. If the driver was Rusty, had he planned on leaving with Flynn? Or were we back to a stranger passing through town, a predator searching for prey?

I glanced at my watch. Ten o'clock. Rusty's office was closed. I wasn't sure if it would be open on Saturday, but I left a message for him to call me as soon as possible. The only number I had for Denny was the real estate office, so I left a message there too. Maybe one of them saw someone pulled over at the traffic circle. Before I jumped to conclusions, I needed to get all the various facts straight.

My imagination started spinning dangerously out of control. I texted Luke:

> Need to talk to you. Tomorrow OK?

His answer was immediate:

> On Duty near U. See U in 5.

• • ● •• •

Ten minutes later we were arguing.

"Alright. So what you're telling me is that Denny and Rusty both lied…"

"Well, they left out details." I still wasn't sure they weren't honest mistakes.

Luke glared at me, strangely annoyed for some reason. "Whatever. Anyway, according to this guy Diablo, both of them may have changed their stories about the last time they saw Flynn. Correct?"

"Correct." Perhaps discussing this now wasn't such a good idea. My police officer friend had been upset since the moment he'd shown up at my door.

"If we believe this Diablo guy, it leaves Flynn outside town hitchhiking into Kingston to the bus terminal. Enter the unknown suspect in the SUV."

"A stranger?" Involuntarily, my hands rubbed my eyes. "That doesn't account for the roses on the gravesite or the place he was buried. How could some stranger stumble on that spot? I've driven that road. It isn't well marked and you'd need a truck or SUV to get up there in one piece."

We both got it at the same time.

"What was Denny driving?" Luke took a step toward my murder board.

"A Mustang convertible."

"No way that thing could get up there."

Of course, Luke was right. "So that leaves…Rusty. He was driving his Jeep that day."

We both moved in front of the corkboard. "Let's see. Rusty was helping his mom with yard work, so he might have had a shovel with him. Maybe Denny dropped Flynn off and went back to the car dealership. Rusty came by, persuaded him to go up to their favorite clearing one last time. They fought. He hit him with the shovel, then buried the body."

"Complete supposition. There's no evidence to support that theory. In fact, it's more likely he was killed somewhere else and the body moved to the burial site." Luke rearranged Flynn's gang on the board. "I could make a case for Evelyn Vandersmitt picking him up and going into the woods for one last quickie. She drove a Jeep back then, too."

"Please, let's get real here."

"You want real?" Luke raised his voice. "It makes more sense to suspect Diablo, a known criminal, of lying to you, concocting a story to divert our attention—when what he really did that day was grab Flynn and bash his brains in. The rosebush you put so much faith in might well have been planted back in the 1800s—leftover from some settler's homestead that the forest reclaimed."

The more he talked, the worse I felt.

Luke picked up the photo of Flynn I kept on the card table along with my markers and pins. "You know, less than two-thirds of murders in the United States are solved. One third of killers literally get away with their crimes. This is one of them."

"Okay. You've made your point."

He hovered over me, angry face set in a scowl. "Gather all your stuff together and give it to the investigators, Kate. Let the professionals do their job."

"All right, all right. I'll bring everything over to the station next week."

After one last look at Flynn's picture he put it back down and turned to go.

Before he could reach the door, I asked, "Luke, you're a police officer. How do you stand those statistics?"

My question caught him up short. When his answer finally came, it sounded clipped and to the point. "You do the best you can. That's all you can do. Accept failures and celebrate success." I heard him take a short breath. "The cases keep coming and coming and coming, no matter what you do. Domestic violence, child abuse, hit-and-run—you name it."

He buttoned up his coat, ready to leave. Our constant bickering was getting us nowhere. His foul mood filled the room.

"I'm glad I work with animals," I fired back at him before he opened the door.

When he spoke, his words gave me the chills.

"You forget, Kate. I work with animals, too."

Luke's visit upset me. I took one last look at the murder board before turning in that night. My gut told me Diablo was telling the truth, but what good was an eyewitness who couldn't remember any important details? I'd promised Luke I'd finish up and turn everything over to the police, and I intended to keep that promise.

One of my Post-it notes had fallen on the floor—Gramps' suggestion to check out the memorabilia left at the original burial site. I tore off a piece of scotch tape, stuck it up and took a step back. The board bristled with notes and drawings and arrows ultimately pointing...nowhere.

I found it hard to admit there would be no justice for this victim.

I also found it unexpectedly hard to say good-bye to Flynn.

Chapter Thirty-five

Saturday turned out to be one of those days that made me wish I could crawl right back into bed. Two weeks before Halloween and the lousy weather had turned extra nasty. Cold gusts of air loaded with stinging ice particles promised snow on the way. No matter how many layers I put on it still didn't seem like enough. The damp cold went straight to my bones.

My staff straggled in with dour looks on their faces. Mari headed right for the coffee, even before she took off her coat. With several sick animals in the hospital I figured the team would work hard this morning so I decided to try to raise everyone's spirits. "Pizza for lunch, my treat."

Instead of the usual cheer, my announcement barely got a grunt.

Cindy arrived, the only dry one in the group since her car had every bad weather item you could think of conveniently packed in the backseat. She immediately took over the pizza order.

"If anyone wants anything other than cheese and pepperoni, let me know."

Finally, I saw a few smiles spread around after wet clothes and shoes were taken care of and the staff gradually warmed up. Even Mr. Katt tried to help by climbing into every convenient lap and depositing a warm layer of cat hair on each unsuspecting target.

Before we got started for the day Cindy asked everyone to gather round.

"I'm not sure if we'll be open on Monday because of the storm. You all will be getting a group text so keep your phones handy. Meanwhile, enjoy your time off with pay."

A short round of applause greeted her announcement.

"Oh, one more quick reminder for this weekend," I said. "You all know that I made a report to state authorities about the bear Mari and I saw at Crazy Carl's place up near Sheckter's Ridge. Long story short—this guy, Carl, was trying to illegally exhibit a wild bear on his farm. He let it go before the authorities could get out there and take possession."

"Another one of his get-rich schemes," Mari added.

"The Department of Environmental Conservation just got back to me. So far, they haven't had any luck tracking the bear."

"What's the problem? Isn't that a good thing that he let it go?" Nick flashed a big smile at everyone.

My technician looked like she wanted to hit him over the head.

"This poor bear may have diminished hunting skills. Releasing him into the wild was as irresponsible as keeping him chained up."

"Is the bear dangerous?" Cindy asked. "Should we warn our clients to be careful?"

All eyes turned back to me. "Black bears normally aren't very aggressive but it's had a bad experience with people. Crazy Carl thought he could teach him tricks by beating him and withholding food, so it might have very unpredictable behavior around humans and their pets." I let that sink in for a minute. What this animal had been subjected to turned my stomach.

"So," I continued, "I think we should e-mail all our clients with an advisory and the link to the New York State DEC website. Remind them to walk their dogs on leashes for now—and that includes all of you and your friends. Oh, and Cindy, please contact Samantha Miller in particular and tell her not to let her big Malamute, Jack, run around in the woods behind her house. Their place is pretty close to Sheckter's Ridge."

"Will do."

"Good news is that when the snow comes, it's likely the bear will search for a place to hold up and hibernate. However, I'd still be careful hiking or snowshoeing for the next few weeks."

"I'm staying in until spring," Cindy said with an exaggerated shiver that made us all laugh.

"I'd like to put a chain on Carl and see how he likes it," Mari announced, anger in her voice.

"My sympathy is definitely with the bear," I agreed. Before we went back to work I had one more reminder for the staff.

"Remember, if you do encounter a bear, don't run away from it. It's a race that you're bound to lose."

Because of the upcoming storm most of our appointments had canceled. Our only house call was a big litter of golden retriever puppies—which made Mari and me very happy. Playing with puppies and kittens is good for the soul.

Once we arrived at the big farmhouse not too far from the office we got right down to business.

All eight in this litter had new homes and would be ready to go at ten weeks of age. Doreen Merced, the breeder, preferred to give her gang a few extra weeks of doggie and human socialization before letting them go, which certainly was a good idea, in my opinion.

Kneeling down in a sea of wiggling puppy bodies made me forget all my worries. Doreen had made our job easier by assigning each puppy a different-colored collar. Sitting quietly I watched the brothers and sisters interact with each other to evaluate their personalities and places in the group dynamics.

I scooped up a little female with a pink collar. "Let's start with this one," I told Mari.

"Great." She opened the laptop and sat down at Doreen's kitchen table. "Ready when you are."

Through trial and error we had found this was the most efficient way to keep track of multiple exams. Not only would I supply a medical history but I'd also try to ascribe a preliminary personality assessment to the puppy. Thanks to Mari, everything went into each individualized computer record that I'd review back at the hospital.

But first I wanted to sniff puppy fur and sweet puppy breath. The little female obliged with a quick lick on the cheek.

I rolled the golden puff of fur over on her back and held her there with the palm of my hand. She stared up at me making no effort to move. However, as soon as I withdrew my hand she stood up and licked my fingers.

As I examined her I called out my results to Mari. "Heart and lungs, fine. Teeth and gums normal. Bite excellent. Pupils responsive. Ear canals clean. Nails and feet normal, body confirmation good. Umbilicus healed. Temp normal." Hugging the puppy close I distracted her with a rub on the ear before using my smallest needle to administer the booster vaccination. Then, after a quick kiss to the top of her silky head, I put her down. Unlike human medical doctors, veterinarians had no restrictions on kissing their furry clients.

Immediately the puppy scampered back to her brothers and sisters. "Healthy puppy. She's got a balanced personality and would make an excellent family dog."

"Got it." Mari typed with one finger while shooing off a pair of puppies attacking her shoelaces. "Next?"

We worked our way through the litter, finding one Alpha personality attached to the largest male and one female who seemed a bit shy. To her credit, Doreen had already noted those traits but we spent additional time discussing methods of building confidence in the shy puppy and reining in the male who thought he was king of the world.

"I wish all breeders were like you, Doreen," I said truthfully, as I observed Goldie, the mom of the group. Watching from the safety of an armchair another member of the family, a large Siamese cat, stared down at the puppies probably hoping they'd disappear.

"That's Simon," Doreen said. "He and Goldie are best friends. The puppies know they can't boss him around."

Before we left we checked each baby golden to make sure there were no adverse reactions to their shots. Simon washed his face and ignored us.

"I'm glad to see the litter gets to interact with a feline who is comfortable around dogs. That makes it easier if their permanent homes include any cats."

The whole gang of golden retrievers followed us to the door but stopped abruptly at the baby gate set up in the hallway.

Everyone's tail wagged a happy good-bye.

I wished I had a tail to wag back at them.

By the time we closed up at two, the entire staff was eager to go home. The big snowstorm loomed over everyone's weekend plans. All my patients had gone home, including the senior citizen doggy in early congestive heart failure. We'd spent a good hour reviewing cardiac disease, explaining each medication. I had given them my number and the emergency clinic's number in case of a problem. Once Cindy closed up, the hospital became terribly quiet. I felt uneasy there, not quite ready to call it a day. I'd gotten very comfortable having Jeremy around and I missed him.

A quick inventory of my fridge showed I needed eggs, milk, English muffins, and a bunch of other things plus Buddy's favorite canned food. Since I'd likely be cooped up in the apartment for the next few days I looked forward to getting out, even if it was only to the grocery store.

The wind had died down but the still cold air wasn't much of an improvement. Dialing the heat up to max in the truck left my mind free to hypothesize about Flynn's mysterious disappearance and to run in useless circles. I'd left messages for Denny and Nate to confirm any part of Diablo's story. This morning I'd called Rusty's office again and left a second message on his voice mail. The only phone number I had for Evelyn Vandersmitt was routed through the high school, so I had no idea if she would get it. What really had me spinning like a top was wondering if Diabolo's entire story was a lie.

Had his hard-luck story duped me as Luke suspected it had?

When I pulled into the parking lot I was surprised at the number of people shopping. The aisles were jammed with seniors, rambunctious families, and harried singles grabbing things off the shelves in preparation for the storm. A few bikers in chaps mixed with the crowd, loading up their carts with breakfast cereal and cases of beer. A frowning Nate Porter from the Country Store walked right past me with a flashlight and handful of batteries, concentrating so hard he didn't even see me.

From the end of the bread aisle Flynn's stepfather, Bruce, glared at me, then said, "Couldn't leave well enough alone, Doc. She's leaving, thanks to you." He looked like he wanted to ram me with his cart.

That encounter caused me inadvertently to back into an employee stacking Halloween candy around a blowup ghoul. When my elbow brushed an orange bowl decorated with a spider web it cackled, "Beware."

What was Bruce talking about? No way was I going to chase him down and find out. Tonight I'd call Mari and get all the details.

Aimlessly moving through the store I added more and more stuff to my cart. Jugs of water, matches, cans of soup, and the store's last rotisserie chicken crowded in together, piling in beside corn chips and nacho cheese. The hospital had an emergency generator so I wasn't too worried about a power outage. Shifting through a stack of DVDs on sale I bought an old Audrey Hepburn movie, *Breakfast at Tiffany's*, before backtracking and adding a few bottles of wine and two gallons of ice cream. Now fully prepared for any emergency I steered my cart toward the crowded checkout line.

Bruce, thankfully, was nowhere in sight.

"Hi, Kate."

I turned to see Shiloh, Rusty's fiancée, next to me, her cart mirroring mine. "Hi. I'm glad I'm not the only one who makes last-minute grocery runs."

"Are you kidding? I've seen half the town here. I was just chatting with Evelyn Vandersmitt, my old English teacher, over by the frozen foods."

We jockeyed into position in the long line. A big guy wearing a motorcycle helmet pushed in directly behind us. Only two cashiers were open and both appeared harried. Our line stalled when a woman in red sweatpants pulled out a huge wad of coupons. The person standing next to her groaned with frustration.

"Looks like we'll be here a while," I told Shiloh.

"It figures. I've been so busy at the office I forgot to stock up. I'm usually much more organized than this." She glanced around as though looking for someone. "So, are you going back to your place and waiting out the storm with your friend Jeremy?"

"Don't I wish?" We both moved our carts forward. "He's in the city on business so I'm on my own until Monday."

"The ice cream will help." She pointed to my cart and laughed.

The man behind her edged a bit closer. I had the uncomfortable feeling he was listening to our conversation.

"Shoot." I'd just remembered something. "When is the snow expected to start?"

"I think they said about five or six tonight. I can check the weather on my phone if you want." She reached into her pocket and opened her cell.

"Never mind. Darn. I was hoping not to have to go out again."

The line continued to inch forward.

"Why would you need to go out?" Shiloh asked.

I hesitated for a moment. "It's nothing. I was going to run up and take pictures of the memorial that's sprung up for Flynn."

Shiloh looked alarmed. "Pictures, in this weather? Don't the police have all of that stuff?"

Again I got the impression motorcycle helmet dude was eavesdropping. "I'm not sure. But by tonight the woods will be covered with snow." I'd finally reached the cashier and started placing my items on the conveyor belt.

"Well, don't get stuck up there." Shiloh put the divider between our items and began unloading her cart.

Once again I glanced back at the biker guy next to her. Odd he didn't remove his helmet in the store. Maybe he had dashed in for only a few items, because all he had in his hands was a roll of duct tape and a bottle of Jack Daniels.

What kind of weekend had he planned?

It would, of course, be easier and smarter to stay in my warm apartment and eat ice cream. However, once I got back home, my restlessness didn't go away. If I had to analyze it, Luke standing in front of the murder board shooting down all my theories may have been the cause.

Both Gramps and Jeremy had said that memorial might be important. I looked out the window. The sky was pale gray but no snow had fallen. A trip up to the gravesite would only take about twenty minutes each way. What the heck, photos of the memorial were the only item left to do before I handed everything over to Luke. At least he couldn't say I hadn't been thorough.

"Buddy," I told my dog, "I'll be right back. Guard the hospital."

Outside the sheet-metal gray sky blocked the sunlight, allowing only a few small patches of blue to peek out. I could smell snow coming in the heavy air. Periodic gusts of wind whistled through the trees. I started the truck and set out for the woods behind Samantha's house where Flynn's body had been discovered. The roads were crowded with people trying to finish their last-minute chores before the storm hit.

Between the music blaring from the local radio station and thinking about making nachos, I almost passed the dirt forestry road that took me closest to Flynn's grave. Tires bounced while navigating the bumpy road. My back and side windows steamed up despite the defroster blasting. A branch scratched across the passenger's side causing an eerie fingernail on blackboard sound. Just past the fence the road veered off to the right but I parked in a forestry service turn-around space farther into the woods. From there it was only a short walk. Nearby, comforting lights glowed in my client Samantha's gorgeous A-frame home. Hopefully, she'd read the e-mail we'd sent about keeping Jack, her curious Malamute, inside.

The ground was mucky with wet, half frozen leaves, causing me to slip when I stepped out of the truck. Opening the cab door I searched for my high rubber boots. Forgotten inside a plastic bag in the backseat, they were still caked with dried bear scat and chewing tobacco spit—a parting gift from Crazy Carl.

With my phone securely in my bag I pulled the strap across my chest to leave my hands free. Checking to make sure I had pepper spray, my Swiss army knife, and a couple of zip lock bags in my pockets, I placed one foot onto the wet muck. Despite the thick rubber soles on my boots I sank into multiple layers of leaves carpeting the forest floor. Something skittered in the brush to my right. Before I could react two squirrels ran past, cheeks comically stuffed with nuts. It got colder and colder the further into the woods I walked. Even the squirrels were smart enough to be safe in their warm nests by now. Part of me wanted to turn back but before I knew it, the makeshift memorial that marked Flynn's grave came into sight.

Everywhere else the land was heavily forested except for this small clearing where Flynn had been buried. A solitary jagged boulder stuck up a few feet away, partially hidden by a gangly shrub. Slipping slightly, I made my way to the memorial. The wind kicked up making a whooshing noise through the trees.

Sure enough quite a few people had paid their respects to Flynn. A homemade cross, the two pieces of wood bound together with twine, had been pounded deep into the ground. Near the cross several photos were held down with rocks beside a bottle of beer and sad clumps of dead flowers. Wet notes and cards jutted out of the pile. A teddy bear propped up against the cross had one of the silver stars from the reunion hanging around its neck.

I unzipped my purse, fished out my phone, and began taking pictures. The light filtering through the trees kept shifting so I turned on my flash. I zoomed in on personal items clustered around the cross—a silver bangle bracelet, a miniature sports car, and a signed baseball. When I had almost finished, something bright caught my eye. Stuck under the beer bottle was a gold candy wrapper. I held it between my fingertips for a moment, puzzled. It looked familiar but where had I seen it?

Another blast of wind whipped around the corner and reminded me I'd better get a move on before the storm hit. One last video recording to document the entire memorial and I was out of there.

Crunching twigs alerted me too late.

A vicious whack on the back of my legs knocked me to the ground. Both my hands reached out to block the fall, but I didn't take into account all the broken branches on the ground. Still gripping the phone in my right hand, my right elbow slammed into the dirt to break my fall. Sharp pieces of dead wood bit into my arms, my legs, and my right cheek.

Stunned, I lay still. What had happened? Was I stabbed?

Movement in front of me compelled me to look up.

Shiloh had positioned herself four feet away, a large purse strapped across her chest and a wooden baseball bat in her hand.

"Why did you do it, Kate? I liked you. I thought we could be friends!" She hammered the tip of the bat on the ground. "I don't have many friends."

"What the hell…?" Pain jackknifed through my body all the way down to my boots.

She was dressed in a red ski jacket and jeans, her voice strident. "First you show up at Rusty's clinic. Next you accidentally run into us at Judy's Place." Her hood fell away as another blast of wind struck us both, setting her shoulder length brown hair floating free. "Then you leave two cryptic messages at the office. Good thing I checked this morning and erased them. I don't know how you figured it out but it ends now." Her bat hit the ground again, harder.

"What are you talking about?"

"Everything. Snooping around. Taking pictures of this memorial. Pestering Rusty. I can't let you jeopardize our future. My future."

Everything snapped into focus. "You're protecting him."

"Damn right. I'm tired of scrambling, counting pennies, never getting ahead no matter how hard I work. Once we're married, all that will change."

"But not if Rusty is arrested for Flynn's murder. That's what this is about." I could feel the damp seeping into my clothes as I lay on the ground. My right leg had gone numb.

"It was an *accident*." Her voice grated. "They got into a fight and Rusty pushed him. Flynn hit his head on that rock." She pointed at the boulder with the bat.

"Then he has nothing to worry about," I lied, sneaking my left hand along my jacket.

"Do you think I'm stupid?" Sudden rage shook her voice. "Keep your hands out of your pocket or I'll smack you again."

I had no doubt she meant it.

"Shiloh, please, you don't have to do this." A prickly feeling started creeping into my leg. A dull ache throbbed behind both knees.

Rage morphed into a chilling burst of laughter. "I don't *have* to. I *want* to. Bet you never figured on that." Her eyes darted to all the keepsakes and dead flowers scattered in front of the makeshift wooden grave marker. "Wouldn't it be funny to bury another body under there?"

Something was terribly wrong with her.

Crazed eyes held mine. Gone was the gentle face she showed to the world. "I'm not going to let you ruin my life. If you think I'm going to jail, you're nuts."

I used a calm voice, like I would with a wounded animal. "Shiloh, if you stop now I won't press charges. We can work something out together."

"Together?" She swung the bat back and forth like a pendulum. "It's too late for together."

"Why is it too late?"

Pretty lips curved into a sick smile. "I'm the one who killed Angelica, not her stupid husband. I strangled that bitch."

Her confession froze me. "Why?"

"Partly payback. She made my senior prom miserable."

I saw Hawaiian Punch spreading across a party dress and a young Shiloh crying.

"After all these years Angelica remembered something she shouldn't have." The bat in her hand swung faster and faster, starting to circle. "Being at the reunion jogged a memory in that stupid brain of hers." She stepped forward, eyes locked on me.

"What did she remember?" I pretended to shift my weight, pushing through clumps of cold wet leaves. Inch by inch I moved away from her.

Her rant continued. She paced back and forth. "That dumb Prom Queen remembered driving past Rusty's car pulled over on the side of the road. She told me she glanced in the rearview mirror and saw Flynn get into the passenger seat. Once the presentation of the Court was over she intended to tell Luke. Said she'd ruin my wedding and fix me once and for all for taking Flynn away from her."

Ten-year-old high school grudges still boiling under the surface.

It had been there in front of me all along. "After Rusty left on an emergency you dressed as a waiter and went backstage." I slid further backwards, accusing her to divert her attention. "You bumped into my chair rushing to get away. All I saw was your back, but you looked familiar."

"My one mistake."

"One?" I had to keep her talking, bragging. "How did you get the uniform?"

"I waitressed at that dump my senior year in high school. All I needed to do was raid the servers' locker room. They keep extra uniforms and shoes in there since half the bozos they hire show up in jeans and sneakers…They never change the lock codes."

Her face took on a self-satisfied air. "I stuffed my dress in one of the garbage bags and snuck out through the kitchen. Didn't run into a soul. I'm lucky that way."

"Wait…that was clever."

She moved closer, her voice now singsong in its repetition. "Lucky, lucky, lucky."

The wind died down. We were so isolated. Could I create a diversion and slip away into the woods? If life was like the movies, I would keep her talking, giving me hope.

But this wasn't a movie.

I did my best to appear understanding. "I'm sure it's been very traumatic for you. A good lawyer could probably help you… but not if you kill me."

"Don't you get it? Flynn's body has been discovered. Rusty is feeling guilty. He was tempted to confess to you the other day, to clear his conscience. I can't let that happen."

"But Shiloh—"

"Enough talking!" she screamed. She shut her eyes for a moment, then in a monotone recited, "Don't worry. You won't feel a thing, I promise. Third time's the charm."

"Third? Who else….?" I baited her, trying to break her chain of thought.

Shiloh's head tilted to the side, eyes up. The bat started to gently swing again. "I hate to boast but I pushed my Mom down the stairs right after we got back from our trip to Colorado. She was drunk. It was almost too easy." She smiled at me.

All hope of escaping vanished.

"What are you planning for me?"

"A big injection of insulin I borrowed from the clinic. Undetectable in an autopsy. Your blood sugar will drop, you'll go into a coma and die." Now she was proud. *Lucky, lucky…*

Another cold breeze whipped around the tree trunks. "Luke will never believe it."

"Yes he will. Because after you go into a coma, I'm going to use this on you." She lifted something out of her large purse and grinned.

At first I didn't recognize what it was. Then the genius of her plan sunk in.

"Sorry I have to scratch up your face but I need to make it realistic." The bear paw in her hand had long curved claws, sharp and deadly. "It's amazing what you can find in antique shops."

I pulled myself up to a crouching position as she calmly stuffed the paw back in her big purse. My right knee shook under me. My heart pounded. "I'm not going to make it easy for you, Shiloh."

"I didn't think you would." Up came the bat. She gripped it firmly with both hands, leisurely took a practice swing.

Swoosh.

My left hand searched for and found the pepper spray. Useless this far away. I'd have to get closer.

Swoosh.

Shiloh raised the bat to shoulder height, eerie anticipation in her stance, her eyes bright.

Branches swayed along the forestry trail behind her but the wind was still. A dark shadow moved between the trees.

"Shiloh, don't move." I kept my voice low. "There's a bear behind you."

"Is that the best you can do?" she mocked me. "You think I'm going to fall for that?"

I hunched further back, my eyes focused just beyond Flynn's memorial site.

She raised the bat again, no regret in her glittering eyes.

"Good-bye, Kate. Tough luck."

A roar shook the trees. The large black bear stood up on its back legs, mouth wide open. Huge white teeth glistened.

Shiloh whirled and screamed, terrified. He loomed over her, paws coming up. Another roar came from deep within his chest, rattling my bones.

She scrambled backwards toward me, slipping in the leaves, waving the bat futilely in the air.

Pushing off with my good leg I lowered my head and lunged at her. I knocked her forward, off balance, still clutching the bat, unable to break her fall. She crashed onto the nearby boulder, the same pointed boulder that had claimed Flynn's life. Something snapped.

The bear dropped down onto all fours and snuffled the ground. Abruptly his head lifted.

Deep brown eyes stared directly into mine.

My fingers dug for the pepper spray. Black bears usually weren't aggressive, but anything could happen. I would fight for my life.

In an instant it was over. With a chuffing sound the bear moved away and disappeared into the trees. Partially healed scars from a chain and shackle were clearly visible on his hind leg.

He was the bear I'd fed in the corral, the captured bear that Crazy Carl had beaten, starved, and tried to teach to dance. Whether consciously or not, he had now returned the favor.

Shiloh lay on the ground cursing, her right arm at a bizarre angle. A jagged piece of bone protruded through her torn ski jacket. Blood slowly ran down her fingers and dripped on the damp leaves. The broken baseball bat lay in pieces amid the photos and dead flowers.

I took a couple of deep breaths, paused to look around, then called 911 and texted Luke.

In the distance I heard the bear move away through the underbrush. Slowly I pulled myself up, legs trembling from pain, and limped over to the closest tree. Shiloh screamed more obscenities, regretting she hadn't strangled me like she'd strangled Angelica.

My phone continued videotaping everything.

In a super-human effort my would-be killer attempted to lift herself off the ground. The scream of agony before she passed out didn't surprise me. Open fractures are a bitch.

Long after the woods became quiet I remained still, my back pressed against the rough bark of a tall pine tree. As the faraway wail of sirens came closer, the first delicate snowflakes of the season began to fall.

Chapter Thirty-six

Safely back home I sipped a hot cup of tea, my dog curled up on the sofa next to me. I nodded as Luke told me in exacting detail all about the arrest. Rusty quickly confessed to accidentally killing Flynn, relieved it was finally over. Shiloh was in police custody, her fractured arm stabilized. Rusty's reaction to his fiancée's arrest was unemotional. In a surprise move he led the police to a suitcase in the garage. Neatly folded inside were waiter's clothes, the Lakeside Hotel logo stitched above the pocket of the white shirt. It seems Rusty didn't trust Shiloh and had fished the stolen clothes out of the garbage. The two former lovebirds eagerly ratted each other out to the police.

Rusty had burned Flynn's backpack, but saved one memento from it, a dog-eared copy of *A Catcher in the Rye* by J.D. Salinger. Tucked inside rested a familiar photo. It showed four teenage boys in swimsuits, smiling into the camera, after a forbidden swim in the local quarry—their entire future ahead of them.

He'd brought his gang with him after all.

Because of the video from my phone, the new forensic evidence, and Rusty's testimony, Chief Garcia reopened the deaths of Flynn Keegan, Angelica Landon, and Shiloh's mother, Serena Alberts.

While Luke continued talking I wrapped the blanket tighter around me. Ice packs were strapped behind my knees to reduce swelling. I'd refused painkillers at the hospital, preferring to let my natural endorphins kick in. The bruising from Shiloh's baseball bat ended up being superficial. If she had hit me from the front, the emergency room doctor said, she would have shattered my kneecaps. Deep scratches on my face and hands stood out against my pale skin, looking like a red Sharpie attack.

A random thought occurred to me. "Luke. Did Rusty plant that rose vine next to the grave?"

"No. Just a wild rose, I guess."

My cell phone rang. I'd received calls from almost everyone I knew but the gauze wrap on my hand made it hard to hold the phone.

"Dr. Kate, this is Alessa Foxley. Are you badly hurt?"

"No, I'll be fine in a few days."

Her normally self-assured voice wavered. "I'm so sorry I didn't tell you everything I knew about Flynn. Gene hired him to help cut down some trees a couple of weeks before he left. I paid him in cash and gave him extra so he could go to California."

Another piece of the puzzle clicked into place. "It was kind of you to help him."

"I believed in his dream. Everyone should have a dream."

Although she couldn't see me I nodded my head in agreement.

"I'm making sure Fiona gets the same chance. Flynn told me his only regret was leaving his sister. He intended to bring her to California as soon as he got settled. Since Fiona is over eighteen now I decided to make his plan come true. We're flying to California on Monday. I've got a girlfriend in Los Angeles with a daughter the same age who volunteered to take her under her wing. I'll stay with her out there until she gets on her feet."

Bruce got it all wrong. Alessa had given Fiona her wings.

Somewhere, I knew, Flynn was smiling. Maybe that had been his plan all along.

Fly away and be happy, Fiona, I thought. Fly away.

Buddy's sudden sharp bark announcing someone at the door woke me from my short nap.

"You dozed off. I'll get it." After a quick look through the curtains Luke opened the door.

Jeremy rushed in and headed straight toward me. Snowflakes glistened on the shoulders of his coat. He bent down. "Are you alright?"

"You should see the other gal."

I knew I looked bad, wrapped tightly in a blanket like a burrito. I'd propped myself up on the sofa with pillows to keep my body straight. Scarlet scratches bloomed on my neck and face and my right cheek was purple and swollen.

His finger lightly traced the curve of my jaw. "You could have been…" He didn't finish the sentence.

"Don't worry. I'm sore from head to toe and have giant black and blue marks all over the place, but I'm fine." My grin did little to convince him.

"Luke?" He twisted his head toward my other visitor. "What do you think?"

I tried to give Luke the evil eye over Jeremy's head, warning him not to say anything. It didn't do any good.

He waited a beat before he replied. "I think Kate is down to six of her nine lives."

With Jeremy to keep me company, Luke reluctantly left. After a shared bottle of wine my aches subsided. For added pain relief we broke out a quart of fudge ripple ice cream and turned on the television. As the storm raged outside I watched a retired couple on HGTV try to decide which house in sunny Costa Rico to choose. My attentive boyfriend refused to let me do anything. Jeremy had declared himself my personal servant for the next few days. After a somewhat awkward bathroom break he'd relocated me to the lounge chair, refreshed my ice packs, and gently tucked me in like a baby kangaroo in a pouch.

"Comfy, Kate?"

"Absolutely."

He tentatively took my hand in his. "Why do you think that particular bear showed up when he did?"

For a second I was back in the clearing, dark animal eyes staring at me. Then he was gone.

"I've got no good answer for that. Let's call it kharma."

"Well," he kissed my fingers, "it would have been unbearable if anything had happened to you before I bared my soul—and told you how much I care for you."

My answer made him smile. "Why, Dr. Jeremy, I barely know what to say."

We clung to each other the rest of the night, his hand resting in mine, as snowflakes swirled outside and the hidden moon rose on its journey past the stars.

Epilogue

The black bear lumbered steadily through the falling snow, climbing higher and higher, putting distance between him and the valley below. Without the heavy chain and shackle on his back leg he moved swiftly, his tracks soon covered by a thick blanket of snow. Day became night became another day and night. Farther and farther he roamed. After pushing past acres of bushes and trees he came to a granite outcropping. A familiar scent urged him toward a break in the stone, into a twisted tunnel hidden in the rock.

Inside it smelled warm and dry and familiar. Comforted, he curled up, thick fur pressed against the cave's smooth wall.

No pain now.

No pain tomorrow.

Time to sleep.

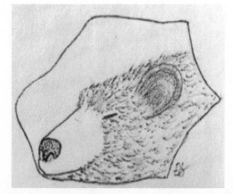

To see more Poisoned Pen Press titles:

Visit our website: poisonedpenpress.com/
Request a digital catalog: info@poisonedpenpress.com